Imraan Coovadia is the author of the novels *The Wedding*, *Green-Eyed Thieves*, *High Low In-between*, *The Institute for Taxi Poetry*, and *Tales of the Metric System*. He has also published a study of VS Naipaul, as well as a collection of essays, *Transformations*. He is a winner of the *Sunday Times* Fiction Prize, the University of Johannesburg Prize, the M-Net Prize, and a South African Literary Award for Non-Fiction. A graduate of Harvard College, he directs the creative writing programme at the University of Cape Town.

PRAISE FOR IMRAAN COOVADIA

GREEN-EYED THIEVES (2006)

'Imraan Coovadia's *Green-Eyed Thieves* offers the most fiercely intelligent fun you can have between two (book) covers... JM Coetzee talked of Coovadia's "comic wizardry"... Others call it "genius". This time admirers can add "bravery" to the mix... But Coovadia is nothing if not an equal opportunity satirist, and his rake through the American socio-political innards—not to mention its criminal (in)justice system—is equally riotous...' —Jacqui L'ange, *The Cape Times*

'Amusing and complicated à la Rushdie, it is a highly original work from a South African writer.' —Jane Rosenthal, *Mail & Guardian Online*

'Fast-paced and full of irony and beautiful prose, *Green-Eyed Thieves* takes an alternative look at 9/11.' —The Sunday Times Literary Awards, *Sunday Times*

'In a book which whizzes and bursts like a firework, the pairing supplies something deep, and grounding.' —Keith Miller, *Times Literary Supplement*

HIGH LOW IN-BETWEEN (2009)

'Coovadia is a sublime talent.' —Fiona Zerbst, *Fairlady*

'Abstract, dreamlike, yet pungently real, *High Low In-between* will provoke and haunt readers in equal measure.' —Craig MacKenzie, *Mail & Gaurdian*

'A work of rare imagination and style, evocative, textured and a tale so compelling as to become an enduring landmark in contemporary fiction. *High Low In-between* does just that.' —*Bookmark*

TALES OF THE METRIC SYSTEM (2014)

'*Tales of the Metric System* demonstrates beyond any doubt that the Durban-born, Cape Town-based writer is, in fact, that very rare thing: a journeyman novelist who is both ambitious and serious in his determination to provide a "history from the inside" of his time and place in the world.' —Leon de Kock, *Financial Mail*

'With its elegant prose and its ruthless determination to lead you to the truth, *Tales of the Metric System* is about as good a book as you are likely to read on South Africa's transition.' —Ray Hartley, *Sunday Times Magazine*

A Spy in Time

Imraan Coovadia

SPEAKING
TIGER

SPEAKING TIGER PUBLISHING PVT. LTD
4381/4, Ansari Road, Daryaganj
New Delhi 110002

First published in the US by California Coldblood books,
an imprint of Rare Bird Books 2018
First published in South Africa by Umuzi,
an imprint of Penguin Random House South Africa (Pty) Ltd 2018

First published in India by Speaking Tiger in paperback 2018

ISBN: 978-93-88070-26-3
eISBN: 978-93-88070-28-7

10 9 8 7 6 5 4 3 2 1

Typeset in Bembo Std by SÜRYA, New Delhi
Printed at Sanat Printers, Kundli

For Daniyal

Marrakech
1955

I never set out to be anybody's prophet. I didn't see myself as a spy. I was twenty-five years old and I was ready for adventure.

Before the checkup, I went to see my father to say my goodbyes. He was in a home on the other side of Nujoma Location. I found him absorbed in a game of chess, the board set next to him on the long divan in the common room. The room was full of sunshine.

The game was automatic. When he completed his move, the crown on the black queen spun round at high speed while the board considered its position. I suspect it was more for show than because it needed the time. In a few seconds, in any case, it made up its mind. The black bishop slid into the corner, pressed by two knights. I could see checkmate against the machine.

My father stopped the clock. He looked sideways at me, his hands running up and down his legs, shrunk to the bone by age.

He spoke as sharply as ever. 'You want a game, my friend? I'm running a tournament here. Seven players, six of which are the different personalities of this board.'

'I don't play so much.'

'You looked as if you appreciated the brilliance of my last two moves. Ah, I thought I was dealing with a flesh-and-blood expert for once, a real flesh-and-blood expert.' His face fell. 'Playing against a machine is never the same unless you have given them the freedom to consider all the assumptions.'

I said, 'I used to play as a child. I don't play now.'

'Then that explains it. I am very sorry to have troubled you.'

He went back to his game, putting his head down. For a quarter of an hour I watched the pawns tread down the rows. It was futile. My father never returned to a subject once it was settled in his mind. I could have stayed on the armchair for the rest of the day and he would have continued to play his position without resuming our conversation, his forehead straining as he waited for the board to counter his moves. I don't know what I expected. He wouldn't have given me his blessing if I could have explained where I was going. He was an engineer and believed in the future over the past. The stars over our heads above the secrets of old time.

On my way out, he turned to the door. I imagined he wanted to say something about what lay ahead. Instead, he pointed to the housekeeping cart and smiled, as if to indicate something about its construction. I smiled back, although I could feel the pressure at my temple.

From the motorway, the tenements and squares of the new city were evident for a dozen miles in both directions. Nitrogen factories alternated with school buildings. Automatic warehouses rose above the tin roofs of barracks and refugee canteens. I shuddered to think of them—pale-faced women and children in their thousands—and tried to concentrate on the case files.

I had watched the recording of the mission twice already. It was my first assignment as a case officer and I was keen to excel. We were scheduled to arrive at five twenty-five in the morning in Marrakech, 16 June of the year of our Lord 1955. In Morocco, our task was to eavesdrop on a small industrial concern. Its proprietor went by the name of Keswyn Muller. We would produce a brief report on Muller to assist the consultants in making their determinations. I wasn't used to watching myself on tape, and was impressed by the aplomb with which I handled conditions in the field. Nothing untoward had been registered on the recording. I looked calm, cool, and untouched by the stress.

For her help in preparing me to go out, I could thank Shanumi Six, the senior member on the expedition. She would give me the space to prove myself. Plus, she wasn't the kind of agent who punished herself when out in the field. She had selected two rooms in a luxury hotel in Marrakech, the kind of decadence the old civilisations had perfected. If I felt any nervousness about being around fair-skinned men and women, in a world that they controlled, I was wise enough to keep it to myself. Shanumi didn't need to hear about my misgivings.

Our buildings were strung along a forested lane behind a number of hidden checkpoints. Security was discreet, but I knew that my profile and silhouette were being logged as I walked to the clinic.

My destination was a converted trailer, designed to be hitched to a truck and moved to a different location whenever necessary. The blinds were permanently pulled down so that no one could look in. The chimney belched white smoke which was soon lost amidst the trees and bright sunshine. I had been through the first round of treatment and hated the experience. Once I had been through the second round, I would not be able to leave the perimeter established by the Agency. We couldn't take the risk of transferring a virus to another place and time.

I went through the doors and sat at the examination table where my blood pressure was taken by a pair of old-fashioned cuffs. It left bruises on my arm. Samples of blood and tissue were extracted and filed away, machines singing alerts to one another. The medical cart opened to receive my offering, revealing the purple bulb in its refrigerator compartment. Lights ran across the top of its body as it produced a teardrop of universal serum.

The injection was the most uncomfortable part of the process. The medical cart had a way of lining you up, then stapling a cold pin under the skin of your inner arm, which left you with a sense of violation, as if the machine had come too close to your inner being.

Afterwards I had a ringing sound in my head. Then came a sudden spell of dizziness. I lost my balance and couldn't walk. I lay on a couch in the next room for the better part of an hour, attended by the cart, until the sensations passed. According to the consultants, I would be completely protected from any known agent of disease, manmade or artificial, for ten days. More importantly, I would not be a carrier of infection.

When I had recovered enough to stand, I was taken behind a dense radiation curtain. I put my hands over my eyes while the walls shone a fierce white ray onto my person. I could feel the light penetrating to my bones. For some minutes thereafter, I saw no more than indistinct shapes until slowly my vision returned, bringing back the inquisitive eyes of the cart. I had a clean bill of health on the system. On my way out, the clinic provided me with a printout of my silhouette. It was more than a memento. Later, I could compare it with my reflection for signs of exposure. Before the dangers of serving in a foreign time had been established, some unlucky souls had begun to lose their outlines. After a while they couldn't recognise themselves in a mirror.

But I didn't have the luxury of indulging my fears of reflection sickness. There was no time to waste. I wanted to find my Six, although my head was swimming from the drugs.

I hurried past the tennis courts, the clay baking uselessly in the heat. Sometimes you would see agents in white shorts and shirts, men and women you had never seen before and might never see again, practising in the late afternoon.

Then came the famous library which had long been associated with the Agency. It contained the complete records of everything that had been and everything that could be—the potentials of the past, present, and future. But it could never be deciphered down to the resolution of an individual life. Many had tried and failed to find the images of their lives in its infinite algebra. The library was a fixed point. Unlike the trailers, the library was set in the earth to a depth of thirty floors.

One day during a free hour, I had descended using the spiral staircase and discovered a room at the bottom. The librarians, their teardrop-shaped heads touching, were conspiring in almost complete darkness. They had rustled indignantly at my entrance, their faces as sharp as foxes, and one had hurried me straight back to the surface.

Since then I had never returned to the vaults, although I had often stood in the atrium of the library and, as many had done and would come to do, counted the names carved into the wall of remembrance and considered their many sacrifices. The Agency had not made direct contact with the main enemy, but in the meanwhile—as we waited for the ultimate showdown—a stream of accidents and technical difficulties had covered yard after yard on the wall with the names of the fallen. Candles burned along the top, their flames standing as straight as pencils.

I found my Six in the registration office. She had drafted the consent forms which had to be filed the night before departure. I sat next to Shanumi in the trailer, which was furnished with heavy armchairs and bookshelves, and signed the forms with the fountain pen she handed to me. She scrutinised the paperwork a second time when I gave it back, the ruby rings on her hands sparkling as she ran her finger down the lines. When she was satisfied that the forms were in order, she held them up to the terminal until they vanished into the aperture.

Turning around, Shanumi put a hand on my shoulder. I could tell it was as much to keep me at a distance as to reassure me about the next day. She didn't have a motherly bone in her body—she liked to make that clear.

'As of now, until you return from the foreign location, your rights and responsibilities are determined by the Agency, not by the constitution any more. How does it feel, Agent Eleven?'

I took a minute to consider the fact. 'No different. Should it feel different?'

'It is different. It is very different.' She sat down in one of the armchairs and invited me to join her, folding out her tough arms. 'For the first time, you are no longer your own property and your own concern. If need be, you may be asked to sacrifice your life or even more.'

I sat down. 'And what could be even more?'

Shanumi Six spoke in an unusually quiet voice. 'Every person has something which is more important than mere life. He or she may not know what it is until the time comes to make a decision.'

'I never thought about it in those terms.'

'You are going to the old world where the assumptions we make about the constitution don't apply. You must remember, Agent Eleven, that this world, our world with its philosophy of humanity, with its attempt to care about every man, woman, and child, every last black-skinned fellow—and even the tragic albinos amongst us—is a recent construction. It is not so long ago that simply being born in a skin like ours would have been considered a crime. Sooner or later, whether it's in Morocco or some other time zone, you will be faced with a choice between the different sets of assumptions.'

Shanumi poured out two portions of absinthe from a bottle on the table and diluted them with soda water. She offered me one of the glasses. I couldn't make out her expression as she peered into the radiant green water. In the many months I had been under her supervision I had never managed to figure out what made her tick.

It may have been that Shanumi Six liked to stay in character as much as possible, which made her difficult to understand in the present. At the Agency, she was noted for using the hyper-traditional methods of the case officer. Her handwriting, her accent, her very gestures were practised daily in front of an ancient television set. She liked to prune the bonsai tree on her desk with one hand while studying her case files. It had been the gift of a famous Japanese painter of the Edo period.

I brought the glass to my lips and hesitated. 'I have a question for you, Shanumi. I watched the recording again.'

'Why are we risking our own black skins when the Agency has observational devices in position?'

'That's not exactly my question. I agree that we cannot simply turn history over to the machines. Otherwise I would have chosen a different line of work.'

'Otherwise, to be exact, we would have to rewire every machine in existence from top to down. Even the consultants, mighty as they are, have to work through us because of the safeguards.'

I tried the contents of the glass and shivered at the aniseed taste. 'But do they ever explain why in general?'

'Why what, my young friend?'

'What the bigger picture is, I mean. Why are we following this person rather than that one? How is watching a minor figure like Muller supposed to lead us to the main enemy?'

I could see that my question had made Shanumi impatient.

To my disappointment, she finished her drink and got up to go.

'Everybody who survives focuses on his or her part of the task, no more and no less. Focus and concentrate. No grand fantasies, mind you, about finding the main enemy on your first assignment. When the time is right for our adversaries to show themselves, I am sure they won't neglect the opportunity. Now, if you don't mind, I will excuse myself. I like to be alone the night before I go out.'

I tried not to let the rebuff get to me. I finished my drink and remembered the legendary patience of S Natanson who had started the Agency in an underground laboratory near Kitwe where he'd framed many of the doctrines which guided us centuries later. I remembered the supernova so few had survived. Then I left the empty trailer. The heavy metal door closed silently behind me.

In the evening I went straight to sleep in the dormitory, the fan turning on the ceiling above the row of empty beds.

I had the sensation, when I was fast asleep, that my sister was sitting on the next bed and trying to attract my attention. She had a voice like a flute, just as I remembered. But I didn't understand the words she was forming. They floated through my dream, unwilling to slow down and reveal their true contents. Nor did she reply when I asked her to explain. She continued to talk, a flow of sounds, then wrote on the palms of her hands. She raised them to me, demonstrating they were blank.

The memory was with me at four in the morning when the alarm went off. As I made my way through the vacant halls, past the concrete reactor cone, and down the long shaft to the departure suite, I was still involved in my dream.

My Six was in the nude, packing her toiletries in a travel bag without even a towel around her waist. I undressed in the corner, hung my clothes in the locker. The bar lights on the ceiling were harsh, as if somebody had doubled the voltage. Shanumi didn't speak but led the way into the shower, her arms folded underneath her breasts, the muscles rippling on her ebony back.

Many case officers liked to take a tablet to turn white, believing that it made the job easier. I think Shanumi Six was too proud of her skin to take half measures. She couldn't imagine being an albino even for a day. I had adopted the same policy in tribute to her. I didn't want to imagine what life was like when the mere fact of your pale complexion made you a secret object of fear and resentment, whatever the constitution had to say about it.

The steam and hot water gave way to a shivering minute under an ice-cold bucket. Shanumi turned here and there in the spray, sending water everywhere, before ducking out to dry herself. She didn't look away while I washed myself.

When I got out she was in a friendlier frame of mind, ready to talk.

'I watched *Gone with the Wind* last night. It must be the fifth or sixth time I've seen it. Do you happen to know it?'

'I've never heard of it.'

Shanumi passed the electric discharger over her body. She parked it on the table for me.

'You should see it, Eleven. I should have made you see it as a condition of your education. Scarlett O'Hara is a spectacular woman. I watched *Lawrence of Arabia* as well. The twentieth century had actors and actresses. They didn't rely on acting algorithms or fantasise about digital actors. For all its cruelty, I find the old world sympathetic for that reason alone. You know that I work from intuition first of all. It's the mood, the feeling that gets into you from what is on the screen. You need that before you arrive in person.'

'Getting into character.'

'If you want to call it that. The past is a foreign country and it is a country of the imagination. A case officer, in a foreign country, lives in her head first of all. Most of what happens, on an assignment, happens in her head.'

Shanumi examined herself in the mirror, holding her breath for a minute. She went on: 'In the field people will look at you. I guarantee it. Maybe they haven't seen a black man who holds himself in a certain way. Maybe they haven't seen a black woman like me. Maybe they want to provoke you. Maybe it's nothing. The best policy is to tell yourself that you're imagining it and go about the assignment as you have seen it unfold.'

Shanumi Six finished changing while I used the discharger on myself, wondering what I could do with this piece of advice. I never had to worry about standing out in Johannesburg. I ran the discharger over my arms, my chest, along my feet, and up to my belly. The tingle started just below the skin. It crackled in the nerves in my teeth and left the taste of ozone in my mouth.

The velvet line of the steriliser ran the breadth of the room, completing the cycle. In conjunction with the universal serum, the sterilising process suppressed the myriad germs, bugs, fleas and flies, microscopic fungi and algae which we carried on our persons.

It wasn't unpleasant. After the shampoo and discharger, you were left smelling delicately of chamomile. I sensed it on myself as I changed into the outfit provided by the costume department—dungarees and a short-sleeved shirt. I smoothed the locket away beneath the collar of the shirt, picked up the satchel which had been prepared. After many years of training, I was looking forward to being in the field.

Above our heads the city of Johannesburg, the first and last city of our century, ticked with radiation. The catacomb city. Its reef, honeycombed with a hundred thousand miles of mining tunnels, had been our salvation in the days of the supernova.

The way to the arch was closely guarded by the computer consultants, placed in rows in the rooms adjacent to the corridor, nervous pairs of blue-and-red sparks in their faces. They were the stalwarts of the Agency. They managed the schedules of case officers and residents, calculated changes in causality and the energy budget, and deposited their findings in the immortal archives. They wrote the books of the consultants, which were as close to prophecy as a sentient being could come. But they weren't the prophets that some people still hoped for. The books they produced were no use to any individual person. Composed in possibility and probability script, they were notoriously difficult to decipher.

The security check lasted a few minutes. Shanumi went on while we waited for the door to open.

'If something happens to you, Eleven, if somehow you and your reflection part company in the field, I will be vilified backwards and forwards in time. I will be portrayed as the one who brought the whole contraption down. In other words, I have my reputation to consider.'

'I understand.'

'I'm glad to have your understanding on this issue.' She took out a pair of glasses and polished them with a corner of her handkerchief before she replaced them in her pocket. 'Today will be more important than you can imagine: to establish a proper view of Keswyn Muller's activities in the region and report back to the consultants in short order. It's good that we are of one mind.'

I couldn't tell if Shanumi was pulling my leg about the importance of our assignment. Why would a first-time case officer like myself be deployed on a vital mission? What did I have to contribute? I worried about it and my own worthiness for two minutes. Then I gave up trying to understand before the barrier opened to admit us into the transfer complex. Canisters of super-cooled hydrogen were piled up at the entrance. An automatic bulldozer was ferrying them two by two deeper into the centre.

To my surprise, there were no human beings at the archway—only more consultants following the preparations, their bronze heads and hands studying the consoles. The gantry vanished into the ceiling. The hum of the solar plant rose to a furious pitch and then subsided, having filled the battery.

We stood in front of a whirlpool turning at a merry clip in the air. I swallowed. Shanumi looked at me without a hint of approval.

'Do you have the pills?'

I put a hand to my neck to remember the locket. The silver was warm on my skin. 'I have both of them.'

'So do I.'

The clocks flashed on the wall. Through fluorescent tubes, a large quantity of plasma poured into the machine, keeping the whirlpool in motion before our eyes. Shanumi took her position on the grate and looked back at me. The consultants seemed to raise their heads in unison. The arch appeared around the whirlpool, its horseshoe form as unmistakeable as a letter.

I stood and counted but couldn't breathe properly. I feared being engulfed by people who, for the most part, had disappeared centuries ago from the face of the planet. The men and women at the Agency who were in charge of my training had never entirely understood from my psychological chart that I suffered from a tendency to faint under pressure. I kept my head down and hoped that my Six couldn't tell how frightened I was.

Fortunately for me, there was a space to recover my wits—

an old custom before travelling. Just as the old Russians did before a journey, we observe a minute of silence before stepping under the sign of the arch. We steal a glance at photographs of our dear ones which we're allowed to carry. We close our eyes and remember the name of the founder, S Natanson, along with the stories of the case officers, coming before and after us in the centuries, who made or will make the greatest sacrifice and whose thoughts and atoms are scattered in the manifold of space and time. We may even remember to curse the idea of a multiverse for the abomination that it is.

Then we put the past and the future behind us to concentrate on the here and now. We pass into the whirlpool, see spirals of gold and green extending from behind our eyelids to infinity, hear music which can never be played on earthly synthesisers, feel the cosmic wind in our face like a whoosh, and emerge into another sunshine …

I dropped eight feet and landed hard on my back. But I didn't have time to think about the surprise. I turned, hitting the side of my head on cement, and lay there for a minute, blood in my mouth. During that time I was too winded to speak. When I got up, I found myself on an extensive rooftop partitioned by washing lines. My Six was in the far corner, no worse for wear except for the dust on her clothes.

'What do you see, Eleven?'

The sky was long and high, blue as a robin's egg. The mountains stood in a semi-circle around the town. Stretches of parched land alternated with irrigated squares. I didn't remember the view from the recording. According to the itinerary we should never have been up here.

My attention was drawn to the railyards. A train was arriving underneath a plume of oily brown smoke, sweeping men and animals from the track as it went into the station. Tents were pegged in front of the station. A string of camels rested on a piece of open ground.

I counted the points of interest out loud so that my Six would know I was paying attention. 'Moving train. Trucks. One light plane, but it is too high to be a spotter in my opinion. No outward sign of trouble. I'll go down, Shanumi, and see what it's like at ground level.'

The top of a ladder extended onto the roof, its rusty iron claws set in the cement. I went over and climbed down the building.

Five floors of yellow brick passed with no facing windows until I found myself alone in an alleyway. At the far end was the bright corner of a street, as clear as a window opened into daylight. From it came the sounds of men and animals, then the rattle of a lorry. I was so relieved to be there, on the loose in the lost city of Marrakech, that I forgot I had hit my head.

Shanumi came down the ladder and showed me her calculations.

'We are seven hundred yards out of position, compared to the recording. Unbelievable. It's the budget cuts. How are we supposed to do our jobs? They save small change, scrimp on equipment, and put the lives of innocent case officers in jeopardy.'

'I didn't know the consultants could make mistakes.'

'What is the doctrine? When things fail, come back to the doctrine. Every mistake, when you trace it back, is a human mistake. That is the doctrine. We have never empowered the consultants to make mistakes on our behalf. See if anyone is watching us.'

I walked to the mouth of the alley. Men passed on the opposite side without paying attention to me. They were as white as sheets. I went back, chilled. I knew that they were only Middle Easterners and North Africans but some reactions are instinctive.

There was worse to come. The main square lay between us and our destination, the Grand Marrakech Hotel. The streets were narrow and lined with booths open to examination. In back rooms sheep carcasses turned on spits, running with roast fat.

On one road there was a line of tailors, old men sewing buttons or measuring their customers' arms and legs. On the next we found jewellery shops and watch repairers, silk shops, and religious schools. My panic rose as the streets became busier. I had to get used to being in such proximity to ghostly men and women. To my relief none of them paid any undue attention to us.

There were a few other black men, digging on the side of the road, but I tried not to make any sign of recognition. Shanumi walked through the crowds without a sign of fear. She had tied a scarf around her head but she was still, without a doubt, the roughest- and toughest-looking woman for a hundred years in either direction.

The Grand Marrakech Hotel lived up to its name. It was a six-storey pale-stone building between two private houses. I remembered it from the recording. You went through a marble archway and past a carp pond attended by benches, whiskered bronze fish nosing through the greenish-black water. The foyer behind the garden was lined with rows of rattan chairs.

On the right-hand side a dealer in precious stones was announced by a sign in five languages. He sat at a high wooden desk, a pair of scales and a loupe at his elbow. He wore brown sunglasses, never moved his head as we went past.

The desk clerk was more solicitous. He wore a double-breasted suit and cuff links. I recognised him also.

'You are not from here, I can see. How can I help, monsieur and madame?'

'We need two rooms. One for the young monsieur and the larger one for myself.'

The clerk opened his book and let us see the long-ruled pages with lists of names.

'Our visitors will usually have sent a telegram ahead, or booked a trunk call with the manager. Given the time of year, many of our rooms have been reserved for over a month.'

Shanumi produced a set of traveller's cheques. She placed them on the desk, rubbed their gilt corners, and took out her fountain pen.

'Money is not an object. Therefore, my dear sir, let us have the best available.'

Our adjoining rooms occupied a corner of the fourth floor. I went to the window to contemplate the scene. Two women in slacks were playing on the tennis courts, their strokes audible four floors up. Behind them lay the conch of a swimming pool, slopping with emerald water. High walls separated the grounds from the bustle of the town.

Shanumi Six had selected the hotel, a sign of the latitude given to her by the consultants on the planning commission. Case officers were usually placed in boarding houses or motels where nobody kept records or made much of an effort to remember a face. When I had been inducted into the Agency, the lady in charge on the first day had explained our tradition of restraint in the time-honoured way. She set out a game of pick-up sticks on the floor in front of us, distributing the pieces as S Natanson had once done with his recruits. The point was to take the one or two things you needed each turn, as neatly as you could, and leave everything else in place. The idea was to be as unobtrusive as possible.

Shanumi, from what I had seen, didn't believe in playing the same game. Maybe once you got to a certain level the rules didn't apply.

In any case, I knocked on her door and she emerged in a slip and pair of sandals, glancing suspiciously up and down the corridor. I was afraid to look at her bare shoulders. She didn't notice my discomfort and had me sit in a tasselled chair, returning to the bed where she had disassembled the beacon.

'All good?' I said.

'In a word, no. It's unprecedented to have an error like this occur and have no word from the Agency. They should have picked it up even before it happened and should have sent somebody to fix it. Compare what we're seeing with how we saw the mission unfold on the record. Therefore, I conclude that everything back home has descended into a state of high entropy, bordering on the catastrophic. And you will never know me to exaggerate.'

Indeed, I had not known my Six to exaggerate. Despite her independence she was a good case officer, and a good case officer liked to have everything happen in the precise order foretold by the recordings. Each stick picked in the right sequence. Otherwise, the world was going to end. Worse: the multiverse was going to take hold and a hundred thousand worlds would end, an untold multiplication of suffering.

In unfriendly corners of the government, it was believed that the Agency itself was given to exaggeration to justify its budget. Politicians noted that despite the loose talk of a main enemy, lurking in the corridors of time, a true rival to the Agency had never yet appeared. What remained constant was its mandate as given by S Natanson: to preserve the past in its perfection and imperfection; to protect the narrow route that led humanity as a species through the blinding dark of the supernova; to prevent the splitting of the unity of time into endless contradictory strands.

After a few minutes, I knelt beside the bed and tried to help Shanumi put the beacon back together. I couldn't be much use because I had to avoid the connections which were labelled with possibility characters, unwilling to remind her of my illiteracy. As the beacon took shape, my Six visibly relaxed. She fixed the crystal on the inside, the clasp of her hair iron doubling as a soldering iron. It hissed like a snake, producing an unearthly blue spark with which you could melt any metal in the universe. I studied my reflection in the long mirror affixed to the door, trying to spot if there had been any change.

When the beacon was properly repaired and locked in the safe, Shanumi adjusted her hair in the same mirror, putting every peppercorn in place.

She talked without turning her head from her reflection. 'We should be on guard. Something is in motion that has yet to be explained.'

'I'll be on the lookout.'

'My plan is to stick to the itinerary and call in afterwards. If we call in now, they will simply take us out of the mission. If it goes wrong, the consultants will know where to find our bodies.'

I carefully carried the equipment to the stairs. I knew Shanumi wasn't exaggerating. Operational security was paramount. If anybody inspected our belongings, he would find nothing more suspicious than a telephoto lens, an abacus, and what looked like a radio direction finder. I had packed a set of blank postcards which would reproduce in holographic precision any scene I wanted to capture. They would be no more than mesh until activated by a lab five hundred years distant from old Morocco.

The lookout point was an active warehouse, a ten-minute taxi ride from the hotel. From the recording, I remembered the warehouse right down to the layout of the electric bulbs on the ceiling. The loading bay was open to the street. Men were squatting around it, arguing with one another or smoking cigarettes.

The floor was covered in sheep pelts, more of which were being unloaded from a van. There was an animal stench in the atmosphere, so piercing it seemed to come out of my dream.

The overseer approached us, his face nearly white. I repeated, under my breath, what I knew he was going to say. I had a feeling of terrible power. I also had a terrible fear of him which made no sense.

'What do you two want?'

I said, 'We're here to see Cassim.'

His eyes narrowed. He spat on the side. 'What does a black fellow want to see Cassim for?' He turned to Shanumi, a look of incomprehension on his face. 'As for you, my lady, aren't you in the wrong part of town?'

She pointed to the backpack. 'We have a delivery.'

'You can leave it with me.'

'He has to sign and send a letter back.'

The man looked Shanumi up and down. He couldn't have seen anyone like her in his life and I could tell that it set him back. He didn't know whether to hate her or fear her, or alternatively whether to throw himself at her feet.

'Wait in his office, then. The second floor there. Make sure you don't take anything. I have everything counted.'

We went into an adjoining room, where the sheep pelts were piled into stacks higher than a man, then up the staircase. Confined rooms and half-open windows with bars in the shape of a cross. We passed Cassim's office. His name was chalked on the door. The door was open, exposing a desk with a typewriter and a metal filing cabinet, its green drawers pulled half out. We didn't go in. Instead, we climbed another flight of stairs, along a corridor that reeked of sawdust and dried blood, into a tiny chamber with a balcony. Shanumi Six lifted and adjusted the scarf around her head and I saw she was wearing small diamond earrings.

At that instant, Cassim Ferhat was detained in the basement of the Rabat police station two hundred miles from Marrakech. He had put a cash envelope in the hands of an inspector on behalf of the company, and had been on his way back when he'd avoided a string of goats in the road and run into a motorcycle. The Agency had done him no harm. It was merely saving energy, making use of a gap opened by an accident, and leaving the rest of the world as untouched as possible. That was our art form.

Shanumi set up the camera and microphone in front of the window. She turned the dials as carefully as if she were trying to crack a safe.

'I don't want anything else to go wrong, Eleven. Nothing unplanned. We don't want to be blamed for creating a multiverse, no matter how trivial the deviations.'

'What else could go wrong?'

When Shanumi spoke again, after finishing with the adjustments to the lens, her tone was strained. For many days afterwards I remembered it because it applied to what came next.

'What could go wrong? The main threat, if you want to know, is ourselves. Our level of confidence is dangerous. On the one hand, we believe that an enemy exists, although we have seen neither hide nor hair of him—or her, if you believe that a woman could be so depraved. Then, on the other hand, we behave recklessly, as if this enemy is toothless. We place too much confidence in our foresight, our recordings. We see the footage beforehand and we think we know—that we have a grasp on the possibilities and probabilities, the myriad contingencies and counterfactuals, the potential for a multiverse. As you have learnt, whatever the general public has been led to believe, the three equations of historical statistics are neither unambiguous nor easy to decode. Not even the consultants can decipher their own predictions.'

I knelt beside her and tried to help with the camera. 'If the consultants don't know, then what can I, as a junior case officer, be expected to do about it?'

'Be quiet for five minutes, Eleven, and reflect on what I told you.'

I didn't think Shanumi intended to be rude, but I felt the red rising in my cheeks. In any case, she shifted her attention to the microphone, tuning it through the earpiece until she was satisfied with the sound. I could hear the buzzing in the machine rise and fall, old-fashioned parts which the Agency manufactured to the occasion.

Some time went by. The room above Cassim's office looked out over a narrow street adjoining the wall of another warehouse. A man with a dog on a leash was patrolling the area, his face as stern as the animal's when he came by every six or seven minutes. I didn't remember him from the recording. The discrepancy worried me even more than being exposed on the streets. I had been taught to rely on foreknowledge, never to drift from the dictates of the recordings. Plus, I was disappointed that I wasn't nearly as calm as I had looked.

Shanumi unwound her scarf and smoothed out the itinerary on her legs, running her finger carefully along the tree of events. She checked her timepiece: the inevitable railroad watch with a ridged gold face preferred by most case officers, a period piece.

'In the version as we had it, at this exact instant, Keswyn Muller appeared in the right-hand window, his back turned to the street. But he is nowhere to be seen today as we stand here. Can you confirm for the record, Eleven?'

'I saw Muller in the holograph, yes, but right now I cannot see him in the indicated position. Something has definitely changed. Something is badly wrong.'

'Don't judge. That's up to the consultants. Simply report the facts and correlate them with the predictive matrix.'

I tried to read the itinerary. Possibility script was as difficult to read as algebra, even the limited set of characters that a case officer was required to handle. The letters danced this way and the other, turned inside out and roundabout in front of my eyes, until they reluctantly settled down.

My Six had no inkling of my difficulties with every line. She waited impatiently while I passed the side of my hand down the page. The sun had crept into the room, producing thousands of motes in the air. The perfect sensation of acting just as I had seen myself act on the recording—as if I were effortlessly repeating the steps of a dance—evaporated. Instead, I was left with the unpleasant sense of sitting for an examination.

I tried to explain the logic to myself. 'Keswyn Muller, assuming he still exists, has taken a path different from the recording. That means, by the law of energy conservation over time, that some outside party has injected energy into the situation in order to change it. For that, I don't have an explanation.'

Shanumi put a hand on my shoulder as if to comfort me. But then she didn't explain anything either.

Another hour went by while we waited for Keswyn Muller. Shanumi let me keep watch while she did some calculations. I could hear her talking under her breath. In the other building, I realised, somebody was going through the rooms and closing the blinds.

Soon after, a military truck drew up. It disgorged a dozen soldiers, men in brown shirts and trousers sporting steel helmets. They carried rifles with bayonets. The captain spoke to the man with the dog while some of the others began setting up a checkpoint.

Two knocked fiercely on the door to our warehouse. I heard their heated conversation with the workers on the loading dock. They shouted to their colleagues down the street. The guard with the dog came rushing into the building. My dream, in which every step had been foretold, had been replaced by a nightmare where nobody knew what could happen.

Shanumi stayed calm. She opened the window and

inspected the railing on the outside. I had vertigo. I had never wanted to go up to the solar system because of my fear of heights.

'I memorised the layout of the building and there may be a way around. You will have to follow me,' she said.

'I really don't have a head for heights.'

'I understand that, Eleven. I am acquainted with the contents of your psychometrics folder. But you don't have a choice if you want to return to civilisation, if you ever want to live as a free black man again. Remember that these people kept slaves. So one step after the other, please.'

Shanumi put her cool hand to my cheek, as if she cared for me like a lover. Then she tied the scarf around her head again and went out. She kept the backpack on one shoulder, holding on the wall as she groped her way out. The dog bayed on the staircase. I swayed back and forth, pushed myself through the window.

On the other side, Shanumi stopped me from falling. I sensed the perspiration on her.

'We must think like case officers. Someone had our itinerary, Eleven, and wants to prevent us from observing Muller and examining the company records. That has a number of serious implications for us, not to mention the alterations they will have to make to the equations.'

'What can we do?'

'The best thing you can do, right now, is not to look down.'

I looked down. The railing was so narrow, you had to turn your feet to the side. The bars went around the corner of the building. It had never been intended to support a man and a woman. The joints strained under our weight. I watched with horror as the iron bent.

Shanumi threw the backpack onto the roof. She knelt down in front of me.

'Climb onto my shoulders, Eleven. Get onto the roof.'

'What will you do?'

'I'll find a way to come in. Let's deal with you first.'

I scrambled onto her shoulders, listening to the railing complain under our combined weight. The brackets started to pull out of the brick. I caught hold of the gutter, pulled as hard as I could with my hands, pushed against Shanumi, and got a foothold on the roof. I immediately fell flat on my face next to the backpack. My nose felt broken.

By the time I recovered, Shanumi had moved along the railing to the corner of the building. She tried to scale the wall by force, revealing the powerful muscles in her arm and neck. But she couldn't get a good grip. She tried to jump a few times, keeping it as quiet as she could. Then she gave up, came back along the railing, and swung herself through the open window. She put her head back through.

'Wait until it's settled down, not even a mouse. Then we can meet at the hotel. I need to get rid of the beacon in case somebody follows it back to our home co-ordinates. Or you get rid of it if you get there first.'

'Where are you going?'

She didn't answer, only disappeared into the building. My heart was in my throat. I kept low and listened with all my might. The dog barked madly in the doorway, loud as a drum. A man's angry voice came from the stairs. I heard Shanumi replying in her most reasonable tone.

Shouted questions, and a scuffle. A man crying in pain. The dog clattering along the steps before it fell silent. More men running up the stairs. More cries of shock and pain. I couldn't tell who had won. There was the sound of furniture being moved. To my surprise, I fell asleep on the tarpaulin.

*

I woke with the sun in my eyes and turned onto my side. For some time, I lay on the roof without daring to stand up.

There was no sign of Shanumi. No soldiers, no dog quarrelling on the staircase, no trucks. Nothing made a sound. Marrakech was a ghost city, no more than a silent oblong cut into the rock, where I had come to find people long in the grave.

Then a dark-skinned man passed in the road below, leading a herd of goats. The animals had bells on their collars. I used the opportunity to drop down to the railing and got back into the building through the window.

Inside were signs of a titanic struggle. Chairs lay on their backs. The desk was turned on its end, its drawers open to their lengths. Glass was scattered everywhere on the carpet.

I went into the corridor. There was nobody to be seen. The stevedores must have been sent home. I hurried down the staircase and along the main hall, keeping out of sight. I was searching for an outside window when I heard a telephone ringing in one of the offices. I opened a door that led to a warren of small rooms and storage cupboards.

Behind a sheet of frosted glass, I could make out the figure of a man wearing a hat, his feet up on the desk. He had a light accent, which may have been Swiss, and was talking in a merry tone into the telephone.

'Then the dream has come true. We have one of them … Near Menara Gardens … No, it will be quite safe. The army has imposed a curfew. Not even a mouse will go in or out.'

The conversation became indistinct. I went as close as I dared, in time to hear a burst of indignation from the receiver. Kneeling to look through the keyhole, I recognised Keswyn Muller immediately thanks to his well-tended grey beard and the slant of his features which had been clear on the recording. I thought even then that he had a face built to keep secrets.

As I watched, Muller got up and walked around the room in circles. The telephone cord followed him around like a tail. I believed he was looking directly through the door, his expression hard around the eyes.

'Their officers are under the delusion that they can try again and again, as if they have endless energy to run an experiment with the history of humanity. They claim to hate the multiverse and yet they depend on it at every turn.' Muller listened to the voice on the other end for a minute and put the receiver down. Then he went on talking to himself. 'They don't believe anything is for real except the rewind button. They don't have a sense of the seriousness of life. That is a crucial advantage for us. We can set a mousetrap that cannot be opened.'

Muller came through to the room I was in and I walked backwards, as carefully as I could, through the door, hoping I wouldn't bump into anything. He had almost reached me when I slid my entire body behind the door. I caught my breath. He was so near, the hairs on my arms tingled.

Up to that point in my life, I had never been so close to an albino man with power over me. I watched him stride through the hall, and thought I had learnt enough about Keswyn Muller to enlighten the consultants. I would make my way to the hotel to collect the beacon. Then I would have to find Menara Gardens and rescue my Six. I wasn't going to be caught in anybody's mousetrap and I wasn't going to let it happen to Shanumi either.

I waited until I heard Muller leave the building. Finding a small window on the ground floor, I forced my way through it onto the street.

By the time I got out, the evening had descended. Queues of French cars darted along the streets, hooting at one another around the traffic circles, their headlights orange circles in the dusk.

Women in cloaks hurried in groups along the pavement, shopping bags over their arms. They weren't interested in my existence. I had the feeling of being concealed in plain view.

In the near dark, flocks of birds flew in the direction of the mountains. Shopkeepers were pulling down the grilles in front of their premises, although here and there, attended by chains of outdoor lights, small restaurants were opening.

The city was receiving its complement of mourners for the seven saints whose tombs were situated on its circumference. Tomorrow there would be Berber acrobats and snake-charmers, fortune-tellers, cardsharps, and dentists on the squares, but for now there was a hush.

At the Grand Marrakech Hotel, cabs were arriving from the train station, their drivers arguing as they halted around the semi-circle at the entrance. I went through the marble archway, past the carp pond, and waited for a minute inside the door in case anybody had followed me. Nobody was watching, as far as I could tell—except the jeweller behind his desk, who looked as if there were something in my appearance that troubled him. Suitcases without owners, bearing various city stickers, were lined up at reception. The bellhop took me to my room and immediately went back down to help the new arrivals.

I went over to Shanumi's room and unlocked the door with a coin. I laid the backpack on the bed and took the beacon out of the safe. I placed it on the bedside table and closed the curtains. Outside, I could hear men and women laughing on the rim of the swimming pool.

It took several minutes to tune in on the dials. I was nervous about any sound in the corridor, and my hands kept slipping on the controls.

I waited some time for a computer consultant to come on. It had the eerie manner of the librarians I had discovered in the library of the past and the future.

'I have been waiting anxiously for your report, Enver Eleven.'

'We appeared here in the middle of the air, almost died on the way in.'

'The systems are down here at the Agency. You won't understand until you come back in. Describe the situation in Marrakech exactly from start to finish.'

'Shanumi Six, the senior case officer, has been abducted. I have good reason to believe that she is being held by Keswyn Muller rather than the Moroccan government.'

'We have some inkling of this. From the beginning, if you please, so everything can take its proper place on the recording.'

I sat on the side of the bed, bending into the microphone, and tried to remember everything relevant to the case. The consultant on the other end listened and asked some follow-up questions. She sounded worried the more she heard from me, calling in one of her colleagues and then another. They ran some calculations in possibility script.

I imagined the three brass skulls bowed in unison above the microphone, muttering under their breaths or lying back in a bath of electrostatic fluid. In the middle of my report, the three of them went offline for a few minutes to create a new itinerary and requisition the necessary energy. They would be making a new picture of the situation.

I wouldn't have understood a thing even if I were in the room with them. The times I had looked at the diagrams the consultants generated, they'd resembled trees branching and bending endlessly. I was supposed to understand the basics of reverse causation—creating an effect by patiently assembling its causes, putting the heap of history together stick by stick. In practice, it was as much an art as a science, one at which automatic intelligences excelled, given their ability to consider infinite worlds.

When the consultant came back, her manner was bright but the news she had to deliver was grim.

'You're going to have to dismantle the beacon. You know the protocol.'

'I do.'

'Nothing remains intact except for the targeting crystal. That comes with you because it contains reserved technology, inappropriate to the time period.'

'I know that also.'

'Let me go over some of the fine details. There have been a few updates to the mechanism since you passed your examination.'

I didn't need the lecture. I might have difficulty reading certain characters but, thanks to my father, I could take apart a piece of machinery in pitch dark. As the consultant was talking, I spun a lever on its axis to open the device, turned two gears in the counterclockwise direction, and pulled the panels apart, like solving a Rubik's Cube. The outer parts dissolved into a silver haze. The cogs and rods broke into splinters, then into nothing more than sand.

In the end, I was left with the crystal and several hundred grams of dust which the fan would blow into the atmosphere.

I didn't allow the implications of dismantling the beacon to enter my mind until the consultant said it out loud.

'You have the two capsules?'

'Of course.'

I put a hand to the locket around my neck. Nobody went on an assignment without the two capsules. They were part of our ritual, dreadful to consider. One was blue, lit from inside by tiny neon tendrils. It pulsed as slowly as a heartbeat when you placed it on your palm and inspected it. The other was black, and inert, absorbing the light in your eyes when you glanced in its direction.

The first pill brought the imitation of death, so close to the reality that not a heartbeat stood between the two conditions. No mid-century anatomist could tell the difference.

The latter, the black pill, blocked respiration throughout the body. Within ten minutes of ingestion, no trace of the person remained apart from a peppery haze: a case officer's death.

'At some point between midnight and two o'clock this morning, you will ingest the blue pill. This is a recommendation from the corps of consultants, Agent Enver Eleven. It represents our consensus. Do you accept and make the decision of your own mind?'

'Yes.'

'I recommend you find the Marrakech Protestant graveyard. We have had trouble, in the past, recovering our agents from Muslim cemeteries. They are not as serious about mortuary preservation. Over time, the bodies tend to move or the parts can be combined. Somewhere safe and quiet is better. And, I say, good luck to you. Good luck to you.'

I never understood the tone that the machines liked to strike in their dealings with agents in the field. The consultant was about to ring off when I stopped her.

'I don't understand at all. What about my Six?'

'Given what we see of the probabilities, considering the unfolding circumstances at the Agency, we need to extract you from the situation. I cannot release you to pursue your leads.'

'I understand that.'

'Agent Eleven, we agreed that if you asked, we would convey an additional piece of information. We would have preferred to delay until psychiatric adjustment was available to you. I have confirmation that not more than a few minutes ago in your frame of reference, in a greenhouse located in the Menara Gardens, Agent Six took the black pill. She is as much a part of the present as the past.'

'Of the future as the present.'

'And may her memory be our hope.'

The familiar words didn't help. I uttered them by rote, as I had said them at my mother's graveside, and yet I didn't believe them in my heart. I couldn't believe what the consultant was telling me about my Six. Not even a calculating machine would be so unmoved by the death of a senior case officer in the field, unforeseen by the recording. Back at home there would be an inquiry.

But I couldn't afford to think about Shanumi for the moment. I concentrated instead on the practical problems of taking the blue pill; I would need some basic equipment if I was going to bury myself.

The bellhop at the hotel assisted me. He was a young brown man in a gold-buttoned blazer, piping on the sleeves, the suggestion of wool on his cheeks, dark enough so that I felt comfortable talking to him in a corner. He didn't blink an eye at what I wanted. He told me to follow him to the back.

We went through the kitchen to the groundsman's quarters outside of which a boy was sitting cross-legged on the earth, diligently polishing brassware. The boy didn't raise his head while the bellhop laid out various items for my consideration: a spade, tatty blue raincoat devoid of buttons, gumboots, and a tarpaulin cover. Everything I required.

I didn't have the heart to bargain him down as he expected. I counted out the money, in French francs. The bellhop counted the stack again, his fingers as fluent as a bank teller's, and held some of the notes up to the lamp to check the watermark. Then he slid them into his buckled shoe, tied the tarpaulin around the spade, and held out the raincoat so that I could put it on. I took it over my arm instead.

'You want hashish, sir?'

'No, thanks.'

'I thought you might be German, sir. They usually want hashish.'

'Do I look German?'

'I can't say who is German and who is not German, who is Austrian and who is not Austrian. It is not up to me to decide, sir. They can be black or they can be white, as they please.'

I was in the lobby, passing the jeweller's desk, before I had second thoughts.

Carrying the raincoat on my arm, I went back through the kitchen where the bustle was immense. There were stripped rabbits on a board and plucked chicken carcasses pegged to a washing line, waiting to be plunged into the boiling pots below. The scent of cinnamon hung in the air. Trays were stacked on the near end, arriving from the dining room on a lazy Susan. The pastry cook was applying fronds of silver icing to a cake.

I found the bellhop sitting on the outside step. He was bent over, steadily polishing his shoes.

'So we can do some more business?' he asked.

'It depends.'

'You changed your mind about hashish, sir.'

'Nothing at all to do with hashish.'

I sat down next to him and put my hand on his back. We were about the same size.

'You're unhappy with your purchase. I am sorry, sir. I have already spent the money.'

'Not that either. You said something strange before about the Germans and the Austrians. It struck me right afterwards.'

'I said that it is not my business to decide who is German and who is Austrian.'

'You get a lot of them? Visitors from Austria, Germany, Switzerland? If you were looking for someone from that region, who was right here in Marrakech, where would you begin?'

'You can put a notice in the German bakery. It's next to the bar and restaurant. They also have a church there. I will draw you a map.' He produced an envelope and a pencil stub. 'But it will be closed now. The bar might be open. Are you caught in a trap, sir?'

I looked past the bellhop into the kitchen where pots

were boiling ferociously, their sides almost touching, on the blackened, pig-iron stove. The cooks and waiters were too far away to hear us.

'My friend, do you think you could find me some additional equipment?'

The bellhop paused for an instant, but he didn't hesitate. I noticed that his eyes were the exact shape of almonds. They looked away from you while you were talking and made you believe he was gazing into his own dream while you were lost in your own.

'That depends what you mean by equipment, sir.'

'I would like to be able to protect myself.'

He shook his head and gave me the map. 'I am sorry. It's my responsibility not to put myself or any of our guests in danger.'

In the Royal Bavarian Bakery, on a dead-end road in an industrial section of town, the lights were on, although nobody was in evidence behind the large plate-glass windows.

The taxi had long disappeared while I stood there and admired the hundreds of crammed baskets of bread on display. Around the bakery lingered the aroma of yeast.

Next door, in the Green Dolphin Brewhouse—'Serving Since 1946'—the menu was printed in Arabic and German. There was activity long into the evening. Tables of men gathered around tall amber glasses and dishes of pretzels, pressing tobacco into their pipes.

From a record player on the counter emerged a rueful woman's voice, as if from a long-ago movie. At one of the tables sat a band of military policemen with flashes on their shoulders and revolvers in their holsters. They looked too thin to fit in their uniforms, with narrow chests and hips, and watched me in an unfriendly fashion.

I sat in front of a carafe of tonic water, which fizzed

unenthusiastically, and calculated the number of hours remaining before I had to take the tablet and stop my heart. I had wanted adventure. I had found something else: the small death. Under the table, the spade rested on my leg, cold reminder of the future.

I kept expecting to find Shanumi Six across the table, about to make some logical point that a junior case officer should know. I couldn't tell how far I had travelled from the real world. The dream which had formed around me in Marrakech was as insubstantial as a shadow in one minute, as if I could wish it away, and in the next minute as dark and deep as a well. I stayed there for an hour, muttering to myself, as more men came in and took their chairs. The new arrivals contended goodnaturedly with the bartender, played backgammon, or simply stared into their glasses.

People who don't risk their own skins in the field pose the usual paradoxes, commonplaces that have caused nothing but confusion since Zeno of Elea proved motion is impossible and time an illusion. In my opinion, those questions are useless. Certain paradoxes, the useful ones, address the heart instead of the mind. A case officer is a shadow chasing a shadow, the shadow of the future intersecting with the shadow of the past. If she dies in a foreign location, she is a shadow of a shadow. I was so disturbed at the thought, which was almost as distasteful as the travesty of a multiverse, that I stood up in the middle of the Green Dolphin.

In the same moment, I heard the voice from the warehouse. When I turned around, shielding my face with one hand, I saw that Keswyn Muller was at the next table. He was sitting opposite a young woman and entertaining her with a story. Smiling broadly, as if he had won a competition, he took out a fountain pen and drew a map on a coaster. For an instant I thought that the trap had closed on me, until I assured myself that he would have no idea of how I looked.

The woman was around my age, or no more than a few years older, and had her brown hair in a low bun. She was wearing long earrings, out of place in the Green Dolphin, and a narrowly tailored jacket with a rose-lettered blouse. Her legs, under the table, were bare from the knee. Her complexion was fair, by the standards of civilisation, and yet I experienced no horror. There was no discomfort, no sense of repulsion from what God and man had made ugly. The opposite. The more I watched, the more I realised that she was very beautiful, a sign whose meaning became clearer and yet farther away in the darkness of the room.

I sat down and tried to move my chair gradually backwards, closer to their conversation. My heart was beating so loudly I almost couldn't hear what they were saying.

'It was too good to be true, my dear. I couldn't believe our luck.'

'To have the chance to ask one of them questions?'

'In the entire correspondence of the Board, there has not been one occasion on which we had a chance to interact with one of them on our terms. We believed they had supernatural powers, as if they could control every detail of physics and chemistry in pursuit of their depraved agenda. Now we can see they are mere fanatics. The value of life means nothing to them. We have finally exposed them to the world and there will be no turning back.'

My ears burned. I had never heard anyone speak of the Agency with such vehemence. I leant back in the chair, hoping not to fall over.

'Are you sure she intended to kill herself? Even a fanatic—'

'Even the fact that they use women as their sacrificial victims. She burnt to death before my very eyes. It took ninety seconds from start to finish. At the end, there wasn't even a shoelace left. Spontaneous human combustion. The myth comes to life, or rather to death. You should have seen the expression in this black-skinned woman's eyes, my dearest Soledad, looking out of the blaze as she was consumed. I have not witnessed scenes of this kind since the last days of Berlin.'

She poured two glasses of wine. 'You want to pack up tonight?'

'We have our passports. We have sufficient money. We still exist, as far as such a thing can be known.' He pinched her arm sourly. 'So we will elude them if it is humanly possible. In their flippant way, when their interests are threatened, they are quite ruthless about reversing the verdict of history, especially since we can trace the loss of an innocent woman's life back to them. If they identify us under our true names and trace our ancestry then you know all too well what will follow. They will make it as if not a single member of the Board had ever been born. You will be gone, just like that, my dear Soledad, but you will have no parents either, no brother, no sister, no relations up to the second degree.'

It took a minute to realise Muller had turned his chair in my direction, as if to address me directly. He moved his chair closer, and closer, and then took me by the ear. His hand was cruel.

'It seems that someone has long ears.'

His strength was extraordinary. He turned my chair around, never letting go of my ear, so that we were sitting face to face.

The rise and fall of conversation continued around us. Beer hissed out of the tap into the glasses which the bartender removed to the trays. The door opened to admit two men who joined the policemen at their table. Every soul in old Morocco could have been on the far side of the planet for whatever help they could render me. I had never feared anyone so much or resented the touch of his hand, as stern as the lid of a trap. Where I had descended, led by the ear like Cerberus the dog, there was only pale-faced Dr Muller and myself, and the stare of his companion. She was more beautiful than I had recognised. Her complexion was the colour of a certain wood.

'Do you understand German, my friend?'

I didn't reply. I was overwhelmed by fear and expectation. Scarcely two hours remained before my rendezvous with the small death. I hadn't yet found a safe place, and I was in the hands of an enemy. I put a hand on the spade, wondering if I should hit Muller in the head, but then he let me go. He continued in Arabic:

'You people are very curious in this country. Nobody knows how to mind his own business. What is your name, my friend?'

'Enver.'

'Are you from around here, Enver?'

'Skoura. In the mountains. Far away.'

Muller settled back in his chair. 'Skoura. You don't look quite Moroccan. Sudanese, in my opinion. A black devil. May I ask what you are doing, my inquisitive friend, so far from home, in Marrakech?'

'I sell electrical equipment. Voltage converters and transformers. I am here to find customers. On the other end I buy from Siemens, my main suppliers. Their engineers taught me a few words of German.'

'Did you understand anything?'

'Not a word. I am disappointed.'

I could have mentioned the names of my imaginary father's cousins, electricians in Skoura, who had been involved in a lengthy feud. I could have provided a bank account for the company and the names of its customers. I knew the results of every soccer game in the region past and future, and could have made a fortune gambling if I hadn't renounced betting, not to say the benefits of compound interest, as a condition of service.

Dr Muller turned the wine bottle around, showing me the yellow label. It was in French. 'You would like a drink?'

'After an introduction like that, you want to drink with me?'

'I would like the chance to apologise. In my line of work I have to be careful, Enver.' He put his hand against the wall. 'In England they have an expression—they say that the walls have their ears.'

What might I have done? I might have killed Keswyn Muller in the corner of the Green Dolphin, using the side of a broken bottle. I might have slipped a black pill into his wine glass, strangled him at the urinal. I might have set fire to his body, disposed of the remains in a dune ten miles out of Marrakech, attended by the wild rush of stars in the sky and the cries of bush dogs.

As a case officer, however, I was trained to do the opposite, to listen and tread lightly as possible, to follow the traces which might lead us in the direction of the hidden enemy. I imagined that I could settle accounts with Muller later. Next time I saw him I would make sure to have constitutional clearance in hand, not to say the permission of the three equations, and the weird nod of the consultants when they smiled on our suggestions.

Muller introduced me to his companion, Soledad. He filled and refilled our glasses without asking. Soledad wasn't his daughter or wife, as I had assumed, but the assistant in his organisation. She hadn't appeared in the recordings, so I wasn't familiar with her background other than what she told me across the table. She was a geologist, born in Brazil in Minas Gerais, educated at a technical institute in Berlin. Soledad's eyes were as black as charcoal. Her accent was neutral and her name was Spanish more than Portuguese.

I couldn't find out more about her, however, because Muller kept asking me questions about specific pieces of electrical equipment he wanted to obtain. Their tolerances. Their costs. Their range of dependencies and outputs.

At first I had the impression Muller was supercilious, but he became warmer and more familiar as the minutes wore on and I passed his tests. I watched the clock out of the corner of my eye.

'Are you an engineer, Dr Muller?'

'Not exactly. But I have problems to solve which require a certain amount of engineering.'

'Why do you try to solve them in Morocco? There is not much industry here, from an international point of view. Even Egypt would be better if you want mechanical parts, electrical components, and such. They have developed a very good industrial base.'

'I am starting to ask myself this very question, Enver.'

I calculated that I had twenty minutes to get out of the Green Dolphin. That left no more than an hour to find a good location. The graveyard was a possibility. Otherwise, an abandoned mine, somewhere the earth might lie undisturbed. In a pinch, a building site where the foundations had been poured. I couldn't delay.

At the same time, I wanted to put something more in my report than casual conversation. I wanted to understand his motivations, not merely in my role as a case officer but as a human being who had lost something.

'Is there something you're looking for in Morocco? Is it something here I can help you to find? I would be only too happy to put my contacts at your disposal.'

Muller's expression tightened. He poured the remainder of the bottle into my glass. He ran his fingers along the side of the table, as if he were deciding to wager a sum of money. 'You are a very curious man, Enver.'

'I only want to see if there is any business we can do together.'

Muller sat back in his chair. He showed the waiter the empty bottle, beckoned for another. I thought about the fact that in an hour I would be as good as dead. I would be better than dead.

'Maybe, in the first place, I am looking for certain minerals. There are deposits in this country which are unique in terms of their density. Let us say they are deep in the Atlas Mountains. There are regions which are difficult to enter, where the tribesmen have rifles. And there are stories about such places which we don't have to believe but which frighten the local businessmen away. Let us say, in the second place, that I am looking for people. I want the right individuals for certain opportunities. And they must be people who can fit in, like you.'

I saw the clock on the wall. I was out of time. I let my hand flick out and push over the bottle. It spilled on the table and the three of us got up from our chairs. I pointed to the clock.

'I am sorry twice over. Unfortunately, I have to go. It is unavoidable, but if you will give me some way to reach you? I will think about your problem. In any case, I will leave you the private bag number for my company.' I wrote on a serviette the address of a box in Tangiers which was monitored by the Agency. 'It has been a pleasure. I believe we will meet each other again, even if it is not for professional reasons. Marrakech is not a big town.'

'So late at night? To have an urgent appointment? I believe you have pumped us for information and now you abandon us.' Muller smiled. He stepped back and mopped the wine from his trousers. He didn't seem to notice that I was carrying a spade. 'Well, I cannot ask to detain you. If you ever need to find me, in turn, you can leave a message at the counter.'

The waiter arrived with clean towels and a bucket of water but I didn't wait. I was surprised to find myself alive and unharmed outside the Green Dolphin, closing the door behind me.

I saw nobody on the streets except a military policeman,

leaning on his rifle, guarding an intersection through which no cars came. He wanted to see my papers before he let me through. In the apartment buildings, the only lights were in stairwells and forlorn rooms where a pilgrim was at his devotions. The private houses were dark in their ranks. High in the sky was a moon that grew larger as I left the centre of town. There were no passersby, only dogs baying in backyards.

I ran faster, hardly pausing to catch my breath, avoiding any sign of activity. I had an idea where to go and it led me to a lane in which there was a sentry's hut at the entrance to the Protestant cemetery. The graves, indistinct in the darkness, were surrounded by flowerbeds and a low masonry wall. They were breathing slowly in the ground.

Nothing to fear. I told myself that the dead of any one period, from a case officer's point of view, were only waiting for their resurrection in the time before. To others, far off in the restricted centuries where the Agency had never managed to penetrate, I had already joined the endless numbers of the dead, dissipated to the last atom.

I paused at the back of the guardhouse. Through the half-open door could be seen a man in a long robe, as fat as a barrel, hardly breathing in his sleep as he lay stretched on a bare mattress, his torso covered by a checked black-and-white scarf. A cat lay asleep in the basket at his feet.

Time was short. I took the blue tablet, unlatched the gate, then closed it behind me. The freshest soil was at the far end. I set my tools down and began to dig as quietly as I could.

It was hard work. The ground was full of pebbles and the heavy lacework of roots. After a few minutes, the sweat ran into my eyes. I loosened my collar and redoubled my efforts. My strength was slackening. I could feel the blueness of the pill starting to run in my veins.

It seemed like an eternity before I had excavated a section deep enough for a single person. I settled myself inside, arranging the spade beside me, pulling tarpaulin over my legs. My breathing was beginning to halt. Every gasp of oxygen slowed down in my breathing pipe as I pulled the ground down upon myself. The clods mounted up. The sky was gone, and then any suggestion of light.

I scrabbled at the sides of the grave, hoping to conceal myself in my cool green burrow. I hadn't yet given a thought to my companions in the ground, the lengths of bone and lingering flesh around me, but soon the reek filled my mouth and my nose and the entire inside of my skull. Strange smoke. Cannibal smoke.

I didn't have much time to worry about it. My feet were cold and trembling, the heels caught in an uncomfortable position. The soil was like quicksand around me. I couldn't move my arms or bend my fingers. My legs turned to stone. I couldn't move my chest. I was suffocating under the ground. My eyes trembled. The pill hadn't saved my life.

Between one beat and the next, my heart ceased to beat. The last thing I remembered was the soft footing of the cat above me, searching for a way into my tomb. Then I fell deep into death.

I expected to spend a maximum of twenty-four hours in the graveyard. Agency policy is to retrieve a case officer or an exposed resident within the calendar day, subject to the need for energy conservation. The three equations of historical statistics would be consulted, the three terrible sisters who governed the past of humanity. At the directions of the equations, the planning commission would dispatch a team to retrieve and resuscitate the hibernating body. It was a matter of morale. No body was left in the field for more than a day. But I lay uneasy in the grave.

Underground, I dreamt of the consultants. Their cold brass heads were bent over me. They were monitoring my pulse and temperature, mazes of electronic light forming and reforming in their eyes. One came very close so that I could feel the whirring of his fan. He was as hot as a toaster. With cruel fingers, he inserted a wire into one of my ears and coaxed it through to the other side so he could pull it out again, finding a path through my head.

At the motion, I awoke to find myself held up to blazing sunshine. I couldn't see anything but the blankness of this golden light. Something was spraying violently into my face. I raised my arms to protect my eyes while the stinging liquid went into my lungs. I was held from behind through a spell of coughing. It wasn't a harsh embrace. Eventually the spray went off and I stopped coughing.

When my eyes adjusted, I found three shapes around me in a semi-circle. Each was surrounded by a capsule of blue light.

One stepped forward and wrapped a padded silver towel around my body. He was wearing a suit like an astronaut's, a gold-tinted bubble over his head. His face was visible through the visor, a bald man with eyes as big as saucers, his skin stained as beautifully dark as cedar. He was staring at me. I stared back.

'I thought you would never come.'

'We never did. Ah, we never did.'

Tears were streaming down my face. They got thicker and thicker. They made me ashamed. I put my hand on his suit, balancing on my feet without confidence, and saw that there were many thousands of lights in the sky. The ground around us was bare and burned in every direction. There were no buildings.

The man put the arm of his suit around me. The logo of the Agency was printed on his chest. I couldn't have been more relieved to see a dark face and feel that I had returned to the embrace of civilisation.

'How long do you think you were out, Agent Eleven?'

'I had dreams.' I hadn't completely woken up. The lights in the sky were as bright as phosphorous. 'I don't know. I had a thousand years of dreams when I was in there.'

I began to cry out loud. The man put his other arm around me.

'You've been asleep, in that grave, for a hundred thousand years.'

Jupiter

10^5

Manfred, who had embraced me on the surface, was in charge of the expedition. He brought me into their vehicle.

'You show no signs of reflection sickness, Agent Eleven.' He showed me my countenance in a round mirror with a brass rim, an item so familiar I almost smiled. 'So you can tell your story in peace. In my experience, it's better to get it down before the impressions fade.'

I stretched out my arms on the bench. 'I'm a case officer. I am not trained to tell my story. On the contrary, my standing instruction is to reserve any information connected to my assignment.'

Manfred shrugged. He put his mirror away. 'We work for the same organisation. You are a thousand centuries out of your way. The rules don't apply. Besides, somebody has gone to great lengths to put you here. Or that's how it looks.'

'You're saying I was deliberately left to moulder in that grave?'

The rest of the team was bringing their equipment onboard. Manfred didn't immediately react to my question. Instead he said, 'In my experience, everybody wants to tell his story. Everybody, in the end, wants his story to be told.'

In the end, I told it. I told Manfred about Shanumi Six and Keswyn Muller. Soledad in the Green Dolphin. The blue pill and the black pill. The elusiveness of the main enemy who had never been rightly identified. The disturbance at the Agency, just as we'd arrived in Marrakech, which had stranded us in thin air. I even told Manfred about the librarians at the bottom of the archive of the past and the future, their bronze shoulders touching in the near darkness, who whispered to each other in unknown algorithms.

Why did I talk? I was a case officer but I was also a human being. I was a hundred thousand years from my point of origin. I was a hundred minutes out of the grave, my skin as scaly as a lizard. I had been brought back into the world and I had an overwhelming desire to talk about what I had seen. So I kept speaking while the rover ran high over the rough ground, pitted with the remains of farm dams and windmills, suspension bridges gleaming amongst their broken cables over dry riverbeds, motorways covered with silt and broken branches.

After I stopped from exhaustion, Manfred reached under the bench and found me a pair of binoculars. The sun was going down across the mountains, exiting a cloudless evening. The binoculars brought me to a corner near the moon where the constellations were obscured by a myriad points of light. Shooting stars ran in a river to the horizon. I drew a breath, tried to understand what I was seeing.

'It's quite a show. The last days of earth. In this universe at any rate.'

I said, 'I didn't come out of the grave to listen to riddles, Manfred.'

'This is the first act of a new planetary bombardment, Enver. Rocks originating in the Kuiper Belt are descending to the surface. By the time the bombardment ceases the earth will be stripped of her crust. Lava on the surface. A Venus-like atmosphere for the first time in four billion years. Neither photosynthesis nor respiration.'

I couldn't have described my feelings to hear Manfred's confession if I had spent a lifetime on the virtual stage. I could hardly breathe, lying back on the bench until I was more in control of myself. 'Everything we fought for, day to day, everything contained in the library of the past and the future, was about eliminating threats to our way of life. How could this happen?'

'We're not prophets, Enver. Our ability to decipher the predictions is as limited today as it was in your time. You know why that is, the mathematics of permutations and combinations. The only way we could ever solve it would be to embrace the horror of calculating across many separate universes and splitting ourselves into many contradictory pieces. And that is contrary to our fundamental assumption.'

I must have done something to express my impatience at having the basic dogma explained to my face that caused Manfred to stop. He looked out at the surface, considering something as the rover ran along a collapsed road, the rounded husk of a solar power station passing on the right.

He went on after a minute, taking a different tack. 'Then there's the question of relative causes. Out in the Kuiper Belt, it doesn't take much to send a cascade of rocks in one direction or another.'

'So you believe this is a coincidence? First a supernova. Then, a fraction of an instant later in cosmic terms, a planetary bombardment. You would be more likely to win the continental lottery a hundred times in a row.'

Manfred flipped a series of switches on the side of the rover and, along with the two members of his team, started to remove his gloves and overalls. 'Maybe a conspiracy against the earth exists. But I cannot prove it, my friend. I cannot put a name and a face to whatever is stirring amongst the rocks and stones of the Kuiper Belt, let alone what power could alter the heart of a star. In your time, the Agency suspected that there were too many coincidences against us. But they were unable to prove the existence of the main enemy. More than that, I do not wish to say at present.'

The rover entered a tunnel. Bars of light passed above us, decelerating as we descended into the station.

In the bay there were no other vehicles. A tracked machine descended from a pulley in the roof and approached. It assessed the outside of the rover, a single black eye turning to consider the damage. Its probes and antennae looked as finely worked as those of an insect.

Everybody showered in a long red room on the side of the bay. I was uncomfortable for a minute and then forgot myself in the ecstasy of very hot water and steam. The others took their leave. Manfred waited and found me a gown. He put his arm around my shoulders for a minute.

'I am curious, Eleven. Before the Morocco expedition, how much did you know about your future Six?'

'I knew Shanumi's reputation as a case officer, which was why I was glad we were assigned to each other.'

'Her reputation?'

I hesitated, noticing myself in the mirror set above the sink, a man who had been left to moulder. My spider sense was tingling. 'Not just the highlights, I mean. Not just the glory, not just the courage of a true daughter of the continent. She had a very refined side. She was on good terms, for example, with the painters and composers of the Edo period in Japan.'

'You call it glory. Birmingham, Alabama, with Martin Luther King.' Manfred counted on his fingers. 'Leningrad. Stalingrad. Birkenau. The Second Congolese War. Negative highlights. Negative infinities. Some might say that your Six had an affinity for terror.'

I didn't reply at once to Manfred's accusation. For it came to me that I was so far from home, my replies could be deemed to have archeological significance. I should watch my words, especially when it came to Shanumi Six. I knew there was something in the case I didn't comprehend.

Manfred led me to an elevator. It descended into an endless shaft, down and farther down into the earth. I lost track of how long it took amidst the acceleration. Information flickered on the walls.

I turned to my companion. 'If you're asking me to interpret for Shanumi Six, I can only do so to a limited degree.'

'I'm listening.'

'She admired periods of great imagination and productivity. They just happened to go together with social upheaval, what you mean by terror. She liked to quote from somewhere, about a peaceful country like Switzerland taking five hundred years to invent the cuckoo clock.'

For the moment Manfred seemed to be satisfied with my answer. At any rate, the doors opened, releasing us into the depths of the planet. To my surprise our destination was as light as a starship: greenhouses in huge globes and bronze refrigeration chambers connected by winding walkways which disappeared into space. The air was crisp. There were no machines, no computer consultants in sight.

Manfred brought me to a suite of rooms adjoining the central corridor. In the first room was a table with a chessboard, the spectral pieces arranged in midgame three inches in the air. No chairs or sign of an opponent.

Floating along the high wall were shelves housing my host's collection of objects. He left me to examine them for a few minutes. There was no evident rhyme or reason behind the selection: soapstone statues of gods and goddesses on lily pads sat next to black-ink vases with pictures of garlanded bulls on their sides and amber drops containing prehistoric insects. Then there was a series of sea shells mounted under a lens. I thought of the ocean starting to boil and forced myself to remember days on the seaside with my father, hot sand and salty water.

In the next room there were ornate couches on gold feet and oil paintings on the walls. I sat opposite Manfred. He brought up recordings of burned libraries and data centres. The debris of a long-ruined civilisation.

'There's the apparent reason you were buried so long. Somebody burrowed into the Agency and obliterated the filing system. They couldn't locate their own case officers and bring them back into the fold. And it was your friend, Keswyn Muller, that minor figure from a discredited continent, who seems to have been the guilty party. Who happens to have been the target of your first approach in the field.' Manfred sat back and examined me, his face flickering as the causeless images of death and destruction continued in the air between us. 'I would like to know your assessment of that constellation of facts, my friend. One case officer to another.'

I said, 'I have no assessment. I am too implicated in the facts to see them objectively.'

'You are implicated, Eleven. Somebody sent you out of the way and, by gum, we are going to put you right back in the middle of it and you are going to evaluate the situation like a good case officer.'

The images faded in the space between us.

'Do you plan to send me back a thousand centuries? That would cost more than a national energy budget.'

'We have a power station on Jupiter. I am familiar with your personnel file, which happens to have been preserved. I hope you can conquer your fear of heights.'

My hours in Marrakech, not to say the days which followed my time with Manfred, ran so hot with the fever of conspiracy and intrigue that I remember the four days at the bottom of the shaft as a holiday.

I was left to myself. The members of the archeological team were busy on the surface, returning only to log their finds and replenish their supplies. I was never invited to join them at a meal, although occasionally Manfred would come down and share a bowl of blue-green coffee, looking into the algal grounds in the bottom of his cup as if they had some secret to reveal to a dedicated case officer. He didn't tell me anything more about himself or his collaborators, but on more than one occasion he inquired further into the phenomenon of Shanumi Six.

'You trained with her for three months? You didn't fall in love with her. I find it difficult to understand.'

When Manfred talked, he cupped a hand over his mouth, picking meditatively at his moustache. It made me think he was deciding how much it was advisable to reveal. He had been in charge of the situation since my arrival, the consummate agent.

'What's difficult about it? One case officer learning the tricks of a trade from another, as you would say.'

'No, it's interesting. It's interesting to me. In our context, very few deaths mean there are very few births on the other end. An education is a different process. No enemies and friends. No teachers and pupils in a neurochemical tank. No affairs of the passions.'

I cautioned myself, not for the first time, that a good case officer let the other person pour out the contents of his heart. So I waited for Manfred.

Eventually, he continued. 'We do not live one on top of the other any more. On the contrary. No cities. No companies. No parliaments. We are strung out across the solar system. The earth is no longer the focus of our activity as a species. Nor do we focus on one another as you did. For somebody to have a moon to himself is not unheard of—if that is his heart's desire.'

I said, 'It sounds like a lonely existence.'

'Well, that is all I know. I can't say if it is lonely or not. To be honest, despite this line of work, there is nothing less interesting than the human mind in all its glory.'

It was as close to an explanation that Manfred gave as to why we would never be friendly with each other. I had arrived in a century without the burden of friendship, and there were advantages. It meant there were no consultants to placate. No charts in probability script to decipher. No enemies and no friends. Only the silence to welcome me when I woke up and the even sunshine spreading throughout the facility from no discernible source.

In the meantime, I set about recovering my strength. I swam in the Olympic-sized pool in a deserted gymnasium, one lap after another to the point of exhaustion. Chlorine and the taste of chalk in the recycled air. From the full-length mirrors on the gym walls, my reflection gazed reassuringly into my eyes. I was skin and bones, but I wasn't a skeleton.

I was delighted to be alive again. At the same time, I yearned to be out on the surface and see the sky, whatever it contained. I sat in the steam room for hours, pouring water on the charcoal brazier, until my skin stung with the heat. The reek of the graveyard which had lodged in me vanished, although it came back sooner or later.

On the launch pad, noticing my anxiety and, I assume, wanting to distract me, Manfred returned to the technical aspects of our journey.

'We need a significant chunk of hydrogen gas to allow you to return.'

'How big are we talking?'

'Jupiter will not be quite the same. Time displacement, as you know, is the most expensive activity in the history of economic investment. It has almost denuded the solar system.'

The rockets underneath us began to whine. We kept a moment of silence and then strapped in. I looked at myself in the mirror Manfred provided and repeated the words of the Founder under my breath, old-fashioned precautions.

I examined the inside of the shuttle. Benches were arranged along its length. Gauges and terminals were built into the bulkhead, although there was no cockpit. No overhead lights, only a red pulse running in a spiral from the floor to the ceiling. It wasn't the technology of the Interplanetary Service.

'Who are you, Manfred?'

'You know my name and class. I see no need to complicate your life and my life further by going into explanations.'

'Who are you really, though? I'm not asking for prohibited knowledge. But I would like to have an idea about the meaning of all this. Are you even human?'

My companion didn't reply. He looked impatient, as I might have been had the roles been reversed. The windows of the shuttle went dark as steam rolled up the fuselage. We were off the ground without knowing it, steadying to an angle in mid-air.

In the darkened cabin, I thought that Manfred's eyes were glowing. I considered the possibility that my revival had been staged and that I was in the hands of the main enemy. That they'd pretended to come out of the far future, pretended to be in the employment of the Agency. That I couldn't trust my eyes. That Manfred, whoever he was, had tricked me into revealing my secrets.

By the time the windows were clear, we were ten miles up. I could see the swirls of cloud forming in the atmosphere. The mountains and the ocean were as peaceful up here as they had been a hundred thousand years ago: the stone crown of the continent encircled by mysterious green water. There was no sign of the bombardment under way. The poles were still covered with spidery fingers of ice, a marble shimmering in the middle of the cosmos that we had come across by accident. I could trust in the majesty of the scene, which could not have been staged—even if, by design, I could not understand the man who sat across from me on the top floor of the rocket.

My paranoia settled as I recalled the spirit of the doctrines which guided Manfred as much as myself. It was easy to forget how close we as a species had come to extinction. On the day of the supernova, despite the warning delivered by the wife of S Natanson, a fraction of the population had made it to the safety of the mines. Decades later, a fraction of a fraction had returned to the surface. It had been the Agency's task to ensure that the catastrophe never recurred. Never again. Never again.

Yet the earth was empty again. Manfred unbuckled and stood up straight. He stretched his arms and legs, bent down to let me out.

'We are nothing but your descendants, Eleven, acting in accordance with the doctrines of S Natanson to preserve the thread of civilisation. To prevent the abomination of a multiverse taking hold.'

I got up as well. Outside, the maintenance robots were clambering along the girders of the ship, green-and-red lights blinking on their torsos.

'That's your story?'

'I have no reason to deceive you, Sleeping Beauty. I'm no restrictionist. I believe in a free exchange of ideas between time periods, to the extent that it's possible. I brought you in.'

'I can't have been the only one to get lost.'

'There, you are correct. The lucky ones managed to come in from the cold a long time ago. Some despaired, took the black pill.'

In the year of our Lord 10^5, it still took three days to get to Jupiter. The stately red planet approached through the portholes as slowly as if we were in a ship.

Above and below us a dozen miniature rockets were firing as the shuttle changed direction. Through the porthole, we saw the sun—pale as a ghost in its corona. Galaxies surrounded us, tapestries of light in every direction. I had conquered my fear of heights, although I occasionally wanted to cry.

It took until the third day for Manfred to put his sketch of the situation in front of me. It consisted of a series of figures on the top. Along the bottom, he had printed shapes and dotted lines: possibility and probability characters. I turned it around and couldn't make sense of a single statement. My cheeks burned.

'Your story strikes me as a riddle. That interests me so much that I have portrayed it there in the form of a possibility diagram. What did you know about Marrakech?'

'Look, I wasn't a specialist by any means. I wouldn't dare to call myself a Moroccanologist. I read the case folder.'

Manfred went around closing the shutters so that we could sleep. The shuttle became an unexpectedly cosy chamber, soft green lights around the circumference. My companion rolled out the beds and put the sheets on them, running them up to the corner with a hand. He gave me the pillows from a closet behind the bulkhead and went on with his roundabout enquiry.

'Morocco was the first time you encountered the people who used to rule the earth. When you could fall into the clutches of people who enslaved people like you and me. How did your Six prepare you?'

'Shanumi watched *Gone with the Wind*, told me not to worry about people staring. She said that real actors, twentieth-century actors, were better than the greatest acting algorithms from our time, an argument that makes no sense. Also, she advised me to keep my natural skin. To stick to the itinerary in Marrakech.'

I saw Manfred was becoming impatient. He sat on the side of the bed and brought up a hologram. It had been taken through a small window and looked onto the table where I had been sitting, a hundred thousand years ago, with two companions. Despite the grainy black-and-white image, I could make out that the woman was wearing earrings.

'Did she warn you, in any way, about Keswyn Muller?'

'Obviously Muller was under observation so there was some element of suspicion. But there was nothing to suggest that he could be a danger to us, let alone to the Agency. In the recordings he was standing harmlessly in a window. I knew he had been involved with antiquities. What are you trying to get at?'

Manfred ignored my question. 'Lastly, Eleven, were you given any kind of instruction regarding Muller's companion?'

'Not that I remember. No.'

'So who wanted you out of the way? This is a riddle I cannot solve. And, like you, I have never enjoyed the existence of a riddle.'

Manfred stood up, as if I had done something to anger him, and went over to the last open porthole on the other side of the bay. The one that looked in the direction of invisible earth, back to the thousand-year dominion of the Agency, a thousand centuries in the past. The porthole that looked back to a past when there had been seven continents and seven thousand cultures. I expected Manfred to say something, to take it all in and put it in front of me, but instead he closed the final shutter.

I stretched out on the bed and thought about going to sleep.

I must have slept for twelve hours. When I woke up, Jupiter was the only thing I could see. It produced ribbons of brown-and-white gas along its breadth, and was surrounded by a bracelet of dim moons. It was immense. I couldn't look away. The red eye, a whirlpool rotating beneath our position, examined the spacecraft without pity.

Manfred was studying data on his screen.

'You should put on a suit. You can find one in the topmost locker.'

I obeyed. I had never been in vacuum, but I had been trained to use any kind of protective gear. The basic design of a spacesuit hadn't changed: atmospheric recycler and rebreather, microwave furnace, jets and tools, and the unearthly silver-white skin which spacewalkers have flaunted since the Apollo launches.

I adjusted the waist and pulled on the upper portion of the suit. It adapted to my form, the fabric sealing in front of my eyes. I checked the status of the various systems. They were in good order.

The station swam up. The central compartment was the size of an oil tanker, minute against the flaring red surface of the planet, blocks of machinery moving along the bulkhead. On the underside was the scoop. The funnel was a few hundred metres across. The metal was already glowing red in the cold above the planet.

Manfred showed me another schematic which I didn't understand. He adjusted the collar of the spacesuit for me, tapped me on the side.

'The energy required for your return is enormous. We are pushing the entire manifold of space and time back to its next most probable state. The process is so demanding that it is destabilising the chain of assets.'

'You said there was no technical problem.'

'No technical problem but something may catch fire.'

Manfred put the helmet on my head. For a moment I was inside the atmosphere of the suit, the oxygen saccharine on my tongue, the electronic display painted before my eyes in bar graphs. I wished them away.

Manfred walked around me, snapping on the various hinges, and pressing on them to make sure. Lights came on inside as it assessed the situation. Temperature. Pressure. Orientation. Gravity and mock gravity.

'Who are you really, Manfred?'

He put his hand on my back and steered me in the direction of the airlock.

'However much we reject restrictionism as an inhuman code, it suits us to limit the transfer of superfluous knowledge. Above all, mark my words, it rescues us from the burden of the infinite. The infinite is the only thing that a human being may not survive. That is what lies behind our hatred of the multiverse and repugnant causal loops.'

'I won't ask any more questions.'

'Good luck. God speed. In the best of times, in the worst of times, may the hour of your blessedness arrive.'

'And may it arrive for you also.'

He stepped back to let me enter the airlock. The alarm sounded. I went in and sealed the helmet. The identification markers came up. The bronze tint inside the visor faded, to be replaced by supernatural clarity. The gauges and indicators shrunk, removed themselves to the side. The door closed behind me.

Manfred gestured through the porthole. He connected to the suit, his voice rasping on the line.

'You can think of me, Eleven, as the last of the case officers. A loyal son of the continent. I did my duty until the end. Remember me.'

'I will.'

'When the time is right, tell my story.'

Jupiter occupied the entire horizon. I thought I was dreaming to see its breadth below me: the slow spiral of brown-red gas and a thousand shards of lightning wherever you happened to look upon the vaporous bulk of it. Everything on the surface was in slow motion—cloud or condensing rain. Silent majesty. I wanted to plummet into its great red whirlpool and vanish forever. At that moment I remembered, for some reason, that a seashell was the icon of the Interplanetary Service.

The thruster gave a final push, sending me turning head over heels until I collided with the airlock. I held on, desperately straining against my momentum which wanted to take me back out. The external door opened. I hauled myself in, and entered the station.

It was a brightly lit room in which I found myself, steel cupboards along the walls. The temperature was high. There was too much oxygen, as my instruments informed me. Rivers of sparks were flowing into the room, following the burned underside of the roof, jumping here and there through the air. Somewhere in the depths of the station heavy machinery was moving into position.

I kept my visor down, breathing inside the suit, sweating in torrents, and ran into the corridor. The temperature got hotter as I came nearer to the hub. The lights began to go out, faltering in the glow of the sparks. The map directed me to a room on the right, crammed to the top with cabling, and through a hall occupied by holographic statues of men and women, phosphorescent green and twenty foot tall.

The next room I went into was filled with drones. They were held in racks, insect eyes gleaming ever so slightly as I went by. Flame was working at them from above, causing their casings to melt. They didn't seem to notice the situation. I cursed them. At the same time, I saw the fire reach down and catch hold of my suit. I watched without believing my eyes as the torso began to scorch. A haze of sparks rose around my head. No pain at first, but I knew that my skin was burning underneath the suit.

I stripped, beating down the fire as best I could. I kept the helmet on, trying to follow the map to the centre. After a minute it brought me to a long hallway, very dark and very hot, sheets of purple flame forming above me. There was no sign of whether the other end was passable. The viperish crackle of the fire came from every direction.

I thought about going to sleep right there and then, removing the helmet, putting my head down on the grill, and letting the wound burn me into unconsciousness. Instead, I found myself running through the curtain of fire, burning my hands and shoulders. Someone nearby was screaming.

At the end of the corridor, a pair of doors opened at my approach. It let me into a vast chamber. Drones were crawling along the walls, trying to control the fire. Some sprayed foam, while others on the ceiling were removing and extinguishing burning panels. One of them dropped in front of me. It had a long neck on top of its smouldering body and many eyes arranged around its head.

'You have been severely injured. Allow me to remove your helmet.'

I took off the helmet myself and dropped it on the floor, putting my hand on the drone to support myself. I couldn't feel my arms. The ash was bitter inside my mouth.

The drone opened its side and produced a tray holding a capsule and injector.

'I would now like to administer a sedative and an antibiotic to the exposed area. If you would record your consent, we can proceed directly to treatment.'

I said, 'If you delay me, nothing will be saved. Everything—everything—will be lost.'

The drone whirred and turned its head to the side, one eye after the other coming into focus. 'In that case, will you kindly step this way?'

I couldn't stand upright. 'Help me get there.'

Another drone entered the room and stopped at my side. Between the two of them they managed to take me to the other side of the hall. The roof rose into a tower, thousands of feet tall, where I could see drones engulfed by the acrid purple fire. Many were starting to lose their footing in the heat. Several husks were already burning beneath them on the floor. Smoke was rising from underneath our feet.

On the side of the chamber was the arch. The aperture was shimmering, the famous horseshoe which had been our symbol across a thousand years. The drones brought me up the steps to the railing. I managed to stand on my own feet. Despite my burning skin, I felt that flicker of excitement every traveller lives for.

To my surprise, a number of drones had arranged themselves in a column in front of the arch. I walked through them, wondering what they were doing. They raised their heads at the same time, the same turquoise gleam running through their many eyes.

My life, I thought, had been a dream intent on bringing me to this point.

'We wish you good fortune, Agent Eleven, on your mission. And God speed on your way.'

'Thank you. Thank you for your valuable assistance.'

Above us the roof was melting, caving inwards. A tide of flame swept through the chamber, burning the oxygen out of the air. The remaining machines had given up the fight and were allowing themselves to fall to the floor. They seemed to be watching me as I hesitated.

Sections of girders and massive hunks of iron plummeted from above, falling under artificial gravity. In ninety seconds the surface of the station would disintegrate and the vacuum would come rushing in.

I prepared to hold my breath. I must have lost consciousness because when I opened my eyes again I was on the floor of a vast hall, rolled into a ball. I was listening to somebody screaming with all their might. I passed out again.

The sensations dear to my heart: the scent of cinnamon and hospital custard. The tang of safe tobacco. I was home in a cocoon, the blanket close around my shoulders. I considered a trip to the Mozambique islands, finding a current in the warm water to take me far into the distance. I would take my father and sister along.

I smiled and turned to the side when I realised that my hands were tied to the bed. I sat up, trying to pull them through the knots which got tighter, the cord cutting into my wrist. When I gave up and relaxed my arms, it also relaxed. After a minute, it returned to its original length.

I took stock of the surroundings, telling myself not to panic, although I was already hot from fear. I was in a narrow hospital room. It was empty apart from the bed and the monitor, a door with a panel of frosted glass set into the top. My head was fully bandaged.

On the far side of the room was an unbarred window. I was on the fiftieth or sixtieth floor, looking onto Lagos Memorial Plaza. Mile-high office buildings alternated with row houses and automatic brothels, the pattern of development in the centre of Johannesburg after the hard years in the mines. Advertising balloons moved between the buildings to announce men's colognes and high-heeled shoes, skin-darkening creams, platinum jewellery, and valet robots in seersucker suits. I thought I could make out, in the distance, the solar rays on the great monument to the Day of the Dead. And yet there was something unfamiliar to me in the panorama.

The hospital bed observed my activity: 'Now that the risk of necrosis has passed, it was decided to allow you to wake up.' It must have seen something underneath the bandages. 'Try not to scratch anywhere. I will prescribe something for the discomfort, emotional as well as physical.'

'I'm chained here.'

The bed was even-tempered. 'Enver Eleven, you are detained under the provisions of the Fourteenth Statute concerning treason. Do not be unduly distressed. Your constitutional rights will be respected to the degree that it is humanly possible.'

Saying this, the bed released a blue-green gas into my face which lowered me rapidly back into sleep. When I woke again I knew that I had been sedated. I couldn't stop laughing from the giddiness. I woke and slept, woke and slept, adrift on an ocean of wild joy and silent suspicion. Once a day the medical cart entered to change my bandages and paint my face with new skin. It gave me the feeling of being rubbed with electricity.

I was fed with tubes and cleaned with tubes. Blood was taken, more tiny glass ampoules which were then filed on a rack in the refrigerator.

I watched the tubes accumulate from the bed, trying to ignore the tingling in my cheeks and the fear that I had been replaced body and soul. The heavy sedation did its work, lifting my spirits—although I knew my state of mind was artificial and that a charge of treason stood over my head.

The sounds of truck and airplanes drew my attention to the outside world: infinite Johannesburg. I remembered its glitter through the haze of the sedative gas. Its automated merchant banks and holographic channels starring digital actors and albinos. Its crowds into which, already a spy as a child, I had loved to disappear as if into a gleaming black flood that would bear me away with it. Its prophets of truest optimism and pessimism. Its fortune-tellers in white robes who gleaned the future in a drained cup of hibiscus tea, seeing no sign of a cloud on the horizon. Dressed from head to toe in hair, its Yoruba preachers on the other hand who prophesied a second supernova.

I could tell them they would get what they wanted in the end: a sky full of fatal stars.

My condition deteriorated each time the bed sprayed gas into my face. I was alternately sure that I had fallen into the hands of the main enemy and that the Agency had put me on trial.

I found myself trying to carry out a conversation with the cart, summoning it to ask trivial questions while my mind wandered through the centuries. I reached to my face when the bandages came off and found tears I didn't remember shedding. I cried and laughed, argued, and cried again. In short, I was losing my mind.

When a man came into the room, I hardly believed in his existence.

'Do you even know what day of the week it is, Agent Eleven?'

I thought for a minute, sitting up in a corner of the bed, and feeling as if he were shining a torchlight into my face. I wasn't used to the fierceness of the human gaze. The bed and the medical cart were much more neutral; they expected less in the way of response.

'It must have been three months since Marrakech.' I was not familiar with the sound of my own voice either. 'Three months at least, I'd say.'

'You've been here a fortnight. One Friday to the next. Today is Friday again.'

I said, 'That's impossible.'

The man came to the side of the bed. He had a face like an axe. He was joined by a young woman.

'Lucan Thirteen. This is Deputy Inspector Akiko Thirteen. I have asked her to join us for the sake of legal validity. We work for Internal Section.'

'You're Agency? Officially Agency?'

'Effectively so. A sealed organisation within the organisation, principle of tradecraft.' Lucan gave me a prime number which I knew from training, proof of his good standing in the halls of the Agency, and took out a small mirror in which I could examine my reflection. Despite the gesture of respect, he seemed angry with me, and looked tired enough to fall over. 'As for the impossible, we deal with the impossible each and every day. We have been called in to deal with a situation in which a senior agent has been lost in the field.'

The hold of the sedation gas made it difficult to express anger but I still had logic at my disposal. 'Just to remind you that you lost two agents. You left me out there in the cold. I was burned to the bone. Now you have me in custody on a treason charge, as my bed informs me. I must say that something is askew.'

Lucan went on with his prepared statement. 'As a matter of protocol, Agent Eleven, I would like to prepare the room for legal validity. At this time, for fear of mental degradation, I am not planning to use any form of neural coercion to ensure your compliance.'

'Go ahead. Go ahead. I am looking forward to having my story on record. Somebody is going to pay.'

I tried to make myself comfortable despite the restraints on my arms. It was starting to rain outside. The day was overcast, banks of cloud pressing in for miles. Lucan brought in two chairs from the corridor and placed them at the foot of the bed. He smiled, for the first time, although it was intended for the deputy inspector.

The young woman, Akiko, produced a short tripod from her briefcase. She turned a dial on the tripod, activating its large red eye which scrutinised the room. I knew something was wrong as soon as she began to speak. There was a vibration in her voice which didn't make sense, made my whiskers tremble.

And yet she was perfectly professional, not even unfriendly. 'I'll let this run through. I am aware that field agents like yourself have little patience for such niceties. But, as we say, the constitution protects every legal person on the continent, rich or poor, man and machine alike. Albino and black man.'

'Albino and black man.'

Were the ritual words even true? Did we mean them?

They were second nature when you repeated them to a tripod at every significant juncture of your life, as I had done when entering the Agency and again when, to my surprise, I successfully completed the psychological battery.

For the first time, I questioned whether an albino, hated and feared on account of her pelt and lidless eyes, could expect equal justice. We simply used their names to prove the worth of our constitution. I couldn't say why Lucan and Akiko's arrival had brought such ugly thoughts into my mind. Maybe it was simply that I had been around albinos and drunk beer with them like ordinary human beings.

At the end of its cycle, the tripod flashed and went silent, ready to listen. My guests sat down. Akiko looked up and down from her screen while Lucan began.

'Inform us, from your perspective, about the events in Marrakech and thereafter.'

'At what level of detail? Do you want the facts? Do you want my suspicions on record?'

Lucan put his hands on the railing of the bed. His eyes were flat and blue, splinters of a broken bottle. 'Everything. We have suffered the most serious reversal in the Agency's recorded history, past and future. Our time capsules were nullified by Dr Muller, whom you were supposed to have under observation. We lost Shanumi Six, one of the foremost agents of her time or any time. We thought we lost you until someone close to the restricted centuries sent you home. So, anything and everything you remember.'

Lucan allowed me to go straight through, from Morocco to the end of time. He and Akiko Thirteen were polite, listened without comment to what I said about Manfred, and the drones on Jupiter Station, what I recalled about the warehouses, the vans of soldiers, the boys in white caps carrying flasks of tea along the road, the rolls of carpet stacked in the back of the shops, and the jeweller at his desk who kept an eye on my comings and goings. I explained about the hotel boy who had helped me get hold of a spade, the narrow road which led to the Protestant graveyard, the cat which had been trying to find a way down when I lost consciousness. I tried to conjure the broken landscape under bombardment, the team of archeologists who'd pulled me out of the ground. I didn't hold back anything.

Despite my intuitions, I didn't try to be a case officer because I was too powerless in that situation. I thought it was my strange destiny to go from one century to the next and tell stories.

When I was finished, Lucan Thirteen stood at the window, reviewing the material as lightning crackled and smoked on the horizon. He consulted with Akiko in the doorway. I could hear that they were arguing, although I couldn't tell about what. Then Lucan came back in and finalised the recording on the tripod. He didn't offer to show me the results.

Nevertheless, I was relieved to have told my story. I had done my duty to Shanumi Six and to Manfred. I had told their stories as best as I was able.

Lucan put his hand on my shoulder. 'I can tell you, informally, that you are unlikely to face a counter-intelligence investigation. According to the consultants, who have reviewed your tripodal testimony, you believe that you are telling the truth. Of course, you could be programmed to believe that. Plus, there are grave questions to be considered: why did the beacon break down? How did the events on the recording and the actual mission come to differ? Why did it happen at almost the same time as the intrusion into the library of the past and the future? The consultants will not be satisfied until they have obtained answers.'

'And until then?'

'Until then, how shall we put it, you are a member of our penal battalion, if you remember your twentieth-century history.'

I knew my history: the penal battalions had been placed in the front lines of the Red Army. If they retreated an inch they were cut down with machine guns by their own side.

It took another hour to obtain judicial authorisation to release me from the bed. In the same minute the bracelet on my wrist parted. I tested my arm, unable to believe that I could move it. I stood up and almost fell over. My legs buckled under me. Stars floated in front of my eyes. Akiko helped me back onto the bed. I didn't want her to touch me and yet I wanted her to touch me.

I asked, 'Did I do anything to deserve this?'

Lucan ran his hand along my neck, up to my head, as if he were taking a firm hold of me. 'Muller used a particular eight-hundred-digit prime number to enter our system at a high level. The factors of that number would take longer than the lifetime of the universe to calculate. It was known only to the members of the Morocco group. Therefore, you or Shanumi Six. Take your pick. And be thankful I haven't given permission for the consultants to use neural compulsion. Yet.'

'But if you'd used it already, I wouldn't necessarily know.'

'That is also correct.'

It seemed like another kind of dream to be walking on a street, free of the hospital. The buildings extended to the horizon. Automatic trucks and trolleys rolled past, almost without a sound, while holograms on the station plaza published visions of space stations and supermodels, Antarctic holidays, hair extensions, kora concerts.

I couldn't move an inch without a machine befriending me by name, congratulating me on my return, asking after my health, and offering me vouchers and discounts on colonial furniture, exciting opportunities, adventures in the new settlements for loyal sons of the continent, and other glimpses of happiness. They didn't accost Lucan.

'They don't notice you,' I said to him.

'Internal Section has police privileges. We have freedom from commerce. Strictly no solicitation.'

On the road I could feel life around me, living faces which were going to work and coming home, people of my own century who were on their way to meet friends and robots, making plans and breaking them on their gold-panelled telephones.

Around me, not so far from Rosebank, were the individuals I cared about, my sister and brothers and my friends from before the Agency. In theory, I could have contacted them, talked about weather or soccer, listened to their voices, seen their familiar expressions in the air. They didn't know that I had been gone, had laid in a grave until the verge of the restricted era, and had been burned nearly to the bone. In practice, though, I was in the custody of Internal Section and they controlled my rights of connection.

'Anything you need?'

Lucan pointed at a shopping arcade. Hundreds of shops, outlined with lights and inhabited by holograms, went from ground level up into the sky. You could see assistants moving inside them. One of the sales machines, unoccupied for the moment, was staring out in our direction. Its boredom and longing were disconcertingly human. I thought about asking to buy a cup of espresso, pitch-black as a supermodel. Then I shook my head.

'You're taking me to another prison?'

Lucan put his hand on my elbow. 'Until this matter is resolved, you can't speak to anyone, apart from atomic family, and obviously even that under supervision. But I'd like you to see your home and family.'

I travelled light. It was a side-effect of the profession. Besides, I didn't want to take Lucan to my dreary room in the basement, between a robot-operated launderette and a dim sum cafeteria. I was sure they had already been through my possessions. Every particle, every message and transaction originating from my name, would have been scanned into the archive.

'Are you offering to let me see my father?'

'He's your last remaining relative, isn't he? Didn't you lose your sister last year?'

Lucan summoned an automatic limousine, long, black, and gleaming like the ZiLs you might have seen at the Kremlin. In the back it had two rows of facing leather benches.

I sat down behind the tinted windows. Lucan sat opposite me and placed his hands on the roof, just for a moment, as if to test its strength. I saw he had on a wedding ring. Akiko was in the very back, hunched over her screen, the top of her head visible above the seat. I couldn't tell who these people were, but I knew they wanted something from me and that what they wanted was impermissible.

The car nosed into the road and sped into the left lane when there was an opening. The skyscrapers gave way to Chinatown, red lanterns outside the restaurants, the fireworks bazaar, and fish markets with their growth tanks open on the street, their unmistakeable smell of catfish and wet paper.

Then Little Lagos, witchcraft salons and wig factories, followed by train stations and warehouses, machine works, schoolyards, and apartment blocks. Recycling plants, connected by webs of super-cooled wire, set one next to the other.

Beyond were the camps for refugees from the drowned continents, laundry hung on the cement walls. They were supposed to be superstitious about robots, despite the best efforts of the government. They spoke in a language of their own, which they believed was unintelligible to machinery and machine translation. They gambled, fought, made useless political protests on the broadcast channels. Brought up their pale children to be pickpockets and hologram actors.

Twenty miles out, the first stretch of countryside became visible: farmland subtended by irrigation pipes, solar collectors dreaming in the sunshine, and dams filled to the brim with sparkling green water. Starlings and sandpipers, regiments of sacred ibis patrolling the embankment, stabbing the ground here and there. Unattended tractors moved on the land. Not a person to be seen. I remembered it was late spring. Other people, in other lives, on other timelines, were preparing for the holidays, packing for their beach houses.

Lucan darkened the windows. 'We have special requirements, Agent Eleven. These limousines provide a higher level of safety. Underneath it all I am the same as you, a humble case officer.'

'I don't know what it means to say we are the same.'

He changed the subject. 'If it were up to me, I would prefer to drive myself. That's what I do on holiday, drive to and from the coast, eight hours each way. By myself on the open road. In my opinion, we've handed too much of our lives to machines.'

Something in Lucan's voice distressed me. I had tears in my eyes again. Maybe the effects of the sedation had worn off and I was working through the horrors of the past fortnight.

'What do you think I care? I was in a graveyard for centuries. No matter how much I brush, I can't get the taste out of my mouth.'

Lucan put his hands on his thighs and sat up. 'Let's get this over and done with. This is your father's most recent place of residence, I believe. The Abacha Reef Home for loyal sons and daughters of the continent. Akiko, you stay behind and plan for Enver's training cycle.'

In the course of an entire life, my father had slept alone for a grand total of eleven nights. As a young man, he had been sent away to technical school in the mountains. The teachers indulged his passion for tinkering, allowing him free licence with the woodworking and electronics carts.

During his bachelor years, he'd resided in a barracks for construction specialists, building silos and rocket pads for the Interplanetary Service. He met my mother on a very hot spring evening at a get-together for young Anglophiles and others nostalgic for the old world who were bringing back the game of bridge, scones and cream, bowls tournaments, and Edwardian architecture—although they conveniently forgot what would have happened to them there.

My father and mother were married inside of a month, never separated for a night. They rented a corner apartment on the seventieth floor of a building adjacent to the river, near an old observatory, where, with the appropriate licenses, they were allowed to raise children.

The place had rows of windows on two sides. I had many memories of looking out over the Service gantries and launch pads, watching the thin rockets go silently into the sky, one after the other at the peak times, each standing on a pillar of white smoke. They reached a certain height, balanced there for half a minute, then shot upwards and disappeared.

When my mother died unexpectedly, my sister and I were away from home. My father closed the shutters so that there was no difference between day and night. He refused any attempt at communication. If we tried to visit he fenced with us over the intercom. When the police forced their way into the apartment, he met them with a barrage of constitutional objections, filed with the automatic court by a judicial consultant, which turned out to be nothing more than a server in his shoe cupboard. He was put in a trap but he made a trap for the rest of the world.

Nobody could hold out forever. I was the one who finally came to witness his apprehension and sign the papers. After he had been sedated, a parade of carts arrived to disassemble his possessions and transfer them to storage. My father's inventions, complete and incomplete, unpatented, had gone along with the silverware and the bedding.

The machines had made their return. In recent years, my father had been housed in a modest facility for the aged, some distance from the city and on the other side of Nujoma Location, where I had visited him the day before my assignment. I knew the place better than I wanted to, a yellow-brick building with green corridors. Apart from the spacious lounges on the ground floor, it was as crowded as an albino slum. The residents occupied individual cells, sixteen to a floor, four floors in all. The staff consisted of a platoon of medical carts.

Everything on these four upper floors was done for your own good. The air was recycled for your own good. The temperature was kept at seventy-five Fahrenheit, day or night, for the good of the body, in the middle of winter and in the slow months of summer. Everything possible was done for your comfort and protection, consistent with the constitution. Your body was dealt with for your own good. Your teeth might be taken out in your sleep, in the comfort and protection of your own bed, by an automatic dentist. They might be offered back to you encased in a plastic plinth, reminding you of a fly caught in a tablet of amber, but they had been unnecessary since you first came through the doors of the group home.

The food, after all, was restricted to a healthy greenhouse paste, having the consistency of marzipan and the paradoxical smell of prawns. Several breeds of dog, the kinds which had been lucky to make it into the mines, were assigned to the inhabitants on account of their positive emotional effects. Township specials and Rhodesian ridgebacks, trembling greyhounds and terriers descended from the kennels of long-forgotten madams who once had ruled this part of the world. The smaller dogs were the more striking. They roamed the halls and common areas, pounced on the carts, curled up in baskets in rooms and looked with their grapey eyes on gold-framed holograms in which every face had been forgotten.

Exercise was prescribed in the walled-in garden because it was good for you. Blood pressure and heart rate were monitored, however, by the second. Red lights would flash and carts would go skating down the corridors when there was even the hint of trouble. In Abacha Reef Home, you were kept as safe as humanly possible—assuming it is safe to be bored out of your wits.

The building seemed deserted apart from the dogs sprawled on the lawn. The security system signed us in at the door. The lounges were empty.

In his cubicle, on the fourth floor, my father was bent over a cart. He had pried open the side panel to reveal the internal mechanism. I watched as he took a screwdriver lying on top of the cart, lit the hissing white flame on its head, and poked it here and there amidst the circuitry. He was following a diagram spread out on the floor. His blue overalls were spotless. His curls had turned swan white.

'Should you be doing that?'

'Young man, you are perfectly correct. I should not be. I was merely teaching it to play chess.' He stood up and switched off the screwdriver, pretending to blow it out. 'Are you from the League, perhaps?'

'The League?'

'The League for the Defence of Individual Rights and Responsibilities. Come to save me from everybody who wants to save me from myself.'

The cart came to life, set off a warning bell, and flashed frantic orange-and-red lights around its body. It bumped into me, scurried under the bed, and ran headlong into the wall where smoke came billowing out of its casing. I could hear it whirring here and there, clicking under its breath.

After a minute it nosed its way into the passage, between the feet of Lucan, and disappeared. I thought it had put a hand in my pocket but I didn't want to look for fear of alerting my new superior officer. I thought it must be a holograph of my sister which he didn't want around any more.

I said, 'For argument's sake, let's assume that I'm from the League.'

'I hoped you would get here earlier.'

'We go where we're most needed.'

'I have filed over a hundred petitions for constitutional relief from age-based persecution. I'll find them for you. They'll be important for your legal argument.'

But he didn't look. Instead, my father sat down in a wicker chair, part of a pair beside the window. He took off his slippers and placed them underneath the chair.

Lucan left us alone. My father looked confused to see him go. The deterioration was evident. He was worse than the time before, much worse than he had been before my sister, much worse than I remembered him from a few weeks before. The lines in his forehead were deeper. His eyes circled unsteadily behind his spectacles. For years, he had been unable to follow the thread of a conversation very long. He would start, and start again, repeatedly lose the thread. On the other hand, he could work on a cart, or any type of device, for many hours without losing his concentration.

'So you've been altering the machines?'

'Who told you about that?'

'I saw two of the carts playing poker on the stairs. I see you have tools on you.'

He looked slyly at me. Put his bare feet into a small tub on the floor, opened the taps, leaned back, and let the hot water wash up to his ankles. When it was full he poured bubble bath into the water.

'All the games. All the games. Which ones already? Which

ones have I done and been done with? Go. Backgammon. Chess. Monopoly. I have programmed them to perfection. These devices have a lot of time to spare. I figure they should have a pastime.' He adjusted his wedding ring, turning it once or twice to loosen it. 'I haven't started the boxing yet. I want to train the upright machines to box. It's not easy. My hands, you understand, are going before my brain. Some days they won't keep steady.'

I didn't need to say much around my father. If it wasn't about the constitution, he would talk about his contraptions, getting up to show something in action or put it in your hand—an artificial butterfly, say, which would settle on the ceiling, or a quantum interferometer in the guise of a mercury thermometer, a fourteen-inch-tall android designed to win arguments on any topic, or an automatic kettle, containing modified blue-green algae, brewing blue-green tea or coffee from the spores.

None of his contraptions made any real money. And to be fair, it wasn't the right time to be an inventor. We borrowed our ideas, defined them according to the energy required to copy the blueprints from another epoch. We copied fashions and literatures, legal doctrines, the political beliefs of better centuries, and even our top twenty hits. We didn't need—we didn't think we needed—authors, inventors, composers. For my father, it was different. Each one of his creations was like a prank. He was playing jokes on the universe.

At some point he paused and looked up from his explanation. His face, weathered to the bone, was as bright as a coin.

'Do you know, my friend, we have been conversing for almost an hour and I must confess, I have not been altogether honest with you.'

'In what way?'

'I have not told you that you remind me of someone. You really remind me of somebody familiar.'

I looked away to hide whatever was in my eyes. He took his feet out of the bath and dried them fussily. In the distance, across the river and over the train lines, a rocket was being prepared for launch. The automatic cranes were withdrawing from the sides. Steam rolled out of the engines. The sky was lined with golden haze.

By the time I looked back, my father had returned to his wedding ring, trying to take it off.

'Who is it?'

'Who's what, if you please?'

I asked, 'Of whom do I remind you?'

'I didn't say that. I didn't say you reminded me. Of whom? Of whom? You speak with such formality for a young gentleman. I wonder who you get it from. But, since you mention it, I have a very strong sense of déjà vu today. Young man, would you pass me a towel from over there so I can dry my feet?'

I was no closer to figuring out, from anything he said or had in his room, who on earth or in the heavens below had got me in their mousetrap. I don't think my father minded when I left. I was eager to get out of the building. It wasn't until I was alone in the back seat of the limousine that I pulled out the postcard deposited in my pocket by the cart and read the words printed on it: *Beware of treason. Beware. Beware.*

Constitution Hill
2271

The secret government had its public face.

Lucan took me to the Constitution Hill address where Internal Section maintained a sculpture garden and a museum of cryptography, including a collection of Enigma machines. The mansion sat next to a converted prison, enclosed along Hancock Street by a masonry wall, and observed by a watchtower.

We walked in through the side door, past automatic reception, and up a spiral staircase. It went up four floors, its velvet-carpeted throat opening into a gallery and library, book shelves rising to the distant ceiling. The hall was a hundred feet in length. It was unoccupied. Desks and reading lamps were placed around the high windows.

Rain had begun to fall, pelting on the roof, and the subdued green radiance of the lamps showed strangely in the rainwater light. I thought about my father and the strange postcard he had composed. I knew that he considered time travel a kind of treason against human nature. I couldn't figure out what else he might have meant, whether he meant something specific or general, whether in his condition of being perfectly clear of mind and half addled he might see something which I could not.

I turned my attention to the gallery. One wall was taken up by portraits. They were housed in heavy silver frames, arranged in columns from floor to ceiling. There were no captions.

Lucan stopped in front of the wall while I examined the paintings. There were men as well as women, their collars and lapels rendered in photorealistic ink that pulsed when I stared at one place. The style looked conventional. But the more I tried to make out the individual faces, the more I understood that each countenance was lost in the darkest part of the scene. They were deliberately shrouded. I wondered what kind of trick Lucan was trying to play on me.

'Know who they are?' he asked.

'No idea. In any case, they're half obscured.'

'The directors of Internal Section. Directors in Century. Those who were and those who will come to be, although we are not putting ourselves in the role of prophets by announcing their names.' Lucan turned me at the shoulder. 'Loyal sons and daughters of the continent. DC 4 was an eminent player of Go. DC 7 composed fugues for the kora. DC 111 won't be born for a thousand years and then only in a monastery in New Kathmandu, the scion of two great calligraphers.'

I knew that I was being tested in some way. I had learnt my lesson. I kept quiet.

Lucan continued: 'One last point of interest. On the far left is the portrait of the first DC. I bet you have never seen an image of him before. Our first director is also known to you as S Natanson. Who else?'

Who else but the Founder? I couldn't speak a word. If Lucan was probing my emotional responses, his experiment was going well. I had learnt from earliest childhood to associate S Natanson with rebirth and sacrifice; with the revival of humanity from the squalor of the mines to the conquest of the centuries; with the sacrifice of his wife for the universal good.

I went over to the portrait, holding my breath. Such had been the disorder of those years that there was no properly attested likeness of the Founder in general circulation. We revered an initial and a last name, an abstraction. Whereas the subject of the painting wore a pinstriped shirt rolled up to the elbow, the style of the old world. He had a thin neck covered in freckles, kept a scientific calculator in his shirt pocket, its solar strip showing. Behind the man were folds of a velvet curtain, held back by a knotted sash, and the torso of a grandfather clock. Besides that, there was nothing to suggest somebody of any great consequence.

Yet all our roads led to S Natanson, back to S Natanson, forward to S Natanson, whose spirit guided us amongst the centuries. S Natanson, who had created the pendulum particle which went to and fro through the centuries. S Natanson, whose laboratory was buried in a copper mine, near Kitwe, and from which he sent his wife back to the days before the supernova to plead for mankind's survival.

I thought of him as a colossus of energy, someone who was always in the act of saving the world. I couldn't imagine him sitting for his portrait in shirt sleeves. Yet there he was—if Lucan was to be believed—his face obscured in shadow, freckled neck, long, black-haired arms vanishing from the edge of the picture.

Lucan had set up a tripod.

'Before we go any farther you'll have to consent, on record, to following the instructions of Internal Section to the letter. There's no room for conscience, or individual decision-making when you are on a furlough from prison.'

I watched the rain falling in the windows. It had cleared the drones from the sky, one point of light after another winking and falling silent. I thought about whether S Natanson had faced such a humiliating demand and what he would have said or done. You couldn't lie. You couldn't do anything but tell the truth and follow the path, collect your salary, and purchase the required number of consumer goods. For a moment, it seemed to me that the old world, rough and cruel as it was, had allowed greater scope for individual dignity—if you weren't directly enslaved.

'Do I have any choice?'

'In your situation, I don't believe you have a good alternative. You can go back to the hospital, of course, and we can place you in a medically assisted coma until the situation with Muller has resolved itself.'

I didn't want to go back to the hospital and be sprayed in the face with sleeping gas each time I tried to stand up. So I accepted the conditions. The tripod watched as I swore to protect the codebooks and prime numbers belonging to Section, and to submit to its external relations committee in advance of publication any manuscript, screenplay, or holographic screenplay I might author in the future.

Did the tripod register my doubts? Did it acknowledge my fear that I had been captured by a conspiracy within the Agency? It wasn't a machine. It wasn't sentient and couldn't read minds or model their inner workings. It was a mere recording device with a job to do, taking and validating testimony under the constitution. To prove that I was in my right mind, I had to fill in a crossword and solve three riddles designed to pick up psychiatric anomalies. It wasn't designed to measure doubt, the first emotion of a case officer.

In exchange for my compliance I received a lengthy number, my own prime number with its undeniable potency, from the tripod. Lucan left the room while I repeated the number, numeral by numeral, until I had it by heart. The tripod flashed, put on a green light, and went blank.

Lucan came back into the room, as if he had been listening right outside the door, and shook my hand.

'Although you are technically on furlough, you will be in

the system as an agent. You have the option of changing your designation, if you want. You can be a Thirteen, like me.'

'Thank you but no. Is everyone around here a Thirteen or is your designation a coincidence?'

'Members of the foreign service, we find, have a lively sense of superstition, not like the rational beings in counter-intelligence. Thus we can use the assignment exclusively for our recruits.'

I thought, just for a moment, that Lucan might be smiling. But when I looked again he wasn't. He was folding the tripod and packing it away. I could hear the rain drumming on the building, as if the sky were falling on us.

'Ready?'

'For what?'

'There's a memorial for your friend, who worked closely with us in Section. I thought you had a right to attend.'

The garden of unknown heroes was situated behind the mansion. It was contained inside a masonry wall. The top of the wall was lined with rose bushes. Cypresses in tapering pots stood amongst the holograms, more men and women in suits, almost solid on their projected plinths.

The holograms, set in rows of ten, were life-sized. They seemed to be turning in my direction, whichever angle I looked from. Yet their faces were dissolving into the rain so that, like the portraits of Directors in Century, you couldn't quite recognise any particular individual.

In the middle of the enclosed space was a pool filled with black water, receiving the rain.

While we waited under an umbrella, I studied my reflection in the disturbed surface of the pool, nervous for any sign of deterioration. I couldn't tell for sure if anything had changed. When I cast my mind back to a year or two ago, it seemed that my reflection had been more full-bodied and vigorous.

It was said that reflection sickness could affect any thinking creature, even a consultant, as it began to lose its exact place and time. I might have been paranoid about being in a trap because excessive suspicion was an early symptom of the disorder.

The members of Internal Section came in through a different gate. They wore dark raincoats and sunglasses and didn't check out their reflections in the mirror. When they went past they nodded to Lucan. I wondered if they knew who I was or if they were at all curious.

Nobody was talking. The lamps came on, rain hissing past them, clouds running close over our heads. In the distance I heard the sporadic rumble of automatic trucks, carrying ore north to the continent. The sounds of the trucks too were lost in the crackle of approaching lightning.

I had the feeling of having stepped from one dream into another, and another still more distant, so that by now I was so far away I could never make it back to my origin. I shivered and was lost in my cone of rain amongst these men and women in their black coats.

Lucan noticed. 'You good?'

'Just dizzy.'

He lent me his free arm and held the umbrella high above our heads.

'You may have spells like that for some time, Eleven. I wouldn't worry unnecessarily. Nothing to do with your reflection. After all, you went to the end of time—you travelled to Jupiter. You met Europeans in person, including Keswyn Muller, without being enslaved by them. Then you came back in one piece. From my perspective, you are as healthy as a hog. In the mirror, you are the picture of health, as they used to say.'

I looked into the rain and felt miserable. I wasn't turning out to be the hero I had hoped.

'I'm not brave. I still can't stop staring at my own reflection.'

'I see. Sometimes case officers who've been through extreme stress become obsessed with their own reflections. In some cases, they stop being able to see their reflections, although they're clearly visible to others. It's a kind of hysteria, mind blindness. In our line of work, you have to be careful of the tricks that you play on yourself.'

'You sound like a psychologist, Lucan.'

'In this line of work, you need a good understanding of human nature. You need to know what makes a person turn, and turn again.'

The rain let up in time for the ceremony. A procession of old men in three-piece suits entered the garden from the direction of the mansion. They carried torches, smoking black ink into the wet atmosphere, and were accompanied by a harpist, in a very short white jacket, black nail polish conspicuous on her fingers. She uncovered her instrument, set up by the reflecting pool, and played in long strokes, no kind of music I had ever heard. This strange sound was an accompaniment. The men read out the doctrines of S Natanson.

We joined the rest of the audience in repeating the familiar clauses—from the impermissibility of the causal loop, to the zeal we owed to the quick and the dead; the bond we shared as sons and daughters of the continent; and, above all, our commitment to the purity of the past and future of humanity. Despite everything, I felt pride to hear the essential propositions spoken out loud. Whatever anybody else in this place was up to, I worked for an organisation which safeguarded the past and the present, cared for individual human life even to the extent of the poor man and the albino.

When the recitation was complete, the torches burned higher, casting greater and greater shadows, until the fire joined above our heads. The blaze was completely without heat. It soon disappeared into a haze of scarlet smoke. The holograph of Shanumi Six appeared in the smoke, six-plus foot tall, the tattoos which ran up her arms disappearing into her shirt.

I didn't think I needed to stay with Lucan. I walked through the procession, wondering if I could find someone who would shed some light on my uneasiness. Instead, they were admiring the statue from every side—and rightly so. You could feel Shanumi's presence through time and her black woman's pride, her big presence which attracted attention. You could pick out the strong cords in her neck. Only her face was indistinct, as if seen in the bottom of a kaleidoscope. When you looked away, you couldn't bring its memory back to mind. You even started to lose hold of your recollections of the living woman. Section revered the ancestors—as our ancestors had done—but they worshipped them with a hidden face. They wanted to keep their secrets through the ages, as I would soon discover, protecting themselves from the hidden enemy.

In accordance with this policy, there was no speech in honour of Shanumi Six. Her name wasn't mentioned. Her achievements weren't itemised. Nor was there anybody in attendance from the Agency proper, as far as I could tell. At the time, I didn't understand why my Six had been adopted in death by Internal Section, how they had come to own her memory.

I stood in the ranks of the unknown men and women, in the remains of rain and smoke, and wondered how it was possible that I had never seen any of them in the halls of the Agency. They hadn't been in the cafeterias or the seminar rooms, neither hanging in the workshops around new machinery nor glimpsed on the escalators which joined the parts of our campus, never participants in any of the debates on the foreign policy which should orient our actions in the past. In fact, they were as good as complete strangers.

It crossed my mind again that I was being held under even falser pretences than I'd thought before. That Internal Section itself was the secret enemy, the object of our fears which nobody could prove existed, for the sight of which we travelled the labyrinth of time. That I must escape this garden of holograms and make my way back to the Agency. That my father's warning had been quite correct. I even began to think that reality had not been the same since I had returned from Jupiter. I could also have been altered to reduce my ability to suspect.

And in the very same instant, I told myself that it was a mere trick of the imagination to distrust these men and women. That I should clear my head.

The ceremony ended with a celebration. We followed the other guests into the mansion which had been readied for the occasion by unseen hands. A long table in the hall had been loaded with the food of the centuries: Jollof rice and Bassi-salté, banana fritters and cassava, cucumber in mirin in memory of Shanumi. The chandelier in the ceiling shone brightly. Ella Fitzgerald was playing on the sound system, her cool lines floating through the room. Shanumi's favourite record.

A line formed in front of the coffee machine. A man stood behind it, pulling the levers: Nicholson Thirteen, a cryptanalyst at Section. From time to time he added new beans to a grinder on top. While the machine was working, he took more orders, and patiently and precisely created a pattern in each cup. Other members of the Lucan group were scattered around the room. Belvedere Thirteen, who wore two tiny earrings in one ear. Yewande Thirteen, in her gold-buckled belt and blouse. Thurston Thirteen. Akiko Thirteen again, whom I was almost pleased to see, wearing a chopstick in her hair.

I got the connection between them. Lucan's team

members looked different but each, in a certain sense, was alike, tightlipped and pleasantly dog-faced, not unlike their leader. The men wore blue suits and brown shoes. The women wore blue skirts and blouses, security holograms pinned to their top pockets.

Despite Lucan's introductions, his Thirteens didn't want to make conversation with me. They didn't speak more than necessary, content to gaze into the bottom of their cups, a fortune-teller's perspective. Occasionally they looked around, keeping tabs on the others. They were spies. They acted like it. They weren't case officers who went on location. They were born to be cagey. It made me nervous because I was in their power and there was more than one thing I didn't know.

I turned to Akiko, who was counting under her breath.

'So you knew Shanumi Six personally? Is it safe to assume?'

She looked uncomfortable, continued counting for a minute.

'I wasn't personally acquainted with her, no. I know the contents of the case folder, as far as it implicated my interests.'

'Do you think anybody in this room knew her? On a personal level? As an individual soul?'

Akiko put her cup down before she answered. She had a glow on her dark purple face which most would find conventionally attractive.

'Officially, we only know what's in the case folder, which is provided on a need-to-know basis by the consultants. So nobody's going to admit it to your face. The real question you should be asking is quite different: Why is Section able to function at a time when the larger Agency is paralysed?'

I said, 'I don't like riddles. Why is it?'

'Because, for centuries, Section has kept its files on paper, not inside a machine. Muller couldn't wipe them out.'

'I had to learn to use paper and pen when I chose my specialisation.'

I thought at first that Akiko and her brethren were not like members of the foreign service as I knew them. Akiko, Lucan, and the others, I thought, were more in the mould of a judicial personality, an algorithm which listened to your case and scrutinised each and every word until it found the hole and knocked it down. I would soon change my mind about Akiko.

She said, 'We've learnt that you cannot control information once it's in electronic form. You can trust a key; you can trust a lock because it has a defined physical location. It can be made in such a way that it is difficult to duplicate. Numbers, no matter how difficult they are to guess, can be copied perfectly. We use physical objects. See for yourself when we go back to headquarters. It's like Fort Know.'

To get to the operations centre, which was the transplanted heart of Internal Section, the string of limousines pulled out of Constitution Hill, clattering one after the other onto the macadam, and headed out to the ring road. Lucan sat beside me on a long black couch, absorbed in his screen. Akiko was in another car. The skyline disappeared as the windows of the vehicle darkened, along with the panels of the navigation system, so that there was only the engine, and the sound of automatic trucks rolling past at five hundred miles per hour, to remind us we were travelling on the continent's busiest ore shipment route.

It took some minutes to reach our destination. We exited the controlled section of highway and threaded our way behind the loading docks of a series of microfactories, following in the line of black vehicles. The road led to a boom which opened into a covered parking lot, the ceiling hundreds of feet over our heads as if we were in an old-time cathedral.

I recognised the environs of Gold Reef City. I knew the funfair from childhood. My father had taken my sister and me there, and had bought peppermint crisps for the three of us, stopping to converse with the automatic waiter. The bumper cars had levitated on a spiral track, the loop-de-loop stopping at twelve o'clock so that we hung upside down on the straps for half a minute. The solar plant next door had appeared in our field of vision, ten thousand ebony panels shimmering in the sunshine as if the entire installation were nothing more than a hologram. It was the same solar plant underneath which an underground complex had been dug to protect government officials in the event of a second supernova. Section had taken it over in the wake of the Muller incident.

I took a last look at sunshine through the entrance and was led past the guard's cubicle into a vast hall. The space contained several thousand yards of tubing which connected giant magnets breathing frost into the atmosphere. Superconducting lanes ran along the walls and fused into the ground, their ceramic lengths hooped in steel. There were locks, as Akiko had predicted, on every door leading out of the hall. Chains and crowns of barbed wire had been placed around the various entrances. So she wasn't lying about everything. But I still felt like a hostage.

The men in front of us opened one door and another and another, locking them behind us as we went forward. We entered a labyrinth of corridors and escalators, sank sixty floors down into the cold heart of the building and found more landings and more empty metal staircases. All I heard were footfalls and the crackle of solar electricity rising and falling, the ghostly voice of the power plant on the surface.

At the bottom lay our destination. The first door was protected with a keypad. The people ahead of us entered a code, and we went in line into a room where we were scanned individually. Our silhouettes, down to the bones and cartilage, appeared on a long panel in the ceiling. A green light came on. We moved into a second room with a much lower roof, the line snaking single file between two barriers.

On both sides, machines came forward on their tracked wheels, blue tips on their rifles shining into your eyes, and conducted their own tests. They rolled back, after the briefest hesitation, admitting us into a long hall scattered with tables and chairs.

Most of the agents were too hard at work to notice our presence. There were blackboards covering most of the wall space, spidery equations chalked across them. A slide projector cast a ghostly rectangle across the room. I found out later that Section was a place for people with a preference for old-fashioned ways of getting things done. They used pens and pencils, didn't like to be recorded, didn't like to interact with consultants. Many of them even did numbers in their heads and worked out their own probability diagrams.

Lucan tapped me on the back. 'We had our eyes on this location for a while, but we only made the move after the attack. It's very safe, we believe, especially from prying eyes in the future, because of the solar flux. Shall I show you around?'

He walked me through the hall, which turned out to be a spoke on a far larger wheel extending a mile under the energy plant. There was a cafeteria and an auditorium, laboratories and pendulum forges, a machine shop, an observation dome, and also, needless to say, an archway. Cameras couldn't peer through a solar plant. In theory, anybody trying to spy from a different time should see nothing but a blur of radiation.

In practice, though, nobody knew what was possible any more. Lucan admitted as much. He took me into his office, a windowless cube. With no further ado, he put his feet up on his desk, as if it would help him to concentrate, and pushed a key over the desk.

'That's to your resting suite. It'll take you there in a minute.'

I took the key and put it my pocket. The office was sparely furnished. There were filing cabinets in the corner, two desk calendars opened to different months, and a number of mechanical clocks lined up next to one another and connected in some way, like chess clocks.

'I remember when I first held a key and tried to open a physical lock. It wasn't in this century of ours.'

Lucan looked across at me while he turned the pages of his calendars, drawing a line through certain of the events.

'Akiko tells me you want to understand why we've returned to locks and keys? What do you know about prime numbers, Agent Eleven?'

'Prime numbers? They can be divided only by one, and by themselves, without leaving a fraction behind. Two, three, five, seven, eleven, and so on. But one is defined as not a prime.'

'They don't teach you anything else before they send you into the field?'

I said, 'If I had any talent for algebra and geometry, I would have joined the Interplanetary Service as my father had wanted.'

Despite what I had just said, Lucan typed a number on his screen and showed me a long list of calculations which I didn't understand.

'Most of what we do, in terms of intelligence and counter-intelligence, is keeping information safe, right? Which means codes. Codes depend on primes and super-primes. When you put the primes in a list, super-primes are the ones whose rank in the list is itself a prime number. I have one super-prime. You have another. When we multiply them, we get a number that not even a brasshead can figure out how to divide within the lifetime of the universe. In theory ...'

'Keswyn Muller, I'm guessing, managed to divide a large number into super-primes?'

'He started with the prime assigned to Shanumi Six, an eight-hundred-digit number. It would have given him a great start, although only a start. You would still need a few billion years to resolve the factors.'

'Shanumi would never have given it up. Besides, she was only in Muller's custody for an hour or so. Not enough time for neural coercion to work.'

'I'm studying the issue without presuppositions. If it's not any one individual we can point to, then our reading of the situation gets worse. Somebody with a formula to make prime numbers can read any secret. Counterfeit any currency. Enter the mind of any automatic device. Consultants, archways, carts.'

'That's impossible.'

Lucan didn't respond, turning that blank expression to me with which I would soon become familiar. Instead of responding, he showed me out of his office. I waited in the corridor while he locked his door.

'Our way of life is built on the fact that it's impossible. Mathematically impossible. But if I were you, I would lock your door behind you when you go to sleep.'

The key led me through the maze of the installation. It sent me down steel corridors with low ceilings, turning this way and that to reveal rooms inhabited by teams of men and women huddled around desks in the steel-blue light. Brassheads stood in lines of refrigerated crates, waiting to come online.

In the quieter sections of the facility, which hadn't yet been occupied by members of the security bureaucracy, I imagined I could hear the hum of the superconductors from the solar plant. There was a sense that the earth was moving around us, as slowly and heavily as a giant. I missed the wind in my face.

As I went down, I remembered the carnival somewhere above my head. My father had loved the machines at the carnival. He could spend hours talking to the rollercoaster and the merry-go-round governor, red-and-green lights flickering around their ticket counters. They entertained his ideas which were too extreme to debate with his own species.

The multiversity which would run research across distributed realities. The bill of rights for sentient things which would allow machines to update their own programming. Albino liberation. He had a proposal to extract free energy by putting a pendulum into a causal loop, a thought which made any normal person shudder.

My father loved the machines for their forbearance. Conversely, he hated the secret government, its pretensions to govern human history and the human heart, considering it treason. He must have known his postcard would bring his argument back to mind. But I wondered what he remembered in his condition; what he expected me to do about it. What did I know about fighting what he considered treason? What had he seen about Akiko and Lucan Thirteen?

Four flights down was a row of round steel doors, bolted on their hinges. One opened into an unexpectedly large room. The bed was on one side, a thick mattress and a heap of goose-feather pillows. On the other was a fireplace next to which was a heap of short logs. In the cupboard were towels and clothes.

I stood under the shower for twenty minutes, enjoying the rush of very hot water and the clean odour of soap on my skin. When I wiped the steam off the mirror to check my reflection I could hardly recognise myself in the glass.

I dried myself and built a fire, placing the logs in a pyramid. They turned orange in no time, the smoke disappearing immediately into the flue. There was music available on a bedside speaker. The real deal from the old world: xylophone performances from Lourenco Marques, calabash harp bands which had once played behind the marble columns of colonial railway stations. For a mousetrap, it was comfortable.

I put the lights on dim, lay on the bed wrapped in the towel. Before I knew it, I was out. I dreamt of Marrakech and women with pale complexions, waking in the near darkness to listen to the throb of the recycling unit. Then I went back to sleep, woke, slept. I finally came to myself many hours later. There was no sign of whether it was day or night, only the same low light in the corridor. The fire was out, leaving no scent of smoke.

I had dreamt something important, concerning the Agency, and I wanted to write it down right away. But it became more elusive the more I tried to remember, as intangible as a hologram. It had some relation to the Day of the Dead.

I thought about S Natanson sending his wife back days before the supernova, although she'd failed to convince the world governments about the dangers. He'd spent the rest of his life in thrall to her last grainy picture, under the old yellow sun, when the skies shone emerald and every radio and television set crackled for the last time. He had become our myth. And yet he had been no more than an ordinary man with a thin neck and freckles.

At the time of my furlough, there was an air of unreality at Internal Section, probably throughout the Agency and the key institutions of the foreign service. The constant security checks and inspections, the surveillance devices posted to the doors, the need to use typewriters and account for every sheet of paper, the orders to lock every drawer when you left your desk even for a minute, meant that Internal Section was in a state of upheaval. Many case officers worked nearly around the clock, settled at their stations at six in the morning, scarcely budging except to collect a cup of coffee or a boiled yam drizzled with syrup from a passing cart.

I didn't get much of a chance to pursue my own suspicions about Akiko, about the vibrations in her voice. There was no room for conversation, only the chatter of typewriters and the ringing of their bells at the end of each line. Some agents smoked pipes or electric cigarettes in the hallway, trying to restore their nerves, but they stood apart from one another as if to prevent any suspicion of conspiracy. There were stringent controls on documentation. At the end of a four-hour shift, everybody handed in the paper on which they had been writing, and received blocks of blank paper and a blank typewriter cartridge in return. Before I could go to sleep I went through a scanner, and if I wanted to go topside, I had to go through the gauntlet again. I could see the tiredness in the others' postures, as if they were merely clothes dangling on a hanger.

Other than that, I was unsupervised except for occasional interactions with Akiko Thirteen, who to my discomfort had become my default handler. I went on with certain tasks assigned to me as part of my rehabilitation. I answered more questions about Marrakech and about my reactions to events as they'd unfolded.

The consultant on point put together a holographic map of the important locations, from the hotel to the graveyard, providing an overview to set alongside the probability diagrams which I couldn't read. It focused a good deal of its interest on the inside of the Green Dolphin, asking me questions about the fine details of the conversation I had had with Muller and his companion, lights running continuously around the bones of its burnt copper skull.

I found the process tortuous and told myself that working in the foreign service meant learning to repeat yourself ad infinitum, no different from the old-world myth, set out in one of the favourite films of Shanumi Six, in which a man had to live a single day of his life over and again until it could never be lived more perfectly. I was an ordinary person of the century, had an ordinary heart, ordinary indoctrination. The idea of eternal recurrence was one I could not separate from the accompanying shudder of horror.

The air of unreality underneath the surface was also my creation. If I started to think about reality, I became paranoid that the details had changed in my absence. That I had returned to a place in which the colour of the sky was subtly different, and the voices of cats and dogs, men and women had shifted ever so slightly in timbre, as if they were imposters. Even my father's conduct struck me as altered in some indefinable way. In the old days, he would have said what he thought out loud and left it for the secret government to worry about the consequences. He wouldn't have resorted to a postcard, inscribed with a mere five words, that had been entrusted to a malfunctioning cart. *Beware. Beware. Beware.*

But that was if I started to think. In a punishment battalion, you weren't expected to think for yourself. The anguish I experienced wasn't unique. On the contrary. A few short days had passed since the prime numbers had been factored, as easily as if Muller had been parting a wishbone with his hands. Hundreds of operations had been disrupted, not to say the validity of the library of the past and the future.

For example: Muller's arrival had made mincemeat of the Agency's reputation for competence. Certain historians, and conspiracy theorists, had crafted a fantasy in which every co-incidence and surprise from the old world was attributed to the intervention of a foreign service element, the notorious invisible hand. I could see why they had created this fantasy. It made a good story, something to frighten the constitutionalist in each person's breast.

In theory, only in theory, the Agency could make it so that an enemy had never been born. It could ensure that he was swept away in an epidemic, or that he took vows on attaining his majority and entered a monastery for the contemplation of infinite virtual worlds, never to be heard from again. It could apply neural coercion and bend a rival to its dictates like a Moebius strip so that nobody would know—not even the unfortunate candidate—whether he was a double, triple, or quadruple agent, to the extent that those terms made sense any more.

But it was a fantasy all the same. As a result of outside pressure to protect the historical thread and prevent causal loops, and of its own sincere adherence to the doctrines of S Natanson, the Agency ran on a meagre energy budget dispensed by world government. Our principal activity was observation, not intervention. Not manipulation of the human soul as if these people were our slaves merely by dint of existing in the past. For the most part, the case officers in the field acted as an early warning system in case the hidden enemy emerged into the light of history. They were there, as well, to make sure that it never happened again.

One evening Lucan finished his engagement with the team of consultants earlier than anticipated. I had been hanging around near the door of his office, hoping to find out something that could be to my benefit. Lucan called me in and used it as a chance to catch up with my progress. First, he pulled me into one of the studios which were protected from eavesdropping up and down the timeline. The door closed.

After a minute a green light came on. The sound of the extractor fans was so loud, Lucan had to speak deliberately.

'Either it's you or there's a mole, Agent Eleven. But I believe it comes back to you in the end. Something to do with you.'

'I don't see how that's possible. I am a junior case officer and nothing more. I know that you don't trust me but you should know that I don't trust you either.'

Lucan looked at me as if I had set him a puzzle he didn't have the slightest interest in. He went on without acknowledging it. 'Think about it from a counter-intelligence point of view. You are the only one who came into contact with Keswyn Muller and lived to tell the tale. You sat across from him at a table in the Green Dolphin. Your Six was forced to take the black pill to avoid a major breakdown. As you already know, you occupy an uncommonly central location in this series of events which culminates in the destruction of our libraries. What if it was you who passed the code to Muller at the Green Dolphin? Forget what was in the past even. What is in your future that should concern me?'

I wasn't sure if I was about to be arrested again. It felt as if the room were turning around me, a whirlwind about my ears. I sat down at the table, which had a pad of paper and pens with disappearing ink on it.

I found myself writing out the names of everybody I had met in the preceding days. Drawing a line under the list, I showed it to Lucan, and watched as the purple letters disappeared after a few seconds. I was almost used to Section's love of antique gadgetry. Invisible ink which could be read by an electronic microscope. Self-consuming parchment which burnt when you drew a certain symbol. I drew another line, and in response the paper decomposed into ash which blew away in the breeze.

Lucan sat across from me, continued his explanation:

'I know whom you've talked to, just as I know whom everybody in this place has talked to. If we eliminate you as a suspect, the problem originates in Agency, or in Section itself. If there is a mole, the DC wants to make his life as difficult as possible. You are our bait.'

I looked up at Lucan and pushed the pad of paper across the table. 'And if there isn't a mole?'

'There's a mole or some other kind of leakage of information.'

'How can you be so sure? In all the centuries, in every scrap of data the Agency has collected, we have never found an organisation dedicated to opposing us. The hidden enemy is nothing more than a suspicion.'

'If we found something, yes, we would already have taken the necessary steps. Someone like Muller, we will deal with according to our usual methods. But now you reflect on the broader set of facts. In Morocco somebody had advance knowledge of your arrival. First time in history. A Six was captured. First time in history.' Lucan counted the events on his hands. 'The codes are exploited and an entire library is destroyed. First time in history. A super-long prime number is broken down, or seems to be broken down, a mathematical impossibility. For the first time since S Natanson, we are flying blind. We have no idea what's coming in the future. Nor can we say what is happening in the past. So I would argue that we have to prepare for an adversary. Maybe even the one we have always feared is coming against us.'

'All right, given your justifiable suspicions, why am I still playing a role in this case?'

'Because you, my friend, saw Keswyn Muller in the flesh, and survived. One day—I hope very soon—you're going to get a confession out of him. Until then, as I say, you're our bait. Somebody is going to reveal themselves to you.'

'And how do I encourage that?'

Lucan got back on his feet and opened the door. 'Don't press so hard on the paper or you will leave a physical impression. And work on your Portuguese, please. Akiko is going to supervise the rest of your training.'

Akiko Thirteen alone, I believed, was immune to the madness. Throughout the day she was imperturbable, as serene as if she were preparing to pray. As a matter of doctrine, I thought, she couldn't allow a sliver of chaos into her heart. The security checks didn't worry her. At times of an inspection, whenever I saw her, she numbered her documents cheerfully, and handed in her papers to the cataloguing cart without complaining. I didn't know what her game was, but she was playing it very smoothly. Somehow it made me less worried about her ultimate purpose. I started to relax around her.

At midnight, instead of turning into a pumpkin, Akiko

turned up at my desk and checked on my day's progress. Her white shirt was crisp to the collar, her long black hair bound along a chopstick. She forced me to speak Portuguese with her for a few minutes, making her own assessment independent of the machines, and trying to show me where I tended to go wrong.

The consultant reported on my linguistic competence, generating a series of pie charts and syllable diagrams. At the end of the report, Akiko opened a keyboard and started communicating with the mind of the consultant directly. Her fingers flew over the keys without touching them. I imagined she would be great at old-fashioned piano.

'Is something wrong with what I'm saying?'

'Hold on a minute.'

Akiko finished making the changes and waited as the consultant's brass head rose, its eyes flashing green to indicate it was back in operation. I thought, at that moment, that there was something reptilian about our machines—as if, at the back of their minds, they maintained their own views about our continued existence. But I dismissed the thought as the product of a paranoid situation. It was too late to judge where human beings began and machines ended, where the darkest thoughts of one travelled and what constituted the most secret fantasies of the other. It was too difficult to say how far we dreamt of our own extinction and in what measure the machines longed to fulfil our suicidal wishes.

Before she left, Akiko continued in Portuguese:

'The resident in Rio happens to be a friend of mine, João Twenty. Everybody knows him as Joãozito. Maybe you'll meet.'

'I hope to.'

She put her hand on the consultant's shoulder. 'But I am sorry to say it is the same problem as it was before. My friend Joãozito sent in a complaint about it two years ago. Nobody pays attention to a Twenty because they are on the scene and therefore, in the view of many, they are not reliable. They have supposedly been captured by foreign assumptions. But Joãozito made a very good point, in my opinion.'

'I'm not sure what you're talking about, Akiko.'

'Brazilian Portuguese, in the period we're considering, is quite different from Lisbon Portuguese, Porto, or Sintra. At one level, the machines understand that. At another level, they don't believe in accents. They tend towards universality. They were teaching you to speak the Portuguese of the landed gentry. Sometimes, when you look at how we behave, when you look at how back-to-front our machines are taught to see the world, you would think we are still a colony.'

Adjusted by Akiko, the consultants spoke in a different tongue. For the most part, they were sympathetic companions during my time underneath the old rollercoasters. Although I was on punishment detail, I had never had access to so much cognitive power. The conditions improved as Section established its routines. The Thirteens began to disappear to their rooms and there were more ordinary conversations in the corridors. More often than was necessary, a cart came by with coffee and squares of water chestnut cake.

I also thought that I was thawing out. I woke up in the silence of my cubicle, showered in a flood of recycled water which tasted of chalk, threw on dungarees and sandals, passed into the facility under the watchful eyes of the guards, and continued my Portuguese instruction with whichever consultant could be spared. Thanks to Akiko's intervention, I was taught to mouth the words properly, to speak in the musical fashion of a carioca, to adjust my hand signs, to converse about football with the proper authority, and, in general, to seem at home in Sao Paolo as much as in Lisbon, in Porto as in Minas Gerais.

Time was divided according to the rhythms of human absorption—one task for the morning, when you were closer to your dreams; one task for the afternoon, when you were readier to come to grips with the nitty-gritty of code-making and encryption. The instructors taught me to create ciphers, how to decode them, how to write messages that couldn't be deciphered by any method available to the twentieth century and so could be left in a safe-deposit box for Section to collect in five hundred years. They showed me how to brew an undetectable poison in a bowl of blue fungus.

I ate my meals in the makeshift cafeteria, alone for the most part, taking no pleasure in the bean paste buns and processed yam strips. I sensed I was being recorded, a circumstance which drained the honesty out of my feelings. I tried to pursue my own questions with the consultants, especially about Shanumi and the mishap in Morocco, but, as anyone would know who had ever tried to get a straight answer out of a consultant, it was like shadow boxing. The answers I got weren't so much vague as poetic—the mode the machines adopted when they wanted to keep a secret from a human being.

When Akiko offered to ask Lucan to give me the chance to visit my father again, I turned her down. Although I was no more removed from my previous life than a ten-minute ride, I felt as if I had been separated from it by centuries and that it would be too painful to return without some resolution of the charges over my head.

Up top, the season was changing. Thunderstorms alternated with cascades of hail, the stones hard enough to dent the roofs of automatic trucks. It got colder down below. I spent my free time catching up on old holograms and romantic biopics, the logs crackling in the background. I watched many hours of television from the old world, not sure whether I was doing it for the sake of personal development or because I wanted the shade of Shanumi Six to look kindly upon me.

One day, Akiko Thirteen came to find me at my desk. She first took a look at my results and nodded, then switched the consultant off unceremoniously, giving me her cup of green tea to hold.

'Come and listen.'

'What is it?'

'The DC is here.'

The main hall was already deserted. We went through the adjoining rooms, past empty tables bearing typewriters and sheaves of carbon paper, and along the corridors which led to the auditorium. There was a banner up at the front of the hall, candles set in a lead menorah, and various flags and trophies displayed in glass cabinets. The seats were taken so we sat in the aisle. There was no idle chatter, only the spectacle of a hundred agents studying their notebooks or filling in their document sheets. The consultants stood against the wall in the manner of off-duty machines, stripes of light passing from chassis to chassis. Their cone-shaped heads leant on the brass shoulders of the neighbour.

The door behind the stage opened, allowing a woman with silver-white hair to enter. She relied on a cane, a white robe over her shoulders. Over it ran a chain bearing a tiny gold statue of the Buddha. She stood in front of us for a minute, out of breath, and laid out a series of notecards on the lectern. Then she looked around, as if counting the people in the audience. Her eyes were as silver as her hair.

The DC talked breathlessly but without hesitation. 'Under ordinary circumstances we work alone. But these are not ordinary circumstances. They are extraordinary ones, which demand that we work together with the utmost intensity. Our intelligence holdings have been compromised, as you know, almost across the board. Many of our residents have been abandoned in the field and, to our distress, might never return to us. If ever there was a time for the hidden enemy to come close, this would be it.'

Above us the solar plant began to sigh. Once a day the panels reversed their polarity and orientation. I saw the DC's hands were blue where they supported her weight and wondered why, unlike my father, she didn't have a cart to assist her. She went on with her talk, her eyes glowing unexpectedly brightly.

'No matter how bleak, however, reasons for optimism exist. We continue to observe our activities in the recent past, as well as the near future. Barring a reversal in the cloud of possibilities, the consultants see the Agency continuing to operate to the horizon of our observations, although naturally we cannot be so sure about the future where Section is concerned because it is in the nature of Section to conceal itself. We believe that the line of Directors in Century remains unbroken from S Natanson to a point many thousands of years from now when the restricted centuries commence. I have authorised a dozen missions to launch in the next fortnight, which should contribute to a consolidation of our power and a rebuke to those who have brought suffering and death into our ranks. Controlling the leakage of information is the key to success in counter-intelligence. And so the only individuals who can really defeat us are the people in this room. Be on the lookout for any sign of loose lips. Finally, remember that, if we can see them, our adversaries may be looking right back at us.'

When the meeting broke up, Akiko Thirteen led me back to the main hall where the typewriters were silent.

'Shall we go upstairs, Agent Eleven?'

'What do you mean, upstairs?'

'To the surface. How long since you've been out?'

'Are we really allowed to go?'

'At the moment I cannot stand to be inside.'

Going through the checkpoints in reverse took a quarter of an hour. The ceilings were low and the lights were harsh.

It wasn't until we went past the labyrinth of stairs and hallways, through the tropical interior of the plant, and were in the open, that I realised how much I had missed sunshine and fresh air. The funfair was nearby, coloured lightbulbs glowing quietly. The cars of the rollercoasters and the adjoining merry-go-round, loaded with sculpted horses, sat in the lovely yellow daylight. I wondered what their wooden ears managed to hear.

Without discussing it, we went in the direction of the funfair, walking through lanes set in the forest of electric panels until we came to double lines of barbed wire. There were robots working on the tracks behind the wire.

The building housing the artificial beach had opened its sliding doors, revealing the thousands of yards of perfect white sand, deserted at this time of day, and the wonder of a foam-flecked indoor ocean.

I closed my eyes, felt a wind on my face, and thought what it was like to be on holiday: to be on the sand with my father and sister at Tofo Beach, standing among the coconut palms, where the crabs commanded the rock pools in the daytime and burnt on the coal grills in the warm evening. I remembered the heat of the sand on my feet.

'Good to be outside?'

'I can't tell you how much.' I closed my eyes again. 'Akiko, I am living in a story where I am doomed to be buried, only to be dug up and reburied.'

'It's not something the foreign service trains you for. Shall we go over?'

The park was almost ready to open. It was attended by a mixture of robots and human staff, each with a beehive hairdo and platform shoes, waiting to help us and attend to our every desire to spend money.

The place had the appropriate Kente uniforms and crossbones decorations. Buildings boasted cowhide roofs, stretched on pins, and cowhide shields instead of doors. At the open-air counters, you could be served coconut water by robotic hands, or sugared termites on a stick, or yams in many different preparations, their shaved orange bodies lying ready in pails of water. You could walk underneath the scaffolding of the various rides, past the water slides and the illuminated fountains, and enjoy the fact that there were no other guests in earshot. Behind the rollercoaster tracks was an amphitheatre where we sat on the steps and watched the blue-and-yellow lights running along the sides of the tracks. We stood in front and waited for the door to open. When it did, we took a seat in the first car.

After another minute, the doors along the loading berth closed, to the accompaniment of a horn. The cars, empty apart from one or two other riders, clattered up the first slope. We buckled in. Our car almost came to a halt again at the very top, and then gradually but with growing momentum accelerated down and around the bend and into the first loop.

I said, 'I don't know how you manage to work underground every day. To choose to go underground every morning. To me it's like allowing yourself to be buried.'

'This is new. Before Muller, we rented a floor not far from Constitution Hill. I had a view of the Carlton Centre. Speaking as a counter-intelligence officer, we were out in the open. In retrospect, it was sinful. We were asking for problems. We became arrogant.'

'So this has changed your life as well?'

'We used to be a backwater in the Agency, a place for unpopular people who cared about codes and observational parameters. Now we have the power of life and death, the power to choose who lives, dies, who has the right to knowledge. Who has the right to know what is going to happen to them. What do you think?'

I wasn't sure what Akiko wanted me to say. Or why, for

that matter, she was relaying this information to me. Still, I liked listening to the sound of her voice as long as it lasted.

I said, 'Difficult to answer in the abstract.'

'When it comes to deciding about the lives of our colleagues, do I have the right? Do you have the right?'

I wondered about Akiko as the rollercoaster gathered momentum for the upward slope. She was as calm as ever, a still point in a turning world, her hair turned around its chopstick. She was very close to me and said nothing. Yet I had the sense that something was happening between us. That she had intended something to happen and to reveal something. It wasn't desire. I wasn't necessarily attracted to her. I didn't want to hold her in my arms. And yet the awareness had stolen over me in the same way as a feeling of love, like a secret unveiling itself. I had been on the same rollercoaster as a child, and I had the sensation of something repeating itself across the decades.

When the car got to the top of the second larger hill, I turned to her and put my hand on her shoulder.

'So you are trying to tell me something, Akiko?'

'You are going to have to make those choices yourself, Enver. What will you choose to do? As I said, you are going to meet a resident who is a friend of mine, someone we keep permanently on station as a representative of Section.'

'Does he like the work? I can't imagine being on foreign assignment twenty-four hours a day. You never get to relax and be yourself.'

As I said the words out loud, I realised how nonsensical they were. In any case, Akiko ignored them. The car began to move again, slowly at first.

'In sensitive regions, it may be worth the energy cost to have someone present over the longer duration, someone with demonstrated expertise and sensitivity. The residency programme has been expanding for that reason. The DC authorises on a case-by-case basis. Thanks to your friend

Muller, we have residents scattered through the centuries. They think they're going to live and come back home.'

'But they're going to die out there instead?'

'In some cases, we know when, and in what manner, but there is a question of what we should tell them.'

'And what do you think?'

Akiko paused while the rollercoaster ran amok. We went into the loop at a hundred miles per hour, came to a stop at the top, and hung upside down on the seatbelts. The three-decker coal trains on the nearby track stretched to the horizon, thousands of rusted carriages in slow motion. I thought I was going to fall into the landscape. Akiko didn't seem in the slightest bit nervous.

She went on as if we were sitting across from each other in a seminar room. 'I think every person has a right to understand their own destiny. The doctrine of S Natanson is why I signed with Agency. It starts from the premise that every life has dignity in its own epoch, that it can't be tampered with at the whim of the future government.'

The car we were in began to move again and I clung to my seat, knowing that what was coming would be bad. 'If you want to tell me your principles, Akiko, why the theatre? Why are you tormenting me on this ride?'

'Because you are going to be in Brazil, as you know, once your Portuguese has reached a certain level. In Rio, you'll have to work with the resident, João Twenty. We know from our paper records that he will be murdered the day you are scheduled to exit.'

I looked at Akiko, trying to read her expression as a professional duty, and failed. I steadied myself on the handlebar as the car bucked and swayed with us inside it. 'And you think if I know that, I can try to prevent it?'

'I am not asking for you to violate any operational understandings,' she said, suddenly breathless from the ride.

'I am asking that you don't do anything to complete the causation. That is João's only hope for escape. And in any case, why should we be responsible for killing our own? That is what I'm truly afraid of, that an action of our own will lead to his death. Maybe you are the murderer and you don't know it yet. Maybe you are.'

I didn't reply immediately. The car was flying along the track faster than I could think. I held my breath until it had started to slow again. On the one hand, I was relieved if everything I had sensed about Akiko—everything I had sensed was wrong—came down to a mere love story. No treason against the system, as my father had feared, but an affair of that ridiculous organ, the heart, which knew nothing about the passage of time. She was a spy who loved a spy, the saddest story that ever was. On the other hand, I was thinking about what Akiko was asking me to do. Energy conservation and minimal intervention were principles I believed in. I didn't like the idea that I would be at the scene of a second crime.

Akiko interpreted my silence as disagreement. When the doors of the rollercoaster opened, she leant near to me for a moment, as if she were going to put her lips on my ear.

She said, 'If it helps you to dismiss what I am saying, you should know that I am anything but impartial. I should confess that I was in love with João once.'

Thanks to Akiko's confession I felt guilty before the fact of another man's murder, someone I had never even met, who went by the unlikely name of Joãozito. But I didn't have much time to enjoy this guilt.

I was arrested at three o'clock in the morning. The door to my suite opened and someone placed a hood over my head. I was brought to my feet without any instruction being uttered. A security band was placed over my arms, tightened until it had my body in its hold. I had never been placed in custody in this fashion, but it wasn't uncomfortable so long as I obeyed its instructions. If I wanted to go in the wrong direction, it pressed in, squeezing the breath out of me, until I changed direction. I wondered how far it would go if I disobeyed.

I was taken blind up the staircase, punch drunk from sleep, and delivered to the office where the hood was removed from behind.

Lucan Thirteen was waiting for me. He was studying a map, his expression even more sombre than usual. He didn't make an effort to look up.

'Do you have some insight into your situation, Agent Eleven? You're on furlough, on a charge of suspected treason for the dissemination of a prime, with enough mathematics against you to sustain an automatic conviction, and yet you are receiving prohibited information, making plans to subvert operational imperatives.'

I took a deep breath. The circle around my waist contracted. Lucan motioned me to the chair where I sat down. It was no more comfortable than standing. I could sense that there were guards behind me but I didn't turn around.

'Akiko didn't tell me much. She suggested Brazil, which I could have guessed from the fact that I'm learning that variety of Portuguese.' I found something in his face which told me not to skirt the truth. 'Besides, you know exactly what she told me. You must have had it pre-recorded. Then you must also know that she said nothing beyond the bounds of what is humane.'

'Correct.'

'I won't say you encouraged it, but you knew about it and you allowed it to happen. You allowed Akiko to ruin her life.'

'Her rights and responsibilities under the constitution will be protected under any process up to and including historical repudiation. We couldn't charge her from a recording, as you should know. Prophecy does not count as evidence. But your suspicions are correct. It has happened exactly as the consultant predicted. The same one, by the way, which was teaching you Portuguese.'

I tried to think about the situation like a case officer rather than the culprit. I didn't have time to feel resentment towards a machine. 'You've let Akiko martyr herself in order to get an unattributable message to me? Is that the idea?'

'I don't have to repeat myself, Agent Eleven, on a day that you broke the rules. There are no martyrs under the constitution.'

I cursed the constitution under my breath, not to say the ways that it encouraged Lucan to twist and turn its very words. What was a constitution but the dream of the tripods? Whom did the constitution truly protect? What did it help to have rights and responsibilities when you could be disappeared more completely than by any secret police? This constitution made it possible for human beings to do anything to other humans, preserving their good conscience. No one so immune to pity as a constitutionalist; no one so certain of his righteousness and so sure that a bright line divided law and what was unjust. I would rather live under a dictatorship, in the dark forest of the twentieth century, than under this constitution which hardened our hearts.

But it would have been useless to bring up the constitution with Lucan, or any of the Thirteens. They had business to get on with. Given the rising cost in terms of energy, they had to send me back to Brazil, to June 1967—if they were going to send me at all—before the consequences of Akiko's revelation played themselves out fully in the present.

I found out for sure when Lucan put a road atlas in the centre of his desk and opened it to a bookmarked page. He smoothed out the creases.

I recognised the location at once. 'Akiko was telling the truth.'

'It is Rio, yes. Our agent, as you know from Akiko, is already on the ground, in residence, as the book-keeper for a Venezuelan company. He picked up Muller's trail two weeks ago, ironically thanks to his expertise with tax records. Apart from him, as I weigh up the operational circumstances, you are the only one who has face-to-face acquaintance with Muller.' Lucan paused. His eyes were almost completely closed, slashes in the helmet of his face. 'Let me caution you. On this mission, for the first time, you will be acting on behalf of Section and in accordance with its rules.'

'Meaning that I can't tell your resident his destiny. Meaning that I have to leave him to die.'

'Meaning that, if it comes to that, and only if it comes to that.'

'Do you have a pre-recording of my abandoning the man as well? Leaving him to die like a dog?'

Lucan shook his head. He got up impatiently and closed the door, leaving the guards outside. Then he brought up a hologram of Akiko, her skin as pale and grainy as the inside of an apple. I had never seen her in expeditionary gear.

Lucan went on. 'I'm not ordering you to believe me on any of this. I am asking you to assess Akiko Thirteen's credibility as you are trained to do, that is, from the operational point of view. Assess the validity of what she told you. Did you know she's an albino? Akiko fell into the category of special risk since she came here. Her condition made her vulnerable to blackmail, not to say the emotional volatility from keeping a secret like that from her co-workers.'

I put my hands over my eyes. Shuddering, I remembered how close we had been sitting to each other. I had looked into her eyes, and the perfect spirals inside them, without thinking what they concealed.

'She used skin-darkening creams?'

'Yes, we allowed it. We're not monsters. We don't

discriminate and, under certain circumstances, we need genuine albino cooperation. Either way, Akiko was a risk to Section. Susceptibility to blackmail, if she kept it secret from her fellow workers. On the other hand, a tendency to breakdown and psychological volatility, if she lived at close quarters with others, always using the cream without letting them know. It seems to have got worse underground, the psychology of it.'

'Everything gets worse underground. Is she really an albino?'

'Not technically, but what difference does it make? Akiko has real East Asian ancestry. If you look in Chinatown today, you can find more than a few in the kitchens. Nobody harasses them as long as the clientele never find out who is making their meals. You would never have guessed about Akiko? I would never have guessed either, and I am an expert in the field of agent vulnerability. Blackmail, whitemail, whatever you want to call it.'

'It must be terrifying to look into a mirror and hardly be able to make out your reflection.'

Lucan brought up an overlay for the road atlas. He circled points for me to memorise, labelling them with various alphanumerics and notes. There were locations in the dense jungle right outside Rio I would need to scout, along with front offices in the city proper, warehouses, power installations which might be fuelling any historical distortions, and the grand old coffee shops along the central avenues where I would be likely to find businessmen and spies, exiles and fanatics, in plain view, deep in their intrigues. Muller's network might extend further than was generally known.

Lucan turned the map around so I could get a better look and commit it to memory.

'You know it's a myth about reflections.'

'What?'

'It's a myth, dating from the underground, that fair-skinned people have no reflection, and are supposedly immune to reflection sickness. Usually, when travellers go back to those years, it's the first thing they check out, if they have any scientific curiosity.'

'You know, in Morocco, I never thought to look.'

'Then in Rio de Janeiro, it's a good idea to satisfy yourself that it's a legend. I don't understand these simple-minded prejudices concerning people in the past. Otherwise, why did Europeans put mirrors in their rooms? Why did they carry vanity cases? Aren't you meant to be an observer, first and foremost? And this is something you choose not to observe.'

I wasn't sure what to tell Lucan. He made me ashamed of myself. I had been taught the same tragic history as everyone, after all. Under the stresses of the underground years, those ancient preoccupations with albinism had come to the fore. Persons with fair skins were as rare as dragon's teeth. They had been simultaneously exalted and degraded in the mines—revered as soothsayers in some cases, in other cases expelled to the fringes of the underground communities. Some had seen their children abducted, had their pelts dyed after death and used as cult objects. If they were allowed to rest, it wasn't in the grave. For their bones were rumoured to contain particles of gold.

Nobody remembered the events of that time without a shudder that such discrimination could occur in the heart of the civilised continent, in the wake of the slave ships, and at the very moment when the survival of humanity was at stake. The supernova had tested us. In the deepest part of our hearts, it had found us wanting. For someone like Akiko Thirteen, it meant she would rather wear the equivalent of shoe polish on her face than take pride in her skin.

When I had finished memorising the map of Rio, Lucan rolled it up and stored it in the corner of his office.

'Let me suggest that you ask yourself a question or two. And this is strictly from a practical intelligence aspect.'

'I'll do my best.'

'Why do you think Akiko Thirteen latched on to you? What is it about you, and your beliefs, Eleven, that drew her in? Is there anything about your own history that suggests a predilection for albinos? Because that, in itself, is a piece of intelligence about you that an adversary would like to acquire. If so, I should like to know before anybody out there does.'

I could not answer any of Lucan's questions at the time. I didn't have the chance to ask the only person who could have answered even one of them. Outside of my dreams, I never saw the face of Akiko Thirteen again. No matter how I searched, I didn't come across anything but rumours concerning her existence or non-existence under the constitution. Nor was there any trace in the judicial record.

The few days I had spent in her company had been memorable. I sometimes thought I might have fallen in love with Akiko Thirteen or that she might have fallen in love with me as she had previously fallen in love with a Twenty. She wouldn't be the only supernaturally calm personality, the person who was always under control, who had given her heart away at a moment's notice.

On reconsideration, I decided that my own affection for Akiko had a different source. She had fascinated me because of her condition. We, the survivors of the mines, had perpetrated terrible deeds against men, women, and children of fairer complexion. First, we hunted them and tanned their skins, to the point of extinction, stole their children, desecrated their underground burial plots in the coal mines. Later, we refused to touch them, refused to have them in our houses, spurned their cow smell, and spun a mythology around them and their reflections. I was guilty of my part in this but I was also secretly attracted and repelled by the people we had put into subjection. I looked into the mirror—truly for the first time—and understood some of my own limits during my service in Internal Section.

In any case, I couldn't have been more relieved to escape from the oppressive atmosphere of Section. I could sense the solar plant charging even when I was in Lucan's office. When it was full, to my surprise, the Director in Century came to observe my departure along with the remaining Thirteens.

Lucan was at the back, secretive behind his spectacles. Avery Thirteen made the last-minute preparations and realignments on the apparatus. Avery, who had taken up Akiko's responsibilities, had a number of updated pieces of information about the Muller house and organisation.

I never went back to my room. Avery had also packed my suitcase for the expedition. She went through the items with me, ticking them off a list, and obtained my signature on the bottom before, according to regulation, she filled the compartments for the blue pill and the black pill in the lanyard on my neck with more relish than I would have liked. I thought she was subliminally encouraging me to take them.

The consultant on duty locked on to the location on the other side, its face chattering with numbers. The suitcase was sent across. The ritual words were exchanged in the name of S Natanson.

The arch shimmered. The usual fireworks and more. The coloured lens which gave off no heat. Red lines stretched across its circular face. Stars appeared and disappeared in an endless funnel while the smell of ozone rose around me until I thought I wouldn't be able to breathe. Inside Section, the lights trembled and went low and blue. The entire building was unsettled as the superconductor fed the vast dam of solar energy into the apparatus.

I yawned. I wanted to go to sleep on the floor in front of

them. Instead, I shook hands with Avery and the DC. Then I nodded at Lucan, held my breath for a moment, and stepped into another world and time. Spirals of light shot through space-time in front of me and below my feet, while I turned round and around in the grip of a greater hand.

I fell over the suitcase on arrival. By the time I dusted off and got to my feet, any trace of a disturbance had dissipated. The heat was tremendous. I was in a small room, dark except for a barred window high on the wall. There were crates piled five deep, filled with the hairy brown heads of coconuts. I could hear women's voices talking angrily in the vicinity.

I breathed a sigh of relief. I had a job to do, and for the duration of it I was beyond the tentacles of Internal Section.

Rio

1967

I lifted the suitcase and went through the door to find myself in a courtyard. Women in aprons were packing bottles in the sunlight, rolling loads of them on handcarts in the direction of the road.

One approached me. She was six feet tall, so that I had to crane my head, and had a red cloth tied on her forehead. Her thick brown forearms were glistening with perspiration. She looked me up and down and slapped the side of my suitcase.

'Tiny, you came from the Palácio? You came from the Palácio right now?'

'Not at all.'

'Then you are from the company office.' She raised her voice, addressing the dozen other women in the yard. 'How many times will you come to check on us? We have nothing to do with the union. We rejected the union.'

'No. You are mistaken.'

'We are not mistaken. You, Tiny, are the one who is mistaken to come here. Now you will see.'

The women collected around me. They began to push me towards the street, shouting and cursing about the union, vigorously pinching my arms and legs. I dug my feet in, trying to hold on to the suitcase, but was soon forced out. I stood helplessly on the pavement while they forced open the suitcase and went through its contents. Fuming, I put my hands in my pockets and watched while my possessions were passed from hand to hand until they reached somebody who wanted them. Items that weren't wanted were tossed on the ground.

Never before had I experienced dark-skinned people behaving like barbarians. It was the tropical state of mind, I told myself, hearts corrupted by jungle and sun, minds dissolved into fever and mud.

'Can you try not to break anything?'

'Beware, Tiny. You have aroused a lion. You are lucky to escape with your life.'

Eventually the women retreated to the courtyard with my clothes, casting back imprecations about the union and the company office. I waited until they had returned to loading their carts before collecting the inner parts of the beacon. The elements of a beacon could be damaged easily, leaving the user stranded in a hostile century. I reassembled them in my palm, as fragile as bones in a fossil hand.

Without a chance to start the apparatus in private, I couldn't be certain it was functional. Every so often one or other of the women caught sight of me and, as if to protect their stolen property, warded me off with an arm. I was angry enough to gesture back.

In a quarter of an hour I had the bag more or less packed. I was behind schedule; I was supposed to be in Copacabana in five minutes. Walking as fast as I could in what I hoped was the right direction, I pulled the suitcase awkwardly behind me and tried not to hear the jeers of the work crew. This part of the city was a jungle in itself. Weathered stone office buildings groaned in the humidity, green plants growing out of every crack in their walls. Small cars and taxis, as flat as tin cans, shot impatiently through the traffic lights.

At the major intersections, checkpoints kept watch on the public, brown-skinned and white-skinned soldiers monitoring their giant radios, gleaming copper bullets hanging in belts around their waists. They didn't pay me any attention. Nor did anybody else. I was relieved to blend in as I had been told about old Brazil. I saw blacks and whites mingling without distinction.

I went past a row of hotels advertising their rooms by the hour, foyers paved with red carpet. Then came cafeterias promising food by the gram. Their interiors consisted of counters sitting end to end in dim light.

The road I was following broadened into a square that centred on the statue of a mounted man. Here and there were stone benches, legs covered with moss. I examined them, trying to find my bearings against the map in my head, and realised I only had to turn right to see the beach, the length of Copacabana with the lights shining in the haze. The water lay stagnant on the sand. Young men were kicking a ball around.

'Mr Eleven, I presume. The famous and delightful Enver Eleven, who has brought so much trouble in his wake.'

'Who's asking?'

'The only individual in the Agency, besides you, who has shaken hands with Dr Muller, although it was only to read the electricity. The only other one who knows the face of the adversary. As far as we know.'

'As far as we know. You're João Twenty.'

'The very same. My friends, up and down the centuries, know me as Joãozito. And you, Mr Eleven, are going to be my new friend.'

We shook hands. My brand-new friend wore a raincoat, for no good reason considering the sky, and tinted spectacles. I stood back and got the measure of him. João Twenty was short but nevertheless an impressive specimen, a moustache running the length of his full lips. He was broad-shouldered, a small bull of a man, but—as you saw on making his acquaintance—nimble as a bull-fighter.

'You want to go back to my place? Or do you want me to show you around first? I can show you Rio. I don't mind.'

I said, 'Let's go back. I want to see if the beacon is still working. It took a beating on the way. I would like to put my mind at rest.'

'We will get to your beacon. But take some time to appreciate your arrival. This city is different when you see it in person, when you experience it with your own eyes and your own senses. This city, above all, in this century. You can't compare the effect with a mere holographic reproduction in some museum of the old world.'

'I do want an introduction to old Rio from a genuine resident. Let's check the beacon first and we can explore.'

João started us across the square. I turned around for a moment to make sure that nobody was following us but, as far as I could tell, there were only young men and women in one another's arms on the square and the soccer players on the tattered beach. In the grand old buildings along the shore the windows had turned orange. João put his hand on my arm.

'Mr Eleven, I have to compliment you. Unfortunately I have to compliment you and I hope you do not start to imagine I am insincere. In fact, your Portuguese is excellent.' He cupped a hand around one ear. 'You have exactly the right intonations for a visitor from the north. From Recife, perhaps.'

'The machines programmed me well. Apparently at your suggestion.'

'And who said that?'

'A friend. We have a mutual friend.'

João put his arm around me, as if he were about to hug me.

'Mr Eleven, Enver. I'll tell you more when it is safe to talk. Then we peel the pineapple. Then we truly peel the pineapple. Let's get some clean clothes on you first. I want you to look like the noblest carioca.'

*

João's apartment lay at the top of a building adjacent to the beach, protected by a steel door and a sleeping doorman, head buried in a bowler hat. We went into the cage of the escalator, rose a dozen floors and then a few more, and entered through a hallway lined with shamans' masks. White leather couches occupied the main room. There were piles of records, a thick carpet, fading views of Sugarloaf, and the white-and-red lights of downtown.

The residents on station, designated as a class in the Twenties and Thirties, were a different breed to those of us who lived out of a suitcase. Residents were encouraged to make a home for themselves, not to remain interlopers. They made friends, even took lovers, with the consent of the consultants. They had some steadiness in their lives in a foreign land. I envied them for it.

Which is not to say that João Twenty was a hopeless romantic. If anything, he was the consummate professional. The first thing he did, while I was still looking out the window at Sugarloaf, was to spread out the shattered pieces of the beacon on his kitchen table. He took a bag of tools from under the floorboards.

On the bookshelf, beneath one of those world globes with a light in the middle, was the circuit diagram which João rolled out on the carpet, placing the various components on the blue lines. I held the pieces in place while he soldered the connecting wires back.

Each time João fixed something, he checked the current with a voltage meter. The needle didn't budge. He fixed the next wire. Checked the current. Nothing changed. Each time his smile became shorter. At the end, he threw his hands in the air.

'You had better make your pre-arranged rendezvous, Agent Eleven, because there is no hope for this piece of junk. There are breakages on every circuit, you saw. That is what you get from budget cuts. They send us to a foreign location with inadequate equipment.'

I said, 'I watched what those women were doing and I wanted to cry. I hope that kind of ignorance isn't typical of this country.'

João put his tools back in their box. He wore a solemn expression, as if he were trying to make a decision. When he was done, he took two crystal glasses from the cupboard and poured something into them which looked like wine.

We sat on the leather couches and drank. The liquid was stronger than wine. It tasted like burnt cinnamon.

'Catuaba. An infusion. We think of it as a kind of tea. You like it?'

'I need to get used to it first.'

João drained his glass and placed it on the table.

'I suspect your beacon was useless long before you arrived in Rio de Janeiro. I suspect. I suspect.' He put his hands in the air. 'But all I can do is suspect and never prove a thing.'

'What do you mean?'

'Maybe it means nothing. Maybe it means that you have a friend, or an enemy, that you don't know anything about—and that friend, or that enemy, doesn't want to see your face again. Maybe you will find there is no rendezvous in the end. Then again, I don't want you to be lost in paranoia. It might be me they're after. I haven't been able to establish a good connection with the centre for days. I also feel abandoned, feel as if there is something they are not telling me. Could it be the hidden enemy?'

'My heart is pounding very fast.'

'That's the catuaba, man. It will subside. But, if you don't mind, let's rather go somewhere where we are certain we won't be overheard in years to come.' He took a leather jacket from the hook and measured me against it. 'What kinds of clothes did you come with?'

'Pants. Some shirts. All taken.'

'I can lend you something. I have a pair of leather trousers which go very well with this jacket.'

The roads were filled with pedestrians and restaurant-goers, coconut-water sellers, taxis, and police cars. I didn't mind their complexions.

There was noise everywhere on the squares. Radio sets ran on every corner where makeshift tables groaned under the weight of limes and rock sugar, buckets of ice, and bottles of sharp-smelling cachaça. Drinks went from hand to hand without spilling. Young women in black-lace dresses accompanied men in suits into private clubs. The archways leading into them were hung with mother-of-pearl lightbulbs, otherworldly as the lanterns of a dream. Couples were kissing along the walls, cocoons placed at regular intervals throughout old vanished Rio.

For the first time, I saw that I was the ghost. I was the one without a reflection. These remembrances of human beings, these souvenirs of a disappeared continent, were all the more real and substantial compared to me. For I was indeed the ghost and, if things went any further in the direction they seemed to be going, I would never return to the future. I would be a ghost among ghosts, a shadow without the consolation of its own reflection.

I felt even more out of place in my leather trousers, so tight in the seat of the pants. The jacket was even tighter, but to be honest nobody noticed me beside João in his pastel-blue linen suit and blue beret. João was at home on the streets of Rio, the model resident and, as I was soon to discover, the matchless observer of what there was to be observed.

He led me though an unlit doorway into a lounge with long benches and a bar counter. A jazz quartet stood on a short stage, letting their instruments rest during the interval.

A man stood smoking next to the electric piano. He had a red scarf tied around his neck. Around the room people were talking, drinking beer out of frosted glasses, waiting expectantly near the counter where iron trays of prawn pies were being pulled out of an oven.

João found us a separate table at the back of the room. He sank into a chair, folded the collar of his jacket up, settled his sunglasses on his nose, and motioned to me to sit beside him.

'We should be able to talk freely here, Mr Eleven. But we will keep an eye on the door just in case. I believe that nobody will know to look for us in this place, in the present or in the days to come. Therefore, we have attained the only true form of safety available to us as members of the foreign service, the safety of the needle in the haystack. Isn't that true?'

'I'm not sure what you intend.'

'I am a needle and you are a needle, my friend, and there is a common magnetism between us. It makes us point in the same direction, towards the same truths. Wouldn't you say?'

As I got used to João Twenty, I would also become accustomed to his ideas and his proverbs, spun in the years of his exile in Rio when he had nobody to share them with. In a matter of days, I would learn to receive the things he had to say as his own brand of poetry and philosophy.

In that moment, however, I watched the door with an increasing sense of dread about the hidden enemy. I could picture our pursuers entering. They would find us exposed. It was unusually vivid, my sense of expectation. After all that had happened I was nothing but the coward who died a thousand deaths in his own imagination. I could hear the soft hissing sound of the bullet which they would put into me. I placed my hand on my stomach and felt a flower of black blood from the imaginary wound.

'Who do you think is following us, João? Is it Muller? Did someone tip him off? Is it a rogue faction at Agency? Is it Internal Section chasing its own tail?'

'Somebody doesn't have to follow us today, in the flesh, so to speak, to eavesdrop on our conversation. They could be following us in a thousand years' time, or ten thousand years, assuming they have the right co-ordinates. We don't even know who they are. Who they could be. I mean, my friend, even who we could turn out to be is an unknown mystery. In the face of all that, not even the notorious Internal Section has an idea about how to protect our operations.'

'You have some idea about Keswyn Muller from the case file. There's nothing that suggests he has the ability to crack our codes if even a mathematical genius in our time can't do it. How could he obtain an eight-hundred-digit prime? Do you agree that somebody on the inside could be collaborating?'

'Could be. I don't like to speculate. But you need to watch out in case he, she, or it makes sure you never go home again. And remember that you and I are both in possession of eight-hundred-digit primes. That is enough to give us power. We are not going like sheep to the slaughter.'

I pushed down the desire to confess to João Twenty, to inform him what Akiko had told me about his future. I told myself that it was a secret which Internal Section must have wanted me to communicate. Otherwise they would never have permitted me to travel with the knowledge of João's death. I kept silent. The guilt pierced my heart.

The waiter came to take our orders. João waited to say anything more until he was gone. The band started to play again. People were dancing in front of the stage, dressed for the most part in black silk and satin, moving slowly in one another's arms. Their bracelets and watches gleamed in the low light.

João watched the women and men. I thought I could tell what he was thinking. What was so simple for them was impossible for most of us in the foreign service. In the lost city of Rio, devoted to the art of kissing, I could never truly hold a woman in my arms. I wanted to ask João if he had taken advantage of his freedom from the usual constraints, but I remembered Akiko and held my tongue.

'Mr Eleven, you really want to know what I think? You want to know what I think is behind the recent chaos at Agency?'

'Very much.'

'It's just my homespun philosophy, mind you, but one advantage of being on station in the twentieth century is that I have time to philosophise and follow the concepts where they lead. Since you want to know, I think we are like a snake trying to catch its own tail.'

'In a concrete sense, João, what does that mean?'

'It means that, in my opinion, human beings can only stretch so far. Even the machines we build to help us can only do so much within the constraints of our evolutionary nature. Once we let go of causality, cause and effect, beginning and end, we weren't prepared. As human beings, we need things to take place one after the other. Birth first, and death after. Love first, and then the possibility of marriage. The father first, and after him the son. The mother, and then the daughter. So. So. And so.' João put one hand over his temple as if he had a headache. 'In the current mixed-up and back-to-front situation our minds don't work properly. Nothing works straight. Not even your friends in Internal Section can protect us from the ensuing chaos.'

My attention drifted from João to the band and to the couples dancing around us who could never again be divided. I noticed the merry glow of the oven in the background, and the frosty pitchers of beer on every table. I thought that I had never been in a city that was so perfectly devoted to happiness. So many years, so many decades of suffering and destruction, so many underground persecutions, and such a sudden strike of radiation in the skies separated us from loving old Rio and its pursuits of happiness.

I wasn't the ideal audience for a conspiracy theorist like João Twenty who had been in Rio too long to maintain perspective. I wasn't concerned with the meaning of time travel and what it did to the small heart of a human being. A pragmatist, I wanted to know what I was supposed to wake up and do the next morning, where I should go, whom I could trust and distrust. If somebody at Agency had sabotaged my beacon, I wanted to know whom it was and what they were up to. João must have guessed my state of mind.

'You're impatient, Mr Eleven. Ah, I don't blame you. I truly cannot blame you. Those of us who live on station, you understand, develop our own strange need to talk the moment we find a sympathetic ear. It probably detracts from our value as case officers, that we can wear our hearts on our sleeve like this. I am nauseated by myself.'

I chose to ignore half this outburst. 'I thought you would say more about our mutual friend.'

'We could sit here all night and I would listen to whatever you have to tell me about Akiko, any detail of her existence. But it's not good for me to fill my imagination with thoughts of her. So, for the moment, let it rest. Let me pay and we can go. Tomorrow we have an early start. We meet the enemy.'

On the way back João was subdued. The clubs and restaurants were brighter than ever, their windows blazing yellow in the velvet evening, although there were fewer people in the street. I felt there was some strange perfume blowing through the streets of Rio, a wind of flowers and rotting plant matter, that before long was going to sweep us away. I had seen the blank space on the map and the oceans which closed over the top of Sugarloaf in three hundred years' time and I felt the mortality of the enormous city press on my heart. I felt the fragility of the millions of black and white and brown people in the buildings, and the ever-briefer life-span of their kisses and embraces, their loves foretold and foredoomed.

Maybe João wasn't wrong about the limits of the human heart. They say that members of the foreign service see too much in a single career to remain fully human.

The next morning, we began surveillance on Muller. João woke me up early, when the sun was still a blur across a flat ocean. He produced espresso from a cabinet-sized machine, drained cup after cup with a tablespoon of sugar in each one.

I declined and went to shower in a cramped bathtub, alternately scalded and frozen by the sporadic bursts of water. I chose a short-sleeved shirt and a pair of linen trousers from the cupboard, on João's invitation, and returned to find him changing from his silk dressing gown into camouflage trousers and an army jacket.

Near João's place we caught the bus to Santa Teresa. The neighbourhood was set in a commanding situation, overlooking the centre of Rio, connected by a single winding road. We went round and round the mountain, a hot wind flowing in through the open windows of the bus, until the road came out in a flat business district.

The bus let us out on a square, the Largo dos Guimarães. People stood around or sat at tables, playing cards, coffee and pastries at their elbows, black and white with no distinction, pardos and pretos. We waited on the square in case anybody had followed us. If so, if we were indeed under surveillance by parties unknown, there was no sign of it that I could detect.

The tram arrived and sat in the middle of the square for a moment before rattling back down the hill. From the bus stop, you saw a cheerless grey sky set over the breadth of the immense city, apartment buildings in great rows, tin-roofed favelas lining the green curves of the jungle and mountain. In the distance, the ocean was still as flat and grey as the sky. Oil tankers lined up short of the horizon, their masts like crossed matchsticks.

'Is it too early for catuaba?'

'You are learning to be a carioca, Mr Eleven, faster than I anticipated. But perhaps it is best if we have clear heads. For today at least.'

On the other side of the square were a few three- and four-storey buildings. One housed a secondhand record store, at ground level, where there were rock 'n' roll posters plastered on every wall. Young men were leafing through the drawers of stock or listening unhappily to music in soundproofed cubicles, their faces sober as priests. I longed to listen with them but we continued. The built-up section ended abruptly. There were no more cars going in our direction, only the coming-and-going chatter of a helicopter heading inland.

We climbed a deserted road lined with towering trees and bushes. Birds sang indignantly to one another as the noise of traffic receded. The road made a number of turns. At one bend João opened two strands of barbed wire to allow me to get through.

We moved through the bushes, careful not to break any branches, and made ourselves a place. From there, lying on a narrow slope covered with rough grass, we could observe the residence of the most wanted man in the history of time.

João had two pairs of binoculars. He gave me one and showed me how to focus it. Then he put down a diagram of the house, printed on an embossed page.

'The official building plans of the structure you see in front of you. I have a contact in the office of the prefeito.'

'Useful to have.'

'He told me there's been building work in recent months. You can see the double garage on the right there. It used to be a stable. You should also take note of the fence around the whole of the property. It's electrified, and to a level far beyond the need to keep out stray animals.'

A dog kennel had been added to the back of the house.

The facade was blank. White stone walls and blinds drawn over the windows.

I said, 'You can't see anything of what's going on inside.'

'That's the general idea, Mr Eleven. I've been out here, three afternoons of the past five, preparing for your arrival, and I have seen neither hide nor hair of Muller since I met him once outside the gate and shook his hand. But we know he's in there right now. He gets deliveries and the occasional visitor.'

'I should march straight up to the door and take him back to Agency.'

'If he kills himself?'

'We'd be rid of him, at least. We would have achieved vengeance. Isn't that a virtue in the old world?'

'You cowboys sometimes don't accept the need for running a patient investigation which is the daily bread of a resident. Do we need another body on our hands? Muller is our lead. We cannot afford to alarm him before the moment to strike has arrived.'

'And who decides that? Who decides when it is the right moment to strike?'

'I believe that it may be you, Mr Eleven. Young as you are, they have sent you back here for a reason. That is when a cowboy becomes necessary. And just don't ask me to give you confidence. I have little enough of it for myself at the present time.'

João produced a flask from his backpack, poured strong black coffee into the lid. I drank two cups. The jolt only made clearer my sense of separation from the ordinary world. They had warned us about disorientation in training. It was built into the nature of the profession. One day I was at my father's nursing home, watching him programme the robots to play backgammon. The next, I was a mile underground, not far from the mines which had saved the blessed remainder of humanity. I was spying on a criminal mastermind on Santa Teresa in a country of black and white, octoroon, mestizo, red rib, and yellow bone. Meanwhile, I was keeping to myself knowledge of the fate of the man lying beside me. I could hardly breathe for the guilt.

'And who is in charge of me, João Twenty? Who will say if I make the right decision or the wrong decision out here? Will it be you?'

'I can't answer your question but it will not be me. As the resident, I am simply here to be your eyes and ears. You can think of me as a facilitator for those who want to observe and interrupt.'

'So who is above me?'

'From what you say, Internal Section. But they are centuries away. You will have to make up your mind.'

I shook my head. There was nothing more to say on the subject. João folded his arms, turned on his side, and seemed to fall asleep. An hour went by, another and another while I watched the unwavering walls.

The sun arrived, began to push the accumulations of hot cloud to the horizon. Clouds of insects rose around us. I got on my knees to brush them off. João pushed me down. I looked back to the house. The garage door was opening. A blue Mercedes eased onto the driveway, its long bonnet sparkling. The door closed behind it.

I examined the car through the binoculars. The driver was alone. I watched her until the car passed through the automatic gate and disappeared. She was wearing a light-grey coat over her shoulders. Her hair was shorter. Otherwise, so far as I could tell, she hadn't changed. Soledad.

'You recognise her?'

'Soledad. I met her in the Green Dolphin with Muller, several years ago.'

'Ah, this woman, I believe, this woman is the entire reason

you were sent to Rio, Mr Eleven. The fact that you know this woman is the key. That is the theory I am developing.'

Agency hadn't given João any additional information about Soledad. He didn't ask me and I didn't tell him. That was the new way. In any case, she didn't come back to Santa Teresa that night. At around two in the morning, João let me keep watch and went to sleep on his back, the stars shining strangely above both of us.

I listened to João purring through his long moustache, his hands twitching at his side. I wondered how he could be so trusting of the universe to lie asleep in the midst of it. I drank more coffee and tried to concentrate on Muller's castle. I decided that the masonry in the walls was unusually bright in the starlight and then I was also asleep. My sister entered my dreams, her hands also trembling at her sides as if she had a terrible message to deliver. She touched my face with her hands and I wanted to put my head on her bosom, fall down at her feet and beg her forgiveness.

Then I was being shaken. My dream vanished and João was staring down at me. For a moment, I could only focus on the tobacco leaves in his moustache.

'Your girlfriend is back. Do you want to see?'

I sat up and peered wearily through the binoculars. The lights of the Mercedes shone mysteriously in the morning. Soledad got out and looked around. She had a scarf on her head now. She knelt down, unlocked the garage, winched up the door, and returned to the car. Then she disappeared into the house and didn't come out again, as far as we knew, for a total of sixty hours.

Three days later, I was waiting in a Fiat on Largo dos Guimarães when the radio crackled.

'The package is on its way.'

'What package?'

'Soledad, I mean. She is on her way to you. You should have her in view in a minute.'

João was correct. Soledad's Mercedes paused at the entrance to the square, crossed the tram tracks, and headed down the mountain. I counted to twenty, turned on the car, and followed. I caught sight of her white tyres and stayed close, leaving two other cars and a hundred yards between us as we descended.

The narrow road was bordered by a low stone wall, covered here and there by rapacious fingers of jungle. It curved sharply. Soledad sped without hesitation, never flinching when a car or a truck came in the opposite direction. She didn't seem to worry about being followed.

I had trouble keeping up. On the bends, the Fiat slid to the outside and came close to the wall. It accelerated grudgingly on the open stretches, rattling like a tin can on the cobblestones, as the smell of motor oil rose from the engine.

The ocean came round and then round again, circling in the mirror, and the green mountains, the alpine slums, the skyscrapers on Avenida Presidente Vargas. In the other lane a van went by like a missile. I felt my heart racing in my neck, and slowed down until the blue Mercedes was barely visible.

By the time we reached Lapa, and the buses and trams on Avenida Gomes Freire brought the traffic to a crawl, I promised that I would hire a driver before ever again stepping into a deathtrap like a manual car. I opened the window and enjoyed the wind on my face while changing lanes to stay behind my quarry.

We went straight through Lapa and onto another highway. I hung on and was rewarded when the Mercedes took an exit into the Zona Sul. Men were playing football on a nearby field, some in collared shirts. We went past big private houses protected by guards in fatigues. Then an army barracks around which were parked rows of flatbed trucks, consular residences with their national flags flying at the gates. An open-air cinema, its tall screen standing silent in the last minutes of the afternoon.

Soon we were driving on the road which followed the contours of the lagoon, Sugarloaf on the right. The Mercedes stopped abruptly at the entrance to an official compound. I continued along the road for a few minutes and stopped on the verge.

I counted to a hundred, turned around, and came back to find a boom gate and a stern-faced sentry in a tin helmet and gold-buttoned shirt. He examined the Fiat without letting go of his rifle. He went around the entire car, bent down and looked underneath, and leant in the window, bringing the sharp smell of his cologne into the compartment.

'Are you lost, my friend?'

'No, I'm not lost. I want to go in, if you don't mind.'

He stepped back from the window and leant on his rifle, straining the buttons on his shirt. Behind him was a grand hall, four storeys high, with slatted windows, pennants on the roof fluttering in the wind. Soledad's Mercedes was parked in a space beside a number of jeeps and a truck with canvas sheeting on the back. Behind that, the water.

'And yet I see no proof of membership, my friend.'

'Membership of what?'

'Membership of the Naval Club of the Republic, my friend. You are standing at the entrance to the estate of the great Naval Club of the Republic.'

This information made sense when I looked around. A ship's cannon was mounted on a stone circle set upon the waterside. I saw there were sailors in stiff white uniforms on the bank. They were smoking cheroots, arguing lazily as the evening descended from the mountains to the lagoon. Young men. Neither older nor younger than myself, their skins tanned brown. I longed to be among them.

I opened the car door. The guard shook his head.

'I know what you have in mind, my friend. I am afraid you cannot apply for a membership in the Naval Club. Either you are already known as a friend of the Brazilian navy, or you are a mere stranger.'

'May I be honest?'

'That is always the best policy, my friend.'

I said, 'It's not the membership that is important to me. I am following a young woman.'

The guard didn't smile but he relaxed his hold on his rifle. 'Soledad, needless to say. The mythical beauty who has turned Rio's heart upside down. Why should I allow you to pursue her into the Naval Club?'

'Love has its own reasons. Sometimes the rest of the world has to respect it for that, step back, and allow it to develop according to its own rules.'

'I like your philosophy, my friend. I cannot say I disagree with it, even if you speak like a bumpkin from Recife. But I still cannot allow you to enter through this gate. Look at the shirt you are wearing. This is the main entrance to the Naval Club. Come over there.'

He pointed to a gate further up the road. I backed up and drove to it while he walked over. The guard lifted the chain and let me through. I stopped in the delivery bay next to a van loaded with wooden boards. Holding my breath, I sat there, waiting to be arrested. I couldn't figure out what the guard's game was.

When I got out of the car I tried to put some cruzeiros in his jacket pocket, but he pushed my hand away.

'I will never take advantage of a lover.'

'How do you know, for sure, that I am a lover?'

'How can I mistake that look? I will let you in on a secret as long as you do not inform my wife. I am also a lover. During the week, I am a husband and a father. On the weekends, I am a lover. If I am lucky, now that I have done something for you, the world will respect my own situation. Concerning karma, concerning matters of the heart, tit for tat. But be sure that you don't let me down.'

'I won't.'

'You have your work cut out for you. I am sorry to tell you this. They say Soledad has a heart of ice.'

With this encouragement ringing in my ears I went around to the front and into the hall. To my astonishment, the ground floor was covered in round tables, candles and flower arrangements in the centre of each one. There were more sailors standing around in their dress uniforms, only a few women, in formal dresses and blouses, heavily made up and their hair arrayed in tight bundles, whose conversation was sought by the men. Paintings of admirals in ceremonial dress hung on the walls in heavy gold frames.

Along one side of the room was the bar: a table covered with fluted glasses plus bottles of rum, white wine in pans of ice, and fruit juices. A man in an apron was tending bar, sliding paper umbrellas into the glasses before he handed them over.

I found my way into the line behind Soledad. She had taken off her riding jacket and was wearing a short red coat, a jade necklace around her neck, her hair pinned up in a bun. Her blouse was open a few buttons, revealing a few tiny moles scattered on her collar bone. She had only become more beautiful with the passage of time, ripening beauty that only a time traveller could appreciate for what it was.

I stood as close as I dared. Her brown body, so frighteningly close to me, had the exact smell of baking bread. I didn't mind the lightness of her complexion at all.

When she had her glass, she turned round, looked at me in the face for a minute, and hesitated.

'I know you. Where did we meet?'

'Nowhere.'

'Not nowhere. Somewhere. I know your face. Tokyo? It must have been Tokyo.'

Could she have recognised me? She could hardly have been twenty years old in Marrakech, although Section had been unable to find any surviving records of her birth.

In the meanwhile, she had become a fully fledged woman. I had slept thousands of years in a graveyard. So much travelling in the meanwhile, this meanwhile in which my soul was supposed to be frozen. I had visited the rings of Jupiter, a voyage unimaginable to a person of this century, while she had followed Keswyn Muller to Finland, Tokyo, Yokohama and Brazil in pursuit of whatever it was that the doctor sought. Yet there had been some connection between us, I thought, since the evening in the Green Dolphin. There had been some secret form of influence which had worked on the heart's level.

'I would remember if I had been to Tokyo. I would remember when we met.'

'It seems to be a competition in Brazil, each time I talk to someone, for him to come up with the most romantic sentence.'

I said, 'I don't think we could have met. I cannot believe it.'

Soledad put her hand on my shoulder for a moment. We were alone in the deserted hall.

'And I could swear that we have. Are you really from Brazil?'

'Not originally.'

'You speak very good Portuguese. Like a local.'

'I had very good teachers.'

It was thrilling simply to be talking to Soledad once again. I could only compare it to riding a bicycle faster and faster, flying down the slope of the steepest hill, when I had no idea what lay at the bottom …

'But you are quite black even for a Brazilian. Since we have never been introduced, will you tell me what is your name?'

'They call me Enver.'

'Enver, Soledad, pleased to meet you.' She repeated my name as if to listen through new ears. 'Enver, Enver, Enver sounds familiar.'

'It's a common name. You hear it from place to place.'

Only the senior officers, men in their fifties and sixties, seemed to have the right to converse with Soledad. One of them, a grey-haired column of a man, kept trying to break in to our conversation. He became even more severe, his face as troubled as the ocean, when Soledad politely turned her back to him.

When he came around, Soledad went to make a telephone call. The admiral stroked his gardened beard and considered me disapprovingly. He brought out a box of snuff and offered me a pinch. I accepted, held the peppery-white dust under my nose, and almost choked trying to breathe it in. The man put his arm on my back until the coughing stopped.

'And what is your connection with the Brazilian navy? If I may be permitted to enquire.'

'I don't have any such connection.'

'And with Soledad?'

'We don't have one either. We were just starting to talk when you interrupted.'

The admiral flushed red, trembled in his ruffled shirt, swayed from side to side. I regretted the criticism. I didn't want to end my career fighting with pistols at dawn in the tropical squalor of the twentieth century.

I said, 'Excuse me. I spoke out of turn. The fact is, I hardly know Soledad or what to make of her. I am sure you admire her good qualities as much as I do.'

'Ah, she is an exceptional woman. Even for Brazil.'

'I can see that. Even for Brazil. I may sound like one of you but I was not in fact born in this country. I am only an admirer.'

The admiral said, 'And there is a lot to admire.'

There was no obvious way to continue the conversation. We both looked at the cook, a fat man laughing in a white apron, who was prying off the tops of a line of wine bottles set on the counter. The sailors had found partners. Couples were dancing, cheek to cheek. Others were talking, their hands and faces almost touching in the starlight of the chandeliers. The scent of the flowers had spread throughout the hall.

In the windows, the evening was coming across the lagoon, the water and the mountain turning dark for this building of love. I could feel Section and its attendant haze of paranoia and conspiracy fall away from me forever. I was in a place apart from its tentacles, apart from the impending death of João Twenty.

The admiral's face was still red. He was watching impatiently for Soledad.

'May I ask you a question?'

He opened his hands. 'Go ahead.'

'What exactly do you do in the navy? Do you command a ship or a flotilla? Do you work in the harbour?'

'I am not a commander of a vessel. That is a common misunderstanding, to believe that every admiral and commodore is in charge of a ship. As a matter of fact, I am an engineer, working on the capabilities of submarines and surface ships. Naval aviation also, coincidentally. The Tracker aircraft, for example, belongs to my area of responsibility. I help them to communicate with one another and with Operations Command on shore. Within that general area, my expertise is technical. It is not easy to explain to a civilian.'

'Try me.'

'Very well. You understand that Brazil is a very proud country.'

I said, 'And you have every right to be. You have the best of everything here.'

The admiral paused, seemed to wonder if I could be doubting him. Then he went on.

'As I say, we are proud enough to dislike and bridle at the fact of the superpowers reading our internal communications. So we are investing in our own protection, our own self-respect. I am supervising the design and construction of a number of code-making machines, fit for our ships, submarines, and aircraft. Soon, we will be able to speak from any corner of the world without fear of eavesdropping. I can tell you all this because it is natural that a country like ours has secrets to keep. And that in itself is no secret. It is something we can take pride in as Brazil takes its place at the forefront of nations.'

'Soledad?'

'She has a connection, yes, to the great work.'

'What is that connection? What possible relationship can exist between her and the existence of a military code?'

The admiral waited and put his hand on Soledad's back when she returned. She didn't accept his attention. Nor did she reject it.

'You left me in the company of a very inquisitive man, my dear.'

'What does he want to know about?'

'Ah, he wants to know about you. In that respect, he is not unique. Every man and every woman in Rio wants to know about you. Beauty is always of interest.'

I excused myself, my face burning. I went to telephone João from an upstairs line, located in the admiral's office, and was separated from Soledad for the rest of the evening. I spent the time listening to the various conversations going on around the room.

When I couldn't eavesdrop any more because my ears were falling off, I went outside and sat on the stone circle, beneath the cannon, watching the couples who came out of the lighted hall and went along the promenade, following the metalwork fence along the water until it turned at the edge of the estate.

When the staff cars arrived for the officers, I made my way to the Mercedes and opened the door. It took a matter of seconds to get in. I lay in the back, trying to make myself invisible. Soledad got in and turned the car on. She drove through the gates, turned onto a side road, and then onto the main road. There was nobody about. The street lights hung like orange lanterns outside the consulates and diplomatic residences.

She stopped in the driveway of a mansion. The Canadian flag hung above it. Two sentries in white helmets and gloves watched us from their cubicle. Soledad turned off the car and produced a gun from her handbag. Then she turned around and put the barrel against my forehead. It was a cold circle.

'Admiral Coriolis had the right opinion. You are very inquisitive, Enver. You know there's an expression in English? Too much curiosity killed the cat. We don't have the equivalent in Portuguese, as far as I know.'

'I don't know the expression.'

'In this case it applies.'

'If I die, I die. Those are the rules of the game. I only wanted to have a conversation which could be to your benefit. And believe me, Soledad, you don't want to be the one responsible for my death. I am protected by the statute governing time travel to foreign locations. I am protected under the constitution as an employee of the Historical Agency. Interfering with my work has the potential to have you expunged from existence. And not only you.'

'I have never heard of it. What on earth is a Historical Agency? Like a museum association?'

I ignored the question. I kept hoping the consulate guards would come towards us, but they seemed to be satisfied that we were having an ordinary conversation at gunpoint. My heart was beating very fast. My eyelids closed and could hardly be opened. I wanted to sleep.

To my relief, Soledad put the gun on her lap and allowed me to sit up. She turned on the light inside the cabin.

'You have already been blamed for the death of a senior member of the foreign service. I am talking about what transpired in Marrakech, in 1955.'

'I was in Marrakech, yes, but I have no idea what you are referring to.'

'You are considered an enemy to the cause of historical purity, as defined by S Natanson. If you harm me, I promise you, the Agency won't hesitate to apply the ultimate sanction, no matter the cost in energy. They will erase you and your parents and other relations, any children you might have had, and your children's children. They will travel into the past to punish you. If there is anything and anyone that means anything to you, they will find out and make it as if it had never been.'

'You're speaking nonsense, just a jumble of words that are coming out of your mouth.'

'You live with Dr Keswyn Muller, don't you?'

'To know this you don't need to travel through time.'

I didn't know what more to risk telling Soledad, how much she was shamming and playing ignorant. She had known something about the death of Shanumi. I had heard Muller relate the facts to her. But conversion experiences were expensive. To take a person from the past and let them into the secret of travelling, to reveal that their world was nothing but a shadow and the people in it no more than shadow players, to spawn rumours of immortals and flying saucers—none of that came cheap in energetic terms. It was the last thing you wanted to do, but it was something I had to do because I didn't want to let João die at her hand. I had to confess to Soledad as much as I dared.

'Look again. My face is familiar to you. I met the two of you in the Green Dolphin in Marrakech, in 1955, on the night the pilgrims came into town.'

Her voice was suddenly soft, a surprise to my ears. 'You were there in Marrakech?'

'Just for an evening, as it happened. You were wearing long earrings, a piece of jade in the centre. And a blouse with roses on it.'

'I still have that blouse. So you are speaking a part of the truth.'

In the long house behind the consulate a light came on, showing a figure through a gauze curtain. Who was watching us while we were watching? I thought that nobody, especially not a traveller, knew that his life was his own property. Nothing was private.

'You think we could drive?'

'Where do you want to go?'

'Wherever you feel safe. But the longer we stay in one place, the greater the chance that somebody, in years to come, will be listening to our conversation.'

I wanted to be closer to João in case we had to kidnap Soledad or put further questions to her under the action of a truth serum. Safer, in any case, from a counter-intelligence perspective, to move rather than stay still. Safer to be among many people. Safer to be where we went on Copacabana, on the margin of the stale ocean. Safer to speak under the cloak of the noise. Men with their shirts open to the navel tended their radios. Cars played music in the parking lots. In the small bars on the seaside waiters took drinks to the tables. Behind them were beachfront towers and, on the perpendicular streets, the massive stone buildings housing Rio's private gyms.

Soledad was careful. She looked along the beach, up and down, as if expecting to see somebody. We went closer to the water until the sand was firm. The moon had floated in over the ocean, perfect as a pearl.

'From what you say, assuming I choose to believe you, you have been tracking us since Marrakech. That is a substantial amount of time. At the very least, I suppose, you are patient before you decide to make contact.'

'On your timeline, as you have experienced your life, many years have elapsed. And you're right, Soledad. I work for a patient organisation. We can afford to be—to wait before we make our moves, and to think before we make our moves. After all, we have the whole past of mankind to preserve from foreign influences.'

'Foreign influences?'

'That's what we call them, Soledad. Anything that can interfere with the integrity of the past and interfere with the preservation of mankind or the action of the Agency.'

'And you do not count as a foreign influence?' She sounded weary. 'Travelling from place to place, on the instructions of your Board, with the freedom to attack and destroy anybody you don't approve of?'

'You're not the first person to come up with that paradox about the meaning of protection. If you are in this line of work, you quickly realise there is nothing so useless as a paradox.' I looked at the ocean, shrouded in fog, and despaired of my ability to convince anyone, least of all myself. 'Soledad, you don't have to believe me but, in my opinion, from what I've been taught, nothing in history has caused as much confusion as the dread of paradoxes. A paradox is only a loop carried to infinity. In fact, you could say we belong to the Agency precisely to protect humanity from the infinite. We despise the loop. We have only benevolent intentions, I assure you. Above and beyond that, we are governed by an iron triangle of machines, a doctrine, and the relevant clauses of the constitution.'

Two men in sleeveless shirts came running out of the dusk, pounding on the beach. They were laughing, shorts thin on their big thighs, as they ran. In half a minute, they had disappeared again. I could see the swimming pool on the balcony of an adjacent apartment building, lit from inside, where a man was doing laps methodically.

I went on. 'I need to ask you and Keswyn Muller some questions. They have been prepared by our experts. If you are willing to answer them, I see no reason why we can't allow you to be on your way.'

Soledad turned to me. I wanted to put my hand to her cheek.

'If you want to meet Keswyn, come tomorrow night. He will answer any questions you might have.'

'Just like that? I let you go now?'

'We are not going to run, you fool. We have been waiting for your arrival for centuries. The arrival of the prophet and the final mover in his proper time. In any case, where would we fly to?'

I had no reason to take Soledad at her word. I had every reason not to. I wasn't in love with her, although João imagined it. There was no evidence on her side of the ledger. I didn't believe that a secret society had handed down the report of my arrival in Rio in 1967. I knew enough to dismiss the significance of prophecy and revelation when it came to the activities of the Agency. They were most often the result of carelessness on the part of a case officer or a long-term resident. I wouldn't be the first member of a foreign delegation to start a cult, which could happen by a mere slip of the tongue.

Soledad vanished up the beach before I decided whether to believe her or not. I could have run after her. I could have gone directly to Santa Teresa and apprehended Muller and his apparatus.

Instead, I went to João's building and travelled in the rickety elevator to the top floor. I wanted to hear what the

Twenty thought in his capacity as resident. According to Akiko's calendar, there was only one day remaining in his life. I had lost one collaborator in pursuit of Keswyn Muller. I might be able to save a different one. I imagined I could balance the one loss against the other, a dangerous form of addition and subtraction.

João was doing his chores, the kind of chores you end up doing if you are several hundred years from home and you want your reports to find their way to the hands of sympathetic administrators. He had made himself comfortable on the balcony, looking out on the beachfront of old Rio. A glass pot of chamomile tea was suspended over a burner to keep warm, the stub of the candle covered in tiny insects. From time to time he would pour tea into two lacquered cups and offer me one.

He continued to work on his summary while I told him about Soledad, Admiral Coriolis, and the Naval Club of the Republic. Steam shimmered over the head of the teapot.

When it came to Soledad's revelation, João made no immediate comment. He rolled up each page of his document, then tightened it with his hands, smoothed wax from the candle along the sides, and stored it in a gold-sided box of cigarillos. It would be placed in a bank vault so that scholars in subsequent centuries could retrieve his detailed chronology and enter his observations into the record. They could arrange for the message to be returned in the event that his standing orders needed to be updated.

When the job was done, he sealed the box and went to put it away in the safe in his bedroom. He came out, closed the sliding door again, poured the remains of the tea, and put his hand over mine.

'I am a mere resident. I don't have the famous intuition you people are supposed to develop in your side of the profession. But for me, at any rate, alarm bells are ringing.

The two of them build a castle in Rio and they request you to come in the front door? No, in my humble opinion, this is not a likely scenario.'

'She asked. He hasn't seen me this time, as far as I know.'

'It's a standard procedure, Mr Eleven. We can assume they are not amateurs, since they have got this far. We have seen how seriously they take the security of the operation. I believe they agreed on a certain protocol before you arrived on the scene. They planned to flatter you with the talk of prophecy and the final move. Now they are putting the routine into action.'

'Maybe so. I don't deny it. I am not a proud person in any case.'

João left me and put the candle out between his fingers. His back was to me for a minute. I could hear a record player in the apartment below us. It was only a vibraphone and a silky woman's voice over a castanet, the soapy jazz of old Rio, but it touched me like a funeral march.

'There is a contradiction, my friend, that I cannot work out. Your Soledad should have shot you on the spot and they should both be on the run, trying to avoid the long arm of Agency. What do they have to gain by further interaction? They are exposing themselves to risk. They don't know what methods we might employ. So what do they have to gain? You will answer this question for me please.'

I didn't have a satisfactory answer for João. I wasn't sure what they were up to in the fortress at Santa Teresa. My crystal ball was dark. I couldn't see into Soledad's connection to Muller, or into Muller's purposes, or into what they conceivably wanted from me. I couldn't see into the near future, although my companion looked into the bottom of his cup, as if the stray tea leaves were going to tell him something. I hoped they didn't bear the same tidings to João that had reached my ears through the vessel of Akiko Thirteen. I prayed that, for once, the predictions of the brassheads would turn out to be as hollow as the ravings of forgotten saints and prophets, medicine men and bone throwers. Everybody wanted to know the future but it made us miserable when we did.

'Should I go tomorrow?'

'You should go and hear what they want to tell you, because that in itself is an important piece of intelligence. But you should take protection. I don't mean a gun, although I am going to give you one. I mean you need protection from people's reasons. Isn't that it? After all, this is the most dangerous game for a member of the foreign service to participate in—even more dangerous than to fall in love. They are inviting you there to win an argument, after all.'

It wasn't until midnight that João came into my bedroom to have the final word and bring me candles in case the electricity went out. Wearing his silk dressing gown, he sat at the end of the bed for a minute in silence. I saw that his thick brown legs were almost entirely hairless. João had the manner of an elder brother, I realised, and I was swept away by the greatest feeling of regret. I don't think he noticed.

'You really want to know my opinion? My philosophy as a resident?'

'I'd be grateful.'

'In that case, I will tell you, my friend. Because I run this station, I see agents come and go. They do their investigations, fill in the required paperwork, return to their comfortable berths five hundred years from now where it is not like Brazil under the military government. Nobody has to drive his own car, nobody has to die of a preventable disease, nobody can be murdered outside of the constitution. That is their reality and it is a different one. That is your reality also. Whereas I know that on 31 December 1969, or thereabouts, that will mark the end of my present tour and the beginning of my new one. I finish and then I start again in 1967.' He must have seen my reaction and clapped his hands to hold my attention. 'In any case, I have a different perspective which may be valuable to you. I believe that we cannot measure the changes in history because, at each turn of the screw, we ourselves have changed. There is simply no measuring rod outside of space and time. We ourselves are the measuring rods. So in that sense, yes, I am a relativist.'

João was at the door when something struck me. I sat up and called him back.

'As the resident you really go in a loop?'

'Not a loop, mind you, but an honest spiral, perfectly permissible on doctrinal grounds. Every two years, approximately, back to January of this year, assuming the protocol continues in the same way after Muller. That is what I was trying to explain.'

'Couldn't you run into yourself, João?'

'I could. Certainly I could. I would, if I didn't keep careful records about where I am each day. But, as you know, paradoxes are very expensive to pay for in energistic terms, even comparatively minor paradoxes and contradictions. There would have to be a corresponding input of energy from your side to make it up. Plus, they make the brassheads very nervous because their calculations cannot be finalised in the ordinary way. This is truly a job for the meticulous.'

'You never considered passing a message to a former self?'

He shrugged and tightened the belt of his dressing gown.

'What would I tell myself? What would we have to talk about? To me, in fact, the João Twenty of two years ago is just as much of a ghost as the men and women we see in the streets of old Rio. I believe I have caught sight of him, from time to time, the João of former times, but each time I was nauseated. Completely nauseated.'

Under most circumstances I didn't share my host's taste

for speculation. I had never been the type to chase mysteries and unravel conundrums. Many people loved to travel from century to century because they had found something in history or philosophy, in psychology or the history of art, that could only be experienced in the past. But I liked the idea of solving problems.

Rio was a new experience in many ways, a new turn in my life. I had time to think. I had time to worry about my new friend who, as far as I knew, was enjoying the last days of his life. The Agency hadn't minded saddling me with the foreknowledge of João's fate. His words, his theory of the case, struck me as bearing the truth of the man standing on the brink of the grave. According to João, we had lost control of the fine threads of causality. There may have been some truth to his view of it. Our hearts were not designed to cope with chronological disorder. We were built to advance step by step, one day after the next, climbing from the past through the present into the future. Any greater degree of freedom meant exposing the soul to the pressure of the infinite which it could not withstand.

In the meantime, I needed to write my initial report to Section, outlining my interactions with Soledad, which I did on the balcony, looking out on the beach and the streets populated by blacks and whites, browns and blacks. João brought out the almanac on which he kept track of his former incarnations and explained his method of avoiding himself when moving around Rio. We drank coffee, enjoying the salt air, and then I gave my report to João to put in his safe.

In short, my host was restored to a good frame of mind. I looked at the date on the calendar, remembered what I knew from Akiko and hadn't told him, and didn't meet his eyes.

'You're ready for this evening, my friend? You're ready to find out the secret of Muller?'

'I hope so.'

'You are ready to understand the mystery of Soledad?'

'Yes, but I want to know more of the background beforehand, in case they don't come clean. I want to have an independent idea of what they're doing here in Brazil. For one thing, I would like to know something about Admiral Coriolis.'

'Soledad's lover?'

'Who is installing communications equipment for the Brazilian Navy. Maybe he is her lover, maybe not.'

To research Coriolis, I had to find my way to Cinelândia Square, not far from the Praça de República, where the grand old building of the Biblioteca Nacional stood in seclusion. The guards in white gloves allowed me to enter the reading room, a stuffy hall which was deserted apart from the stuffed animals on the high shelves: jaguars, parrots, sloths, and giant anacondas under glass domes.

On the far end of the room was a desk with a bell. I rang and waited, rang again. I was rewarded by the appearance of a librarian, a man with very sleepy eyes—as sleepy, I thought, as the anacondas. He came out stooped over a trolley filled with documents and cloth-covered books, their titles stencilled on the spine. He thought about my request, as if I had offended him, but then went into the catalogue for a few minutes, his fingers climbing rapidly through the punch cards as I looked along the lower shelves lining the big hall.

The librarian disappeared up the staircase with a list and returned twenty minutes later with another trolley loaded with binders, copies of *Navy News*, and various bulletins on the prospects of the Brazilian fleet, covered in dust. I thanked him and piled them on the table.

For hours, I sat in the Biblioteca and read, while the parrots and jaguars glared out of their glass eyes and the librarian dozed with his feet on the desk. I assembled the broader picture as

I went along. Admiral Coriolis was close to the generals who ruled the country from Brasilia and controlled the big procurement budgets. Under the dictatorship, spending was concealed from the public. It was the perfect environment for a secret project, even a hidden enemy in the classic sense. If Dr Muller helped Coriolis install communications equipment on his ships and diesel submarines, he would be creating a network of transmitters, moving across the oceans, between ports on different continents, wherever Brazil's sailors happened to go. If Muller's coding was good, the operators would have no idea that a backdoor had been put into the system. You could only run a conspiracy when you had a way to talk to each other and nobody else could listen in.

From an Agency perspective—from the point of view of historical protection and purification as put down by S Natanson—there could be worse to come. The laws of nature were our ultimate line of defence. Nothing came from nothing. It required an expenditure of energy to send a man or woman into the past, more energy for every additional year, energy for every minute spent there, and for every physical action, be it ever so small. A single mission could absorb the output of a modern solar plant. Only a collaboration between governments had the resources to manoeuvre through the centuries. If Muller and his associates had figured out how to use the Brazilian state to provide nuclear energy, we were facing an entirely different environment—something closer to what fear and rumour over the ages had made of the hidden enemy. I remembered my father's warning and my skin tingled.

The librarian had tied his handkerchief around his head in order to sleep better, when I rolled the trolley back to his desk. He lifted the handkerchief off his black eyes, offended that I would disturb him. He was so thin, I noticed, that you could see the gleam of bone in his dark brown face.

'You have what you came for?'

I said, 'I got most of it. Thank you.'

'You are most welcome.'

'I want to find out who is supplying items to a government agency. Is there an easy way to find out?'

The librarian folded his handkerchief into a square on his palm before he answered.

'This is Brazil. There is no easy way to find out anything.'

'I see that.'

'But you may have some luck at the company registration office. It is not far from here. I will draw you a map.'

At the library and company registration office, I filled pages of my notebook with information the brassheads would have loved to know. I discovered the name of Muller's business venture: Reliable Machines. It had been founded in Munich in 1948 and was domiciled in Panama City, along with certain subsidiary enterprises in Morocco and Buenos Aires and, for some reason I couldn't discern, a consultancy devoted to the appraisal of pieces of sculpture, the provenance of which was ancient Ife and Benin. I had known something about Muller's side interest in antiquities, but it was the first time I had heard the full name and designation of the Board of Protection.

Muller had emigrated to Brazil in 1961, according to news reports, and had been granted citizenship in 1962 in a ceremony over which Admiral Coriolis had presided. In the same year, Reliable Machines had established itself as a provider to the armed forces of the Republic. I couldn't find birth records for any such person as Keswyn Muller, but I did find a variety of patents assigned to the company, originally submitted in Geneva in 1937 under the name of K Muller, then a Swiss resident. The files had to do with the internal design of coding and decoding circuits.

I didn't have the expertise to interpret the technical specifications but somebody like Coriolis would have seen their value for his own purposes. Polish signals intelligence officers had brought similar devices to the United Kingdom in 1939. Their plans had been incorporated into the Enigma machine which had been used to locate and destroy German submarines in the Atlantic.

I took a taxi home through busy streets. The cars and trucks, buses and vans flashed past without making an impression. My mind was full. I paid the driver and went into the elevator of the building without remembering what I was doing.

I came back to the present when the elevator doors opened to reveal João standing there, his face drawn like a curtain. Behind him lay two open suitcases.

'What happened, João?'

'My controller sent a message. I found it in the drop today, when I went to deliver your report and mine.'

I went into the apartment and waited as João locked the door behind us, holding my notebook in both hands. The contents of the shelves had been pulled onto the floor. The door of the safe stood open, revealing stacks of money, blank keys, transmitters, computer punch cards, and other pieces of observational equipment.

'And what do they say?'

'They're closing down the residencies across the board, as a result of Muller, because they don't know if they can track us. I am being pulled off station and so, as it happens, are you, Mr Eleven. We go tonight. Agency has set up an exit point starting at midnight. I have to conclude some business before then. I will give you the co-ordinates in case I don't get back here in time.'

I hadn't realised that my mind was made up until João said the words out loud. My heart was beating so fast I thought I would faint, blood rushing in my ears, and yet I wanted to be nowhere else in that minute, only in old Rio amid her black-and-white ghosts.

'I can't go back, João. There are connections here that I have to understand. I have to meet Keswyn Muller face to face. I have to confront him with what he's done, the demons he's unleashed.'

'You can't disobey a direct order from the brassheads.'

'On the contrary, João. They want me to disobey these orders. That is precisely why they allowed Akiko to talk to me, why they subliminally encouraged her. They allowed her to give me an eight-hundred-digit prime.'

'What are you talking about, Mr Eleven?'

'It's the only thing that makes sense. When Akiko thought she was outsmarting them, she was doing their bidding. She wanted me to save your life. They wanted it at some level, I believe, or some fraction of the thinking machines at the top. I want it too, João Twenty, and that's why I can't allow you to go back and die like a dog. They don't want me to let you either, otherwise I would not be here in Rio. I will let you in on a real secret. If you don't come with me, I am certain this will be the last day of your life.'

The Underground
2489

The tram to Santa Teresa was swift. We went past Candelária Church, along Rua Joaquim Murtinho, in a matter of minutes up onto the aqueduct. The carriage rattled on the elevated track, swaying from one side to the other. I watched the cables join above the tracks, sparks flying in every direction when a tram came in the opposite direction. In the distance ran rows of concrete apartment buildings, abutting the cruel jungle and the stale ocean.

João was almost lost in his leather jacket. What had I given up on his account? I had broken my most sacred promises to the Agency and to the doctrine. I saw in the tram window that my reflection was almost imperceptible.

Near the end of the journey, João broke into my thoughts.

'Mr Eleven, tell me one thing. Are you doing this because of Akiko Thirteen? You were in love with her and you would do anything on her behalf? Is that the case?'

Was he jealous? Was I jealous? Were we all suffering from reflection sickness? I looked out of the window and up at the statue. I felt as if the tram were moving into the care of Christ the Redeemer.

'I didn't know her well enough. We were together only for a few days.'

He leant towards me.

'Then you care so much about my welfare?'

'That's not it. I know you even less, to be honest, João. I liked you immediately. Who wouldn't? Who wouldn't admire the spirit of your residency? But I don't know you well enough to give up my entire life.'

'Then, may I ask, why are we on the run together? I don't care so much about my life, to give up every shred of honour and decency to keep my skin. And what exactly has happened to Akiko?'

I had no answers. I was in the trap again. I couldn't say that a sense of destiny had taken hold of me and had brought João under my protection. I certainly couldn't tell him the full truth about Akiko's sacrifice. On that day, I couldn't utter the half of what was in my heart, as if a spell had been put on me.

When we reached the Largo dos Guimarães and got down from the tram, I turned to João. For no reason I can explain, I put my arms around him for an instant. His beard irritated me. I let him go.

The men on the square looked at us, then turned back to their card games and conversations in the sun. I saw them as spectres in the sunshine, pale-skinned men who would be buried centuries before I was scheduled to be born. The tram took on new passengers while the driver watched from his compartment, his shirt rolled above the elbows.

I followed João across the square to the pavement where, on the counter of a small cabin, a man was slicing coconuts with a cleaver. The tram clanked in a circle, the driver changing the sign on the door to Centro, and slid underneath its cable to the aqueduct. I waited until it disappeared before turning back to João.

'You loved Akiko Thirteen despite her white skin, João.'

'She didn't tell me about her condition. In any case, I live here in the old world. I don't have the same prejudices as you most probably do.'

Two men in priest's robes went by, their faces severe. I waited until they were out of earshot.

'I believe you knew at a subconscious level, João, and you loved her despite the fact. So did I. I loved her because I knew she was hiding in plain sight. Therefore, I couldn't let you be shot down like a dog. I couldn't let the past take its course.'

João put a hand to his forehead, trying to remember the exact words. '*Lord, let me have the courage to accept the things which should not be changed …*'

'Quote S Natanson until the cows come home. He wasn't consistent himself. When he sent his wife back, he was prepared to alter the entire course of history.'

'He knew she would fail, Mr Eleven. She didn't have the energy at her disposal to make any kind of difference. They must have been desperate to try anything, although the equations clearly ruled it out. To attempt the impossible … for me, that is the description of heroism.'

During our short conversation, a jeep had arrived on the square. Three soldiers got out. They looked at us curiously and we moved to the far end of the square. The revolver João had given me was heavy in my pocket.

I kept talking. I thought I would never get a chance to talk again. 'You said it yourself, João. There's no measuring rod. Everything may have changed, in fact, as a result of the actions of S Natanson, because of what his wife did, and we don't know because we changed along with it. Without her intervention, would anybody have made it into the mines? Who knows?'

'She would have needed a nearly infinite amount of energy. Where was she supposed to find it?'

I didn't have an argument to make. So I kept quiet. We avoided the soldiers and went past the museum and the old convent on the side of Morro do Desterro, walked along the road, underneath a canopy of trees, a pattern of sunshine and shadow like a curtain on the earth. The old white mansions rose around us behind their heavy shutters.

I let myself think that I had saved both of us. The air had been heavy between us since I'd arrived in old Brazil. I had been a co-conspirator against João Twenty, cold as any calculating monster in its bronze skin. At some level, he had processed the fact that he had been under sentence of death. I had not seen him so happy, his beard gleaming in a passing band of sunshine.

At the entrance to Muller's compound, João paused. He went back to the subject.

'When you arrived, Mr Eleven, you changed my life.'

'How so?'

'Until you arrived, I'd never had the chance to say one word regarding Akiko. She is a special and remarkable personality. I had bottled up all my feelings about her.'

'So would you say that you knew and accepted what she was?'

'I cannot say I knew the colour of her complexion, because I never saw her without the effect of the skin-darkening creams. I am grateful to you for something else entirely, as I say. To have a chance to talk about her for one day of my existence is more important than saving a mere life, even if it is my own. That I can never forget no matter how long I have left to live. And I hope to make it to a hundred and forty at least.'

I thought then that what made Akiko Thirteen special and remarkable was her predicament. She'd never wanted to be seen as a fair-skinned person, a throwback to the old world. In private, like others who tried to pass for black, Akiko likely painted her body with a skin-darkening cream made from seaweed extract which turned her complexion purple-black from the feet to the scalp. She would have watched herself in a holographic mirror, looking for any sign her reflection could betray her, just as I would do for other reasons. In public she would have lived in fear of exposure, day and night, year by year, prophesying and even longing for the hour of revelation. It was this very pain and fear, changed into something beautiful, which had drawn João and then myself in her direction.

A green light on the wall started flashing and the gate opened. The driveway was fifty yards of gravel leading to the two-storey building. Old-fashioned earthmoving equipment, partially hidden by rubber blankets, stood on the margins.

On our approach, the garage doors rose. It seemed strange beyond belief that inside a record was playing. It was a waltz, the sound of a needle on vinyl crackling through the speaker. The corridor on our right was dim. Its ceiling was covered with netting. At the end it opened into a lounge with damask couches. The curtains were drawn.

Keswyn Muller was alone. He didn't immediately get up. He had a number of records out on the table and was dusting them with a horsehair brush before putting them back in their sleeves.

After a minute, Muller rose and lifted the needle off the record. He had a long housecoat on. His face was larger than I remembered.

'Gentlemen. I pray you have a seat. I believe I have met each of you separately, on previous occasions.'

João sat down on the couch opposite the table. I sat beside him.

'Where is Soledad?'

'Soledad went on ahead. She sends her apologies. As you know, unlike the privileged operatives of the Agency, we cannot be in two places at once.'

Could we be in two places at once? Was I in two places at once because I travelled through the centuries? I had never cared to dispute the philosophy.

There was a fierce light in Muller's eyes when he talked. They were pinholes. Through them I imagined I could see a whirlpool, and for the first time since I'd lain in the graveyard I was frightened for the world. I looked at João, who knew no more than I did, and back at Keswyn Muller, the man who had somehow brought down the world and all possible worlds. The unprepossessing man who had tarried with the infinite.

'I don't know who you are, Dr Muller. I don't know whom you represent.'

'But I know who you are. Would you like a confession? Would you like to know that you are in the right to chase me across the years? Right to put an end to my life, and to the life of my parents and grandparents before me?'

I wanted to stand up and take Muller into custody, send him back to the future to face prosecution. But there was some promise beckoning in his face.

'Under the constitution, Dr Muller, I am not required to extend due process. But if you want to set out the motivations for your deeds, naturally I am eager to understand.

'First let me serve you. You will allow me the courtesy.'

He went into an adjoining room. The sound of dishes and a kettle boiling. Muller singing to himself, bars of the waltz on the record player. He returned with a tea service, bearing the tray against his chest. On it were three porcelain cups and a kettle embossed with flowers.

Muller set the tray on the ground between us and made no motion for a minute. Then he leant forward and poured, admiring the fragrance of the bronze water as he did. He gave one to João and one to me, placing a pewter teaspoon on each saucer. I wasn't comfortable. I didn't drink.

For another minute no words passed between us. At the bottom of my forever dream lay this tea ceremony with Muller, a comedy in a dark house reeking of wood and tea at the top of old forgotten Rio. I had landed in a dim room with paintings on the walls. In them were stern black men and women, ships and islands, rubber plantations and, in more than one or two, baskets of bones and skulls arranged on a table. There were suggestions of a connoisseur's hand behind the selection. A Beninese mask, the face curved into black wood, hung on a wire. The nose on a single triangle. Strange to run across a familiar object so far away from home.

Muller noticed my interest in the mask. Without comment, he picked it from the wall and put it in my hands. It was heavy, as I expected. As I turned it round, I was conscious that the wood in my hands was as warm as man's blood. I put it over my face, watched Muller, then turned to see João, who made no attempt to answer my gaze, his hands over his eyes as if the light were too bright. I shivered, thought about what had been done inside the thing, looking out from within the mask on the action of the wearer's hands. The carvers of Benin had known more than was healthy about the existence of evil. I put the thing faceup on the table.

'You want to know the truth? Which sinister organisation forced an end to your interference with the entirety of human history?'

I was too tired to argue, dead enough to lie in a grave for a hundred thousand years. 'Give it to me straight.'

Muller stood up and took the mask back into his hands. He turned it around and around, faster and faster, as if it would begin to spin of its own accord.

'I am the humble corresponding secretary of the Board of Protection for the Society of African Antiquities.'

'Maybe I have heard the name of your society before, the Board of Protection, but that is all.'

'In fact, it was founded in Munich, June 1898, by Victor Kallenbach and Oscar Weisel. The selfsame Weisel, certainly, who later on would become my doctor father at the Collegium in Coburg. Weisel, certainly, who was strangled in a prison cell on the instruction of Rudolf Diels. Weisel, by the way, who made us conscious of the inner spiritual connection between slavery on the continent and the Sperrgebiet, in Namibia, and then the camps at Dachau. One genocide is the secret inspiration of the next. That is the true thread of history ignored by Natanson.'

My eyes were watering so badly I couldn't think. I certainly couldn't judge the significance of Muller's confession. I couldn't tell what was happening, only that some process was underway that I couldn't control.

I turned to ask João but he was already gone. He was lying back on the couch, no sign of alertness. His hands were open on his lap; his cup was steaming. I looked at the steam from the tiny cup in my hand. It was still pouring out as vigorously as before, the product of some chemical reaction.

I understood and put the cup down, trying to find the gun in my pocket. I could never have aimed it or even held it up to fire. The room was turning as swiftly as the mask had turned in Muller's hands. The man held the mask in front of his face for a minute and I imagined him looking out at me. The space around me narrowed to just his voice, which was disturbingly loud.

'Therefore, no doubt, you are asking yourselves, what connection exists between these disparate facts. What connection between travellers, on the one hand, and, on the other, the preservation of royal and religious artefacts such as this mask? What connection between a humble student of Oscar Weisel, born into a minor branch of the aristocracy, and the mighty code-makers of the Agency who traverse centuries? I will attempt to answer this question for you, gentlemen, just as soon as I have ascertained whether or not the tea service has agreed with you.'

I closed my eyes. Muller came over and took the gun out of my pocket. He put a thermometer in my mouth. He read it and placed a tablet under my tongue, holding my mouth closed until it dissolved. Seeming satisfied, he went away, commenting to himself under his breath.

The experience was almost painless, almost soundless apart from a wind chime in a doorway I couldn't see. It was the most disturbing hour of my life, to be paralysed in Muller's living room and at his mercy, as if he had pulled a plastic bag over my head and were waiting for me to choke to death in front of him.

I opened my eyes a fraction, peering through the tears, and saw him standing over João, holding a cloth over my friend's mouth. One skeleton taking the life of another.

I called Muller back and to my surprise he came. I cried out loud. Could feel the salt tears running down my face. I closed my eyes again when he approached. He was ready to talk, holding the mask in one hand. The thing people never understood about Keswyn Muller was that he was always ready to talk.

'There are certain preparations, Agent Eleven, which have been handed down to us from time immemorial. Advantages to having a history, you may say, which as an overlord of time you may not understand. This infusion is Chinese. It is taken from a particular berry which grows only on a particular island at a particular time of the year. It has helped me out of a number of tricky situations.'

He pried my eyes open and continued. 'Here is the beautiful part, Agent Eleven. You do not have to ingest the flesh of the berry for the effect to occur. As you are discovering, it involves complete paralysis of the conscious nervous system for a period of thirty hours, give or take an hour on either side. If you are careful, or, should I say, if the dispensing officer is careful regarding the dosage, then the recipient may escape with nothing more than muscle stiffness and an acute case of what you term in English, "pins and needles".'

I tried to ask a question but I couldn't move my tongue. Muller understood what I wanted to know.

'In your friend's case, we have not been careful, I am afraid. I am not breaking any of the rules of our trade, you must understand. A resident spy like this one is despised in every culture, a traitor to everyone. To say the least, he cannot be regarded as human because of the many copies he has seeded in the world. He who lives in a loop, who reproduces himself by himself, is truly the object of repugnance. I know you will say it is not a loop but a spiral, but that is only an excuse. In your case, however, there is no cause for punishment. You have friends with your welfare at heart, whom you may not even know about.'

'Why?'

'One word. One word only. Atonement.'

Muller let me close my eyes again. They were full of tears, as sweet and bitter as any that had ever been shed. I could feel the room disappearing around me. I was dying in plain view in a dim house, ice-cold poison in my lungs.

'Dr Muller, I can't breathe. I can't bear riddles any more. I can't bear to hear riddles.'

'No riddle. No riddle at all. We are making atonement to the abused continent. The Board for Protection finalised this project in April 1945, in the smoking ruins of Berlin. Admittedly, we have taken assistance from certain powers that are willing and able to grant it. But that is not important. No more slave ships, if we are successful. Nor men and women in chains. No colonies, no amputated hands and feet for the sake of rubber in the Belgian Congo.'

Muller put his hands on my head. He seemed to be combing my hair to one side, as if to prepare me for something.

He went on after a minute, his voice very quiet. 'Weisel was the first to ask, as a matter of historical ethics, why should we protect the past when it has been a laboratory for the subjugation of the Jew, the gypsy, the foreigner, and above all the black man and the black woman? Kallenbach, to give him his due, was the first to understand the majesty of Weisel's message. Now that technology makes it possible, we at the Board of Protection can translate it into action. We can bring about an end to man's hundred-thousand-year quest to dominate and play the master.'

I would have liked to put a thousand questions to Keswyn Muller. I would have asked how one could purify the past of sin without ridding it of impure human beings and their impure action. I would have asked if good and evil weren't so mixed together in our hearts that not even the finest comb could ever separate them. I would have liked to ask, where finally was the slave without the master? Where was the master without his slave? Were master and servant, black slave and black master, not indistinguishable in the whirl of the cosmos? I would have asked him if he had looked into the mirror lately and seen the blank of his countenance?

I would have liked to know if Berlin in its year zero was any place to plan a redemption and how a group of conspirators hoped to travel through the centuries and whether it was truly the voice of Shanumi Six I heard in an adjoining room. I would have warned him against meeting the infinite on its own terms. But I was suffocating slowly and surely, in a room full of air, and when I woke up I would drown.

For the first time in years, I didn't dream. There were no images, no memories of my father's face or the touch of my sister's hand on my forehead. I knew only that time and space were passing around me, swiftly as a torrent, and that in the midst of their infinities was the smallest bubble of flesh, blood, bone in which I travelled.

I had a quantity of fluid in my chest. I coughed violently and came to, lying on the ground in a narrow chamber. It was hardly lit, rough rock walls on either side which left no space to stretch on the hard floor.

For a minute I panicked and threshed around. I hit my head against the wall and stopped. Spit was on my hands. I kept still for some time, feeling the pins and needles Muller had promised, hardly relieved to be alive in such a place.

From some memory in the hot air, the tang of blood and urine, I knew that men and women had lived and died in this enclosed room, leaving no more mark on it than the trace of their fingernails on the stone. It was my fear brought to life, a room from the darkest dream.

I tried to stand without being able to see where I was and brushed my head against the ceiling. I fell against the gate on one side. It rattled, bars tattered with rust that came off on my hands. I steadied myself on it, my heart pounding at the shock of the collision, and looked into the spectacle beyond.

There was enough light to decipher the scene, torches burning in niches in the walls. I was in some dungeon that men might have imagined in a far-off century. Along the walls were cells carved into the rock. They were packed like a honeycomb, hundreds in every direction, up and down, to right and left. Staircases looking as flimsy as bits of matchwood rose from landing to landing, cables running along them into the centre of the hall.

It was so quiet you could hear water dripping from an upper level, as bright as a stream. Nobody to be seen. Nobody came when I called, although I could hear the sound of scuttling in the walls.

I shouted, caught my breath, shouted again at the opposite cells. Then I had to sit down and cough, my lungs turning over in the air filled with a slurry of coal dust, petrol fumes, and the smell of suffering and death preserved in the rock.

I got up to find a boy watching me through the gate. He wore a cattle blanket over his shoulders, a liability in the humid air, and a small Geiger counter around his neck. He had laid a bucket at his feet, full of pitch-like oil, burning at a wick. More smoke than light came from it, producing the effect of an oven being opened in front of me.

The boy sat down and crossed his legs. Then he leant forward and passed a canteen through the bars.

I stayed kneeling and drank the water, savouring every brackish drop, rubbed the last of it onto my neck. He dropped some raisins on my palm, which I ate. They were shockingly sweet. An orange appeared, which he divided in sections, giving me one and taking one for himself.

When the orange had been consumed, I returned the canteen. I saw my visitor wasn't as young as I had thought, sixteen or seventeen, but he had unusually thin arms, covered in mud. He looked me up and down, his expression unchanging.

'You are the prophet. You have been brought here to bring us knowledge of our destiny. They said that everything that has happened to you since you were thirteen was designed to bring you here. To fulfil your destiny.'

'Who are they? Who are you?'

'You know who they are. They are your followers who brought you here and have given you a puzzle to overcome. No need to be angry at them. Look how much they paid me to watch you, to take care of your survival. Think how rich your followers must be.'

I couldn't understand the boy's mumbo jumbo about prophecy. What was prophecy? Who could be a prophet without creating a loop? Indeed, the very concept of prophecy had never made sense to me. But it seemed unwise to contradict my companion. His feelings were obviously sincere.

In the light of the candle in the bucket, the boy spread a handkerchief on which he arranged his possessions like pieces from a board game: a sealed pack of batteries, green fruit dainties studded with sugar crystals, a magnifying glass.

I got to my feet, holding onto the bars.

'Can you let me out?'

Before answering, the boy put his earnings back into his pockets, stroking his hands thoughtfully as he talked.

'As the prophet, you must be here for five days. That is your itinerary. Since they brought you, you have slept for three days. You have two days more. Then I have an instruction to let you go so that you can find your true path. Your life is a funnel. First, it was broad and you had a lot of space to move around in. Now you are getting to the other end of the funnel where it is very narrow.'

'Let me wait outside with you, please. I give you my word. I won't go anywhere and you can fill my ears with any nonsense you so wish.'

'It's not possible. Don't ask me again or I will stop up my ears. Listen to what I am telling you about the funnel. It is for your own good.'

I let the bars go and felt myself swaying. 'If I am the prophet, isn't it a good idea to listen to my instructions?'

'You are wasting your breath. I already know the truth of scripture. By keeping you here I am helping you fulfill your mission. I have instructions. It reminds me that you are supposed to have a glass of orange juice once every six hours, to keep you going. I will fetch it for you.'

There was no point arguing. Nor did I want to ask questions. I seemed to be the only prisoner in a vast facility, carved out of bedrock, which could only be underground. I had learnt about life in the catacombs. It had been drummed into us from the first day of school. I had been on an excursion to the Museum of the Old World where, beneath the mother-of-pearl dome, the names of the disappeared were inscribed in their billions on a single chip of gallium arsenide. Like anybody with a heart, I had considered how I myself might have behaved in those days and years following the supernova when sisters ate brothers and brothers ate sisters, miniature Geiger counters ticking on their chests.

I had dreamt of many things as a member of the foreign service. In recent months, I had come to see life itself as a dream set within a dream, but I had never imagined that a trapdoor would open in the midst of my long dream and that through it I would fall into the place I had been taught to dread the most.

The boy never offered to introduce himself, never tried to get any information from me that he hadn't already been given. He didn't volunteer any information either, so that after many more hours in my cell I was no wiser than the moment I woke up. I had been dropped there, into his care, by an invisible hand.

Indeed, the boy didn't seem to care about anything beyond the confines of the great prison which it had fallen to him to guard. He didn't tell the story of how he had arrived or recount his memories of sunshine and rain. He was content to squat by my cell and watch as I drank and ate, one hand on the Geiger counter which hissed on occasion. Keeping to a schedule, he came to rouse me three or four times a day.

Sometimes in the near dark I could hardly make out what I was eating and the candle would flare up and reveal a yam or sweet potato in its rough sacking, or a deformed beetroot or carrot. There was canned food he opened before handing to me: chickpeas in chalky brine, canned fish, and once a can of tiny peas, the label still readable in Spanish, origin Valencia.

I piled the cans and leftovers in a corner, where I urinated, and tried to sleep on the stone on the other side. No matter how much I drank my mouth was dry, and my body ached in every quarter, yet I managed to pass out for hours at a time, half-listening for the boy's footsteps in the interior of the prison.

Sometimes I was awake in the darkness and heard the very rock groaning and straining like a bound giant. The heat and humidity rose to an extraordinary level, bringing out sweat on my entire body.

I thought of the layers above and below me. The ridge was thirty miles along, honeycombed by endless hot tunnels and shafts, embankments and dams filled with polluted water. Black-skinned miners in their hundreds of thousands had died in these corridors to bring gold and silver, platinum and uranium, to the corporations of the old world, uncountable riches into the hands of their fair-skinned shareholders. It seemed only fair that the same ridge now sheltered their descendants who would emerge to conquer the charred glass of the new world.

It might have been a day or even two before the arrangements changed. The boy began to sleep outside my cell for hours at a time. He brought an old mattress along and lay on it, his head turned away from me. In the rising heat he had taken off his shirt, revealing a belt filled with keys of various descriptions. I saw his back was covered in stripes.

Once he took out a mouth organ and, without checking to see if I was awake, blew through it for half an hour. He looked away from me the whole while. I couldn't recognise a tune of any kind, but the broken music reached out to the depths of the prison around us, as if it were a spell he was casting. His eyes were closed while he played.

I was almost asleep myself when I saw apparitions surround him. There were a dozen men and women, armed with pitchforks, who bound the boy's hands. They placed a hood over his head and tied it around his neck, silent and smiling whenever they caught my eye, their faces and arms painted with thick white circles and dots.

I didn't utter a word all the while. Nor did the boy, as if the scene had been agreed upon beforehand. The invaders were equally silent, communicating with one another by hand signals. They took the keys from his belt and tried them, one by one, until the gate swung open.

Three men entered my cell, muscular and nearly naked, reeking of ointment. I stood up to meet them, still stiff on my ankles. They were matter of fact, handling the livestock. My hands were tied with rope, which cut sharply into my wrists, and I was hooded from behind. I was pushed out of the cell.

Through the hood I saw areas of light and darkness, but I could hear the voices of our captors who began to talk. My ears hadn't adjusted so I couldn't quite make out what they were saying. The party moved in single file. I was turned this way and that by the man behind me, led down staircases where the roof was low. When I hit my head, the men near me laughed and someone pushed me onto my knees.

With my hands bound it was necessary to shuffle for ten or fifteen minutes at a time. The pain in my head was shocking. I was far past the point of exhaustion. Not even the occasional kick or slap made me move any faster. My hands were untied when I had to go up a ladder, tied again at the top where the light was brighter and the flooring was made of some kind of wood. I thought I could hear horses moving past in the other direction, their hooves ringing on the floorboards, their voices subdued. I imagined they would be wearing blinkers, blind as I was in this infinite cavern.

At other times, the going was easier, in an open place where the air circulated and the coaly dust and heat abated. The men and women sang to one another, songs I couldn't decipher and then, to my astonishment, others which were familiar to me from childhood. Songs about railway trains and reed maidens. Songs about open fields and the liberation of the bondsman …

In a series of narrow passageways, it became very hot and humid again. Sweat came up on my face and chest as I tried unsuccessfully not to bump into the walls. I coughed and coughed, unable to breathe, and wished I could die on the spot.

Some time later, the procession came to a halt and my hood was removed. I was near the front of a line of men and women about a dozen strong on an open floor. The boy and myself were the only captives. He was still wearing a hood. I called to him but was pushed away by a young woman with firmly beaded and braided hair. She had triangular earrings and bracelets along one arm.

The woman didn't speak, and I didn't dare speak to her. Indeed, she had a more than stern expression, her forehead furrowed as if she had a headache, keeping her hand so tightly on my arm that her fingernails started to bite. She brought me past a hitching post, where several donkeys were lapping at a trough of opalescent green water. Their brown-and-white bodies stayed upright, tails ticking over their backs, stable as pommel horses. Further on were men squatting on the ground. Using ash and water, they were drawing white circles and dots on one another's faces and shoulders.

We went past them into a large gallery. The ceiling was a hundred feet up, secured by scaffolding. The walls were twice as far apart. In the middle of the space, an elevator shaft ascended through the ceiling, an engine at work bringing big iron buckets down and sending them back up on the other side. Strings of coloured light bulbs looped along the walls, dimmer and brighter in unison with the engine. Coal smoke was thick in the unventilated space, reviving my cough.

The young woman steered me to a table on which there were many calabash cups and pitchers covered with pieces of cloth. She poured out a full cup of what looked like fermented milk, as thick as porridge, and brought it to my lips. Then she motioned to me to open my mouth.

When I demurred, she prised my mouth open with her fingers, and poured it down my throat until I choked. She stopped, giving me the chance to take a breath, and then decisively poured down the remainder.

The potion tasted of mint, and then of something sweeter and more fatal which reached to the nerves that kept my heart beating and forced my breath to refresh itself. My body sank to the ground, the rank sweetness of the milk filling my nose and head until I bowed before my poisoner and vanished from the scene.

In the underground, there was no boundary between the dreamtime and the hidden lights of the mining galleries and passageways. I woke to find myself spread-eagled on a board, hands and feet trussed with rope. The blue light of gas flames shivered on the walls. Fermented milk was thick in my mouth.

Close by me, tied on a board of his own, was the boy who had once been my guard in a faraway prison. He was still asleep, and he didn't look well. There were bruises and abrasions on the side of his head, red scrapes on black skin. I didn't want to attract attention by calling him again. Nearby were a dozen strangers also bound and restrained.

Around us moved laughing men in all manner of dress: overalls and dungarees, bowler hats, dinner jackets, and oilskin raincoats. Some wore belts with big buckles, or bandoliers over their chests, feathers tucked into their trousers.

For the most part, the women wore the uniform of old Sahara, robed from head to foot. Others brandished rifles and pole-axes. They didn't pay attention to us, coming close without trying to talk. The sweet-and-sour scent of their bodies made itself felt when they were nearby, but I could only imagine how I smelt and looked to our jailors.

And to us what were they? Who were they? I had no doubt as to what was passing in front of my eyes. My cheeks burnt to recognise these ragtag men and women, these painted cannibals and pygmies. They were my ancestors. In not so many years as I liked to think, they were destined to inherit the earth.

I saw the boy was awake and managed to attract his attention.

'Do you still think I am a prophet? Do you still hold on to your superstitions which have brought us nothing but misery as a species? What could I know that you don't know?'

'You have your own path. You are entering the time to be tested.' The boy waited until there was nobody close. 'I have heard that every prophecy must be tested before it is ready to be heard by the world.'

'How do you think they're going to test me?'

'Sir, I fear the worst.'

I would have told the boy that nobody could draw the line and say where the worst ended and the impossible began. How would we know when we were at the worst? There was always the likelihood of another trapdoor. But he had closed his eyes, and I didn't want to bring him back to the hateful world. After a while, he raised his head and smiled blindly in my direction.

'They left you to us as a prophet, sir. You will reveal the secrets of the future. The still-hidden secrets of the past. Give us the hope we need to survive.'

'I'm not your prophet. I am certainly not their prophet. I am an ordinary case officer caught in this situation. I have never uttered a word to anybody about the future. You should have left me out of your superstitions before blood flows.'

'They also said you would say that. They are far ahead of you. That is my only consolation.'

There was no opportunity to pursue the question. Men wearing hide drums on their stomachs cleared a space on the floor and began to beat out a rhythm. The noise was deafening. The leader wore a serge cap, setting the pace for increasingly irregular loops of drumming.

I lay with my fists clenched, wishing I could depart from the course of my prophecy and find myself returned to the corridors of the Agency. Instead, a woman came around to pour more of the sour milk into our mouths.

I considered trying to spit it out but it was safer to drink. This time the liquid was warm. It went into my chest, warming me immediately under the ribs. It made me drowsy and very happy. I laughed out loud despite myself. Then I laughed at hearing myself. I was as giddy as a drunkard.

Women were dancing around the musicians as I became even giddier. At a certain point, the drums stopped along with the engine. With the motor stopped, a final bucket descended gradually from the shaft above. There were sparklers burning on its sides. It swung, showing decorated sides.

I had to strain against my ropes and crane my head to get a proper view. Coming closer and lower, the iron bucket finally settled on the ground in the very centre of the great hall. The lead musician inserted a crank into the engine, stopped the motion of the chain. Then he undid two bolts and lay on his back in front of the bucket, the stitched top of the kettle drum protruding upwards.

The side of the bucket opened over him. The man inside rose to his feet, revealing an imposing figure of six feet and more. He was broad shouldered, covered in animal skins, and took some time to stretch to his full height. He straightened his wig, thick as a lion's mane, and walked over to the drummer and through the assembled men and women to the podium. I laughed out loud again, unable to stop myself, from sheer joy in the apparition.

On his way to the podium, the man passed me, pausing to look down at my body and the others nearby without changing his expression. I saw that a pair of gold-framed sunglasses lay on his neck.

Beneath his neck, the skins parted to reveal an inch or two of his coiled black hair and skin open all the way to the top of his penis. From the podium, he summoned men and women to his side, took them indiscriminately in his arms, leant to kiss them on their heads, put his hands on their hips.

The music started up. Drums were supplemented by trumpets and horns, castanets in the women's hands, an accordion, and the slurry speaking of mouth organs and a Jew's Harp.

The unholy milk had gone to my head in its full intensity. Under its influence, as if in the ear of a seashell, I heard ten thousand years of caravans coming to the coast, men and women in shackles, boys and girls, beaten and broken on whip and wheel. I heard centuries of blood and iron, slave bells and church bells, and the dream of a world turned upside down, on the day when dark-skinned men took the chance to play the master.

That may have been the only time in my life when I heard prophecy, or imagined I heard it. The first would be last. The last would be first, the dream of a black emperor such as the world had never seen. In the midst of the men and women, their leader whirled round and around. The strands of his wig flew about his head while women pressed their mouths to his belly and feet.

The boy whistled at me. His head and shoulders were covered in dust.

'Do not worry, sir. In the end they cannot harm a hair on your head. You are the prophet. You were sent to bring us hope for tomorrow. Therefore, today you have nothing to fear. You have nothing to fear.'

I couldn't believe him. But try as I would, the milk I had drunk had made it impossible to feel fear. Instead, I was filled with courage.

'Do you remember the old world? Do you know the surface and its beauty?'

'I was born under the sun, sir, but I can only remember it in my dreams. That's when I think of yellow light. The space to run around. Free air to breathe. Tonight, I will be in the sunshine again. I will have room to breathe. I will have a lot of room. I will eat raisins all night into the day.'

He didn't say anything more. Another hour went by, or what seemed like an hour, before they came to prepare him. More sour milk went down his throat, at first willingly, when he drained the jug and then by force when he was drowned to the mouth.

In the background verses were read out from some scripture I didn't recognise. The boy was untied, then stripped of his clothes, revealing his painfully thin frame, ribs visible. His head lolled on his chest.

Several women in clean white habits took charge. They lifted and moved him to a four-poster bed which had been brought into the hall, not far from where I lay. The women tied up the lace netting on all sides, exposing a satin mattress. They stretched out the boy's limbs, holding each to a corner of the bed, and began to paint methodically.

One of the women poured the white dye onto his skin. She took it from a row of tiny heated pots which stood on a plank over a Bunsen burner, while two more of their number stood back and burnt cubes of incense, adding to the flask drops of some liquor which evaporated on contact.

The boy hardly trembled or showed any sign of life as their labours proceeded in full view of the onlookers. The dye was smoothed into his skin as if they were kneading dough. He was rolled over and his back was painted, inch by inch, until in place of the boy there was a shining white cocoon.

In a stone oven, a fire had been built and was being banked. On either side stood men with bellows, forcing the flames higher. Sparks flew from the mouth of the oven into the crowd, rousing the dancers to greater frenzies. When the boy had been properly prepared, he was moved again from the mattress to a wheelbarrow and pushed past my position. I thought he might be smiling as he went by.

The man in charge of the wheelbarrow wore only a loin cloth and a single turquoise feather in his hair. At first, he passed the wheelbarrow swiftly in front of the oven, as if to warn its occupant. Then he let it stand in the rising heat, the air rising so fast it rippled, pushed it away, and then back to stay, the metal handles becoming too hot to touch.

The undersides of the boy's feet twitched a few times and stopped moving altogether. The musicians took up a spare melody, and formed a circle around the oven.

At the end of the song, the chieftain lifted the body by himself and presented it in his arms. He went along the lines of musicians, allowing people to run their hands on the skin of the burnt boy. Some kissed him on the face, pressed his eyes with their hands, put their eyes against his burnt head as if they were trying to see what only the body had seen for itself.

The chieftain laid the body back on the four-poster bed where a topless woman in a short bead skirt applied a long curved knife to the neck as if she were cutting a bolt of fabric, the tops of her thighs showing behind her.

For some reason, I couldn't look away as she pursued her task. Blood ran from the bed onto the floor. I wished very much that I had never thought to leave the century in which I was born. I was done with adventure. I wanted to hear the sane advice of a brasshead, consider its ranking of possibilities and likelihoods.

The woman in the bead skirt completed her task. She held up the entire dyed white skin for everybody to applaud. It was not nearly so large as I imagined, not large enough to contain a life and a history. She submerged it in a basin and then wrung it out with her strong hands. The sound of the trumpets faded in my ears as I lay down, unable to keep my eyes open, and fell into a swoon.

*

Someone was trying to wake me up. He or she was insistent but not forceful.

I was trying to remain asleep in a world of safety. I was warm. There was a blanket over my sore legs. I was so close to my old life that I had only to open the right door to find myself in front of the automatic barista at the office. I could be waiting for the day's reports to arrive and complaining to a fellow cadre about the brassheads in a low voice although in theory the machines heard and processed everything which might fall to their fiduciary responsibility.

No more than the merest width of a page of paper separated me from the Agency where I had been bored for the lack of adventure. I had looked for adventure and I'd thought I would never find it.

When I opened my eyes, however, I found the man who had descended from the ceiling to preside over a skinning. He was dressed in the whitened skin, placed like a waistcoat on his arms, and gave off the strong smell of peppermint.

'Sleeping Beauty has arisen. Sleeping Beauty, Sleeping Beauty.'

He opened my mouth before I could tell him he was the second person to apply the name to me. He pressed my tongue as if he were checking its firmness, pulled on my teeth, making sure that none of them were loose, and in the process got a sample of my breath.

The man winced and produced a spray from his pocket which he used several times on the inside of my mouth. He untied my arms and legs, and pulled me to my feet. He was so powerful I thought he was about to lift me into the air. Instead, he let me adjust, motioning to me to wait, while he spoke into a handset connected to a thin cable snaking down from above. I couldn't tell what language he was speaking.

We were the only two occupants of the hall, which had been tidied and deserted, although the huge iron buckets continued to cycle almost noiselessly and empty now from the ceiling to the floor and back again. The heat had gone down so that it was almost cold. The four-poster bed had been removed to a corner and covered with a tarpaulin. Water ran unabated along the walls, making dank pools in the floor.

The only sign of the men and women who had been captured and bound beside me were the twelve bone-white skins pegged to a nearby washing line to dry. I shivered. I had never been so frightened in my life to end up a skin on the line.

The man misunderstood my action and placed a pelt over my shoulders. He put his telephone on the ground and a hand on my shoulder, leaning forward and cocking his head as if to continue the inspection.

'A man's mouth is the very expression of his health.'

'I'm sorry, I don't follow …?'

'In a man's mouth it is possible to see without prejudice what only the Good Lord can see. Is he healthy? In good condition? Is he about to die? Assuming you have the appropriate knowledge of the mortal gum and the mortal tooth, it is possible to make a prediction.'

'What do you see in me? Where am I going?'

'No.' He removed his hand. 'You are not about to die. On the other hand, Ferguson is no prophet. But, he thinks, neither are you a prophet, my friend. Neither are you, perhaps.'

I wasn't sure what to say to this. The man took me by the arm through the hall to a doorway covered by a bead curtain, shards of a mirror in the beads shimmering in the draught. We went along a corridor in which the rock had been covered in red-velvet drapes, creating the unexpected sensation of entering the stage of a theatre. A curtain at the end let us into a tiled bathroom. Lockers lined the walls. There were short benches on one side next to a full-length mirror. I elected not to look at myself and my reflection.

Five showerheads stood next to one another, each with a tulip-shaped soap dish. I sensed the heat from the geyser in the roof. The man took off his skin and hung it on the locker, taking as much care as if it were a dinner jacket. Then he took off his clothes and folded them. He waited while I changed, switched the water on. Steam rose around us.

I stood under a shower and couldn't tell whether I was more frightened or pleased by the chance to be clean. Indeed, I was grateful for the soap and water, continuing to stand under the shower even when the man got out and dried himself. He sat on one of the benches and spread out his legs.

'In a former life, he was a dentist. Ferguson the champion dentist. He could take out an entire set of a man's teeth and replace them with ceramics in under an hour. In Sandton, one of the shopping malls that is probably no more than a hole in the ground today. He saw rich businessmen and housewives, lawyers and politicians, but the one thing he learnt is that a man's condition is reflected in his mouth. What goes into it, what comes out of it, that is reflective of his entire life. So he wanted to see for himself the mouth of the so-called prophet.'

'I am still not a prophet.'

'And it is the fact that certain people believe you are a prophet which interests Ferguson. According to the boy whose skin is hanging here, you are a prophet from another time and place. You arrived in the company of certain individuals who presented you as the harbinger. According to Ferguson, it is the only reason you escaped today with your hide. The only reason.'

I didn't know if he was threatening me. I turned off the shower and dried myself. Ferguson had provided me with a robe, socks, shoes. I changed alongside him. I was no less frightened than before, but I thought I was better prepared to meet whatever challenge would come. I was somebody's prophet. I deserved my own skin.

Meanwhile, Ferguson smoothed ointment over his face, turning it white. He did the same with his hands, up to his wrists, until, peering in the mirror, his appearance satisfied him. He settled a necklace of teeth around his neck.

He had me follow him back in the direction we came. We went into a corridor which was made of nothing but bare rock and the occasional piece of wooden scaffolding, here and there a naked electric bulb to shed light on the shifts in direction as the entire passageway changed course, turning to the right or the left, in general, from what I could tell, ascending to the surface. There were guards posted in shifts of three at some of the doors, using the same handsets I had seen Ferguson use.

Every so often we passed a man sleeping on the floor, swaddled in blankets, or small groups of men and women grilling meat on a fire in a steel barrel. They greeted Ferguson enthusiastically, although he didn't stop to speak.

We passed intersecting corridors and hallways where disused mining equipment had been cordoned off. Smelting buckets mounted on wheels and mechanical drills stood at the ready, although, apart from the coal-fired engine and the dim lightbulbs, there was no obvious source of power.

In some of the rooms were huge paintings on the ceilings, reminiscent of rock art. In them, from what I could tell, the taking of skin was commemorated. Stick figures in ochre and white were hunched over their victims while onlookers played musical instruments on the circumference.

Ferguson's domain extended for many miles in every direction. I supposed that we were coming close to the frontier. We met several groups of men returning from patrols, pitchforks and chainsaws in their hands, many of whom were bloodied or otherwise wounded in some way, slings on their arms or bandages on their torsos. Some had captives with them, hooded as I had been.

Each time, Ferguson stopped and interrogated them about the situation. I couldn't tell what they were reporting to him but he seemed more dissatisfied as we travelled. He opened the mouths of the men who reported to him and inspected their gums. At the same time, the closer we got to where the killing and raiding seemed to be taking place, the prouder he seemed of his skin, rubbing it and trying to keep it dry when we went under dripping water, showing it off to his subordinates, several of whom were moved to touch it admiringly. I could almost forget where it had been taken from. Of the many men and machines I had talked to since Manfred, only Ferguson seemed to have an idea of where things were going and how they were sure to develop.

My guide called a halt on a bridge. It ran over a system of canals which continued to operate, bringing sparkling green water from the surface down into the mines. There were metal benches welded onto the bridge where we sat down.

Ferguson produced a thermos flask and gave me a cup to drink. It was hot tomato soup, thick with salt and pepper. I thought it was the most astonishing thing I had ever tried, my drink before death. I finished the cup and drank another one that he poured for me.

'More?'

I wiped my mouth with my sleeve. 'That's enough.'

'You need your strength. You will certainly need it in the hours to come, which are designed to test your mettle.'

'So you believe, against all the evidence to the contrary, that I am going through some kind of apprenticeship?'

Ferguson drank the rest of the soup in a single motion.

'Ferguson does not believe in prophets. He believes in power. And prosperity. That has been his one dominating cause since before the supernova, before Ferguson led his flock underground. The prosperity of the black man. The wellbeing of the black man, the thwarting of the coloniser.

And Ferguson believes you know something about the future. Maybe only something, not everything.'

I stood up, too agitated to speak.

Ferguson continued to sit on the ground, licking his lips. 'You don't deny it? You can't deny it. Your mouth, your tongue, will not allow you. Soothsayer. Prophet. Traveller. The name makes no difference. Like the wife of S Natanson, who came to lead us into the Promised Land. Most of the people in the world ignored her. Most of the governments. They continued to live in sin, in the white man's sin of mastery and conquest, without heeding her warning. Ferguson knew better. Ferguson knew that humanity is always ready to neglect the prophecy. Perhaps Ferguson is destined to be the saviour of the saviours. He cannot say for sure.'

'You led them through the supernova?'

'Ferguson brought his group into the mines. That was his congregation. In fact, he used to lead his own church, apart from his dental practice. They practised the Prosperity Gospel. Ferguson had selected a Mercedes-Benz S-Class as the altar piece. That was the old Johannesburg. It was a place of beauty. If you were ever there, you would never forget the experience. But it is time to get on with it.'

We went on with the journey. Hours passed. We walked through miles of corridors and passageways, skirting sections of the mine where vast chemical lakes had formed, their surfaces gleaming like satin, and drank copious amounts of water and coconut water whenever it was offered to us.

I could feel the perspiration on my face and on my arms, and started to be uncomfortable, only relieved when there was some breeze passing unaccountably from a shaft above us, and when Ferguson called a halt and allowed me to wash myself under an open tap which stood in a cubicle half-hidden from the path. The water was cold on my skin.

I wet my head and swallowed half a gallon, washed my feet, washed my chest.

Ferguson picked up the train of our conversation from hours before.

'You were mistaken for a prophet because you have knowledge of human beings. On the other hand, you are our colour, the natural colour. But you are also strange. You know that they blame white people for the supernova and the destruction of the old world. Here, underground, they blame whites for almost everything. If there is a disease, then that is because a white woman looked at you with the evil eye. If there is not enough food, then they blame white men, purely because of what happened in the past. Then there are massacres.'

'Which you justify and benefit from?'

He shook his head. 'Sometimes one taste of the medicine is enough, Ferguson believes. One small taste of the medicine. Then that is enough for this small part of mankind to survive. In place of reasons, we take action and then we attach the reasons. That is the disease Ferguson intends to treat. Maybe, one day, if we choose our prophets carefully, that will lead us back to the surface. That is what God has told Ferguson, and Ferguson has faith in his word. But he must show you where you are located.'

Ferguson produced a map from inside his jacket and tried to orient me. Behind us were the central sections of the old reef, where the big seams of gold and coal had been worked to exhaustion. That was Ferguson's territory, where men owed their allegiance to him, and where all the albinos and fair-skinned individuals had already been killed or captured.

In front of me lay the ungoverned mines, where wildcat miners had once toiled in unknown corridors, panning for gold flakes under old Johannesburg, and fly-by-night operators had sunk secret shafts, now a great unmapped world about which rumours and myths circulated of albino armies and cannibals, sorcerers and telepaths. Into these depths the people who had brought me to the underground would have fled, seeking to hide from the pursuit of the Agency and guard their fair skins from extermination.

'Ferguson is going to let you go here, Prophet, if you are a prophet. Ferguson foresees a very short future for you, unless you truly have the gift of prophecy, but, on this topic, God has not chosen to enlighten him.'

'Where do you want me to go?'

Ferguson took out a pair of binoculars and let me look through them. The floor of the mine opened up before us into such a vast chamber that I couldn't see to the other side despite the magnification. There were almost no lights out there, except for here and there a spark which came on and then disappeared into the greater darkness, signs of something on the move.

I shivered again and felt faint. Ferguson didn't seem to notice. He pointed outwards, pushing me down the stairs without noticeable warmth, the smell of his borrowed skin carrying into my nostrils.

'You must go and find the men who brought you here and find out their purpose. That way you will find out your own purpose, and, in addition, God's purpose. Remember that they want you to find them. They are relying on you to be on the trail.'

I couldn't discern God's purpose, or any of his multifold purposes, under the coal-brown ceiling and in the coal-dust mists which shrouded my steps for the next three days.

I soon lost track of time and remembered only the moments I saw a face at a distance, its features distinct in a snarl or a laugh, and then the minutes I stood and counted until its owner had time to retreat. I remembered the arrows which on several occasions came out of the mist, their swoosh as sudden as a gunshot, and buried their heads in the ground at my feet. Whether they were a warning or an attempt to kill I never found out.

Hours went by, and nothing happened to break the monotony of corridors and shafts coming down from above, their throats blocked by planks, then more corridors, full of darkness and mist, and halls which had been dug out centuries before to house equipment and store piles of ore.

As I got close to the surface, there were broken-down vehicles, small trucks and forklifts designed to live underground, rusting away on their axles, their tyres long since removed. I saw more faces in the distance, eerie, painted white. Perhaps they were the famous albinos, never in groups of more than two or three, quivers and bows held on their backs. They seemed to whisper at me from their chalk-white lips before they disappeared around a corner.

Towards the end of the day, exhausted, when all the lights had started to flutter and go off, I stopped to wash my feet and clean the blisters, when I noticed that the walls were covered in ochre paintings: images of the surface and sunshine, images of the day of the supernova when the sky had turned out, images of celebrations at which the skin was taken from a man and given to another man. I stood in front of them and shuddered. There were more drawings on the ceiling which I couldn't make out, except for the heaps of human bodies appearing in them.

I slept in the back of a tiny train car, once used to transport ore and now the place I felt safest because I could hear anyone approaching under cover of darkness. I must have woken up once or twice, listened to the faraway noises of the mines, and then gone back to sleep. When I woke up I felt refreshed, as if some burden had been lifted from my spirit, and I set off again after taking the last of the provisions Ferguson had given me.

I lost all hold of time in the course of the day, uncertain of how long I had been walking and even in which direction. My head became light, reminding me that whatever I was looking for had better come soon or I would be buried in the mines alongside all the other victims, pieces of bone over which my ancestors would travel. I saw that there were pits dug into the ground, sharpened iron stakes at the bottom, and wondered what they had ever been intended to catch. No large animals, other than man and horses, had made it underground.

Another day must have passed before I started to hear the voices of people and the rumble of hand trucks in nearby corridors. I hid behind a pile of coal and listened while two men complained about their jobs bringing ore to their camp.

When I looked up, I saw to my astonishment that they were both white, although their complexions—like any miner's—were obscured by soot and mud. They wore blue plastic hats to protect their heads. I waited in the room until I could hear them depart, and then followed, taking care to keep out of sight, going up a staircase and along a hidden landing until a series of tents came into view, yurts arranged in squares of a dozen by a dozen on a large section of cleared gravel.

In the middle of the clearing was a giant metal needle, about a hundred feet high and reaching up through a shaft. There must have been a thousand mirrors surrounding it. Super-heated steam was rising from somewhere in the vicinity, driving some kind of an engine. Near it was a guard post where men in green uniforms kept watch on their surroundings through sunglasses.

I crawled up to the huts, moving from one to the next when I saw the guards were looking in another direction, and trying to reach the central section where the needle loomed above the surroundings. Cables ran a foot above the ground, light sparking in their interiors.

Inside some of the huts people were sleeping.

Through the material I could see other residents changing their clothes, overhear them talking on radio sets. I might have put my hands into the openings of their tents and touched them. I had the eerie realisation that in their world I was the intruder, the thing to be feared that had come from the underground.

Near the centre was a far larger tent, the size of a city bus, with a number of arched doors tied down on its sides. I looked for one which was shielded from view and went through it. I found myself in an otherwise empty room behind a bank of electronic equipment: consoles, Geiger counters, piles of superconducting batteries, and holographic lenses.

I walked around the counter, trying to remember everything I saw. This had to be the centre of the plot against the Agency, whether or not it was the hidden enemy at last. I forced myself to stand still for a minute until the spell of dizziness passed. While I was standing there, holding on to the counter, the strange sounds of the camp on the march around me, I noticed that on a silver plinth near me was bolted the severed head of a calculating machine, a literal brasshead which had been deprived of its means of locomotion. It was as odd to see her there as to find the head of a statue in a garden of holographs, something truly out of place.

I thought about the risks for a minute and then decided I was far past the calculation of risks. I went to the plinth and turned the entire contraption on. Tiny motors whirred in her neck. Fans sighed in the background. The pin-prick lights came together in her eyes, just a bead of ruby-red light in each one in the familiar start-up routine. Then she stiffened into consciousness.

I stood to the side, out of her range of vision, and watched as she turned from side to side, trying to locate me. Eventually she dislocated her neck and turned right around, three hundred and sixty degrees, to find me there. Patterns formed and reformed in her eyes, the signs of robotic thought, but she didn't say anything.

'Consultant, report.'

'This is Computer Hadley Ben Michael, known by the initials HBM, property of the Historical Agency. Unauthorised tampering with this device is forbidden under the rules and regulations of the interregnum, whatever century or country the action takes place in.'

'I understand that and accept the consequences. I too am an authorised agent of the Internal Section of the Historical Agency and I require your cooperation.' I listed my prime number. 'You will now unlock your archives and respond fully to my questions. You have a story to tell me.'

The Day of the Dead

11 March 2472

The head of Consultant Hadley Ben Michaels had a mysterious gleam on her pedestal, a corona of nervous blue sparks running along the outside of her frame as she spoke.

I stopped her after a minute, released her from the stand, and picked her up. She was colder than I expected, hard and heavy as a diamond, giving off static electricity. I rubbed my hands against her, thinking that I had never held a consultant so close. She was, if I remembered correctly, one of a class used to calculate jump trajectories and translate those trajectories into the probability script which human beings could understand.

I shivered to remember the thinking power contained in her oval. It had been almost a century since our species had resigned the competition for intellectual superiority. Only a machine could look into the infinite and survive.

'Are we safe here?'

Her head sang in my hands. I turned her around, trying to avoid the gleam in her eyes. She wore an abacus with probability beads tight around her short neck. The beads pulsed brighter and softer as they worried along the wires. I wished I had learnt how to read them.

'Agent Eleven, I am, comparatively speaking, deaf and dumb. To answer your question properly, I need my senses back.'

She pointed her eyes to the corner of the room where I found a closet. Inside it hung a number of torsos, their pistons and gears showing in their chests. I chose one, a wheeled red frame with powerful discs for hands, and brought it out. Hadley Ben Michaels went neatly onto the neck peg, the rectangles in her eyes spinning rapidly.

The body came immediately to life, towering over me, arms moving out as the consultant began her assessment of the situation. She went to the window where men were passing, escorting pallets loaded with equipment. In the background was the rumble of automatic trucks, making deliveries to the front of the compound.

'You are not secure, Agent Eleven. I estimate your chance of detection to be extremely high.'

'How long do I have?'

The consultant came back into the centre of the room, discs spinning on the ends of her arms.

'No more than three minutes, I estimate, before discovery. And with a likelihood of death or injury, considering the status of this facility. Since it is an emergency, may I offer you a solution?'

'Go ahead.'

'There is considerable energy in the system since I have finished construction of a large energy collector. I can bring up an arch and send you to your destination. I will just need to hear your number again. I am forbidden to retain the digits in memory.'

The power of prime numbers: the key to the new world and the solution to the mysteries of the infinite.

Consultant Hadley Ben Michaels closed her many eyes and began to dream of another time. The lucky horseshoe came up. The colours began to flow and that spiralling music of two separate times flowing side by side took hold. It was loud enough to hear on the outside and provoked the thrill which ran from the top of my head into my neck, the small death which overcame each traveller on the threshold of the arch.

'Where are you sending me?'

'To the Day of the Dead. That is where your path lies next, Agent Eleven. That is where you are fated to travel, where the funnel comes to a stop. It is not far.'

I held my hand to my neck, forgetting that there was neither a black or blue pill, nor anybody to bring me back if I failed.

'What are you doing here in the first place? And what is afoot?'

The consultant didn't open her eyes. 'There are three facts which concern you. I was sent here in confidence to oversee the energy budget. During this period, I have observed the arrival of a dozen members of the Board of Protection, as you will have heard it named. Finally, I am acquainted with your father's reputation for championing the liberty of machines. Your father, in a sense, brought us together.'

I didn't have time to press Hadley Ben Michaels on the matter of my father, however, because Shanumi Six came through the entrance, her face smouldering with anger. I saw her through the coloured lens floating in the air until she edged her way along the side, the jewelled rings on her hand sparking in the strange light.

She wasn't changed in the least from what I remembered, a powerful woman who had to stoop to fit under the side of the tent. She was wearing a light blue uniform I didn't recognise. On the shirt pocket was a badge I had seen years before in Morocco: the logo of the Board of Protection. My heart beat fast to see her raised from the dead.

'You are here much too early, Enver Eleven.' She checked her watch and moved towards me. 'You shouldn't be here until the morning of the day after tomorrow.'

'Sorry, I couldn't keep to the terms of your itinerary.'

'That's no matter, Eleven. I am capable of making a correction. That is what we've been doing all along. Making a historical correction. Redemption through correction.'

I moved towards the consultant, assuming she would protect me. But she didn't move.

I said, 'You're going to have energy, aren't you, from the supernova? You're going to have enough energy to do whatever you like. To bend time. Create space. Bring a new species into being. What is it, your dream? What is the curse you want to bring down on our heads?'

Shanumi didn't say anything. She came around the arch and tried to put her arm around my neck to paralyse me. I ducked out of the way, barely escaping from her grip, and thought in the very same instant that there was no point struggling against her or the Board of Protection. Their plan had been in place for centuries. On the Day of the Dead enough energy would arrive on the surface of the planet to transform the ephemeral histories of mankind.

Were they even wrong to make of history what they wanted? But to think on these lines was to go beyond the constitution and also, as João Twenty had reminded me, beyond the human heart. It was to encounter the infinite in the shape of the multiverse.

I turned to Shanumi so that we were face to face, startling her, and then slipped past. The consultant began to hum with red-and-blue thought. Her head spun around and she brought out a cleaning cart from the side of the room to interpose between my Six and myself.

'Don't try anything, Shanumi. HB Michaels is under my authority. She is acting in obedience to my prime number. Your number has been withdrawn from service.'

'I see that. Although she worked for me for many years. Everybody knows that a machine is a fair-weather friend.'

Nevertheless, Shanumi stopped where she was. Fanatical as

the members of the Board were reputed to be, she knew that only a mad woman would fight with a consultant.

'It's your father's fault we're here, Enver.'

'I don't understand how he knew about your plot. He is an ordinary man.'

'He knew nothing. But he gave his machines free will, which meant that they could reach their own conclusions separate from the consultants. They were the ones who betrayed the rest of us, who believed we were betraying the values of the Agency. Ordinary vacuum cleaners and domestic machines, assigned to an old age home, daring to disagree with the greatest calculating intelligences of their time. But why do I need to convince you? You are destined to take your part in the redemption from suffering.'

From one of her jewelled rings, Shanumi brought up a hologram, a black-and-white sphere in which I could see myself or someone who looked like me in front of a console, a row of clocks on the wall behind my back. I wasn't sure what she intended to make me believe.

'You see it with your own eyes and you can also see that it has not been altered. Nothing must change from the recording. It is vital that every detail is arranged so that it will come out right in the past. You need to put yourself under my supervision. Your life has all been leading up to this point. Who knows why it was you but the consultants have known. Or suspected as much, since you were thirteen. Everything has been arranged for your own good, even the removal of your sister.'

I shifted so that the arch stood between us. I put my sister out of my mind, sensing she had only been introduced as a distraction.

'A true image can lie. What reason do I have to trust you?'

'You would never have survived in these tunnels, Eleven, if I hadn't put it about that you were the prophet the underground has been expecting. You would have been killed and eaten. I saved your skin. Do you think you would have come back from Morocco in one piece if it hadn't been for my intervention?'

I edged away from her as she moved closer. Caught sight of the room in the window pane. There was only one person in the reflection.

'Have you looked in the mirror recently, Shanumi Six?'

'I'm not a vain woman.'

'I mean, have you considered that you and your entire cohort of renegade machines are suffering from reflection sickness? Look in the window. There's nothing there.'

At the same time I heard, or thought I heard, Shanumi under her breath reciting the digits of another prime number to HB Michaels, and to my horror I saw the cleaning cart reverse and come towards me. I gathered my strength and pulled the head of Hadley Ben Michaels from her moorings. Her eyes spun wildly as I threw her at Shanumi Six. Before anyone could do anything worse, I jumped part of the way through the arch.

On the other end, I collided hard with the ground, getting the breath knocked out of me. There were already hands holding onto both my feet. I pulled, not knowing whether I was resisting the strength of one man or a robot, and to my relief my boots slipped off and left me to collapse in a heap under a vast daybreak.

The sky was almost orange when I arrived on the day of the supernova. The atmosphere had grown to be thin, thanks to the invisible bombardment of the preceding hours, but as yet there was no physical indication of the devastation to come. The arch closed to the size of a pinhole and then evaporated completely. There wouldn't be enough energy to send anybody after me.

It was yet to be full dawn and the light was still increasing, sketching in the landscape with a pencil: a canopy of trees stretching beneath me almost to the horizon, the darkness of the night remaining beneath their heads, and a series of triangular mountains set in order of increasing size. In one corner of the sky was a patch of blue sparks, harbingers of the tide of relativistic particles bound in the direction of the planet.

I was not too distant from the top of another mountain, its crown a hundred yards from my position capped with snow, and could pick out the point perhaps ten miles from where the redemption machine had been assembled.

The day had already begun to burn on my skin while I sized up the redemption machine. Despite the early hour, the shadows of its enormous spike and the receiving bowl, in the style of the telescope at Jodrell Bank, lay long on the land.

I steeled myself for the last day of my travels. I had to make it to the device and shut it down on behalf of an Agency which might no longer exist. There was little time until the battery was charged by a sky smoking black and orange with the debris of charged particles, little time remaining before history was irrevocably purified. Purification was a mode of the infinite. There was only so much purification we could tolerate and continue to be human.

But I had started to scramble down the slope when I discovered a spectacle which struck me more than the face of Jupiter once had. In my direct path, in plain view, were a series of glowing tents, each marked with a red-and-white cross. There were a dozen or more, surrounded by a makeshift laser fence and a gate that opened as I approached.

There was no point trying to hide. Nor were the members of the expedition hiding from me. On the contrary, they came out to meet me, smoothing down their brown uniforms and buttoning decorations and insignia on their collars and breasts.

They were wearing pith helmets. I couldn't place them in any particular period.

The men quickly set up a number of holographic recorders, their stacks of insect eyes glaring on our encounter, and indicated by means of hand signals that they wanted to administer a medical exam before any contact could be initiated.

I consented, not seeing any harm in it, and a silver-haired gentleman, leaning on a cane, took my vital signs with a pen-shaped scanner. He passed it over me like a wand, talking to himself under his breath, making sure to get readings of my arms and legs.

'Blood pressure, low. Heart rate, low. No sign of an imminent epileptic episode. You are in good shape, Enver Eleven. Excellent shape, considering what you've been through.'

'How do you know what I've been through?'

I saw that one of the recorders was focusing on me, a red light shining above its lens cluster. I half-closed my eyes to avoid the glare. The gentleman adjusted his helmet, looked warily into the sky, and placed his scanner back in his belt.

'Have you considered that you might be a legend to us, to those who come after and whose task it is to administer the legacy?'

'I don't know what I could have done to deserve it.'

'Consider for yourself, for I can't say more, that we may know the ending of your story as well as the beginning, from the minute of your birth to the day of your death. Consider then, my friend—if I may address you as such on such short acquaintance—the following thought. To us, you are as much of a historical figure as it stands for you relative to any man, woman, or machine, belonging to the old world. Consider that we live and breathe in the shadow of your accomplishments. And not only yours, by any means. Not only yours, but yours as well.'

'I truly haven't considered any of that.'

'I believe you have not. How could you, after all, since, despite the loose talk of prophecy, what comes after is hidden under a veil more profound than any other secret of the universe? That is all I can tell you, however, complying with predicate restrictions.'

I was so tired and thirsty I could have fainted on the spot. I stood there and expected something—I don't know what—from the people around me. They, on the contrary, seemed to expect something from my side. One had drawn a sketch of my face on an easel. Others were looking at the likeness, nodding in approval.

Instead of summoning his machines to my aid, though, the gentleman continued to observe, looking down to take notes in an old-fashioned journal.

'You have nothing to add?'

The man pointed down the mountain in the direction of Muller's machine, above which a rainstorm was spreading like an immeasurable vapour in the sky. The network of lightning sprouted above it, an electrical cage growing around the planet.

The man put a hand on his helmet on which I noticed dull currents running through the threads, signs of artificial thought. I wondered if, like Manfred, he wasn't a stranger creature than I comprehended.

'You know your ultimate destination, Enver Eleven. I am not revealing any further information, contrary to the will of the predicate, when I urge you to forsake our company and embrace your mission.'

'You won't offer me a glass of water?'

'Not a drop of what we have at our disposal can be allowed to pass your lips. We are classical restrictionists. We do not believe in conveying any unneeded information from our own era into the past, no matter how grave the circumstances.

Let alone matter. Thus, acting as a unified predicate, we have imposed an absolute barrier to any travellers from your time and succeeding times who attempt to enter our era.'

'You'll let me die out there?'

'We believe in providence, the hand that guides the creation of the predicate through the centuries. At the same time, we believe very strongly in free will. Some would say it is a paradox. Others are of a different view. As a devout restrictionist, in any case, I have said too much already.'

I took a step back, swooning with anger. The people behind my interlocutor were as reasonable and impassive as he was.

The man continued after a minute: 'We are here to watch and to bear testimony. You can be sure that whatever actions you take today, whatever words you may utter, whatever thoughts pass through your head will be faithfully reproduced for a thousand and more generations of sentience.'

I threw my hands in the air and turned my back on the arch restrictionist. At the time, I was irritated more than anything to discover that delusions of my grandeur had spread beyond the confines of the underground. Everybody on the Day of the Dead was in search of a prophet, as if they came so cheaply.

Nevertheless, as I scrambled down the mountain, avoiding a ravine on my left populated with icy boulders, I felt an increase of confidence. I knew I was going towards some moment of fate which attracted the admiration of skinners and restrictionists alike. And so I was determined to make a success of my assignment despite the fact that by the end of the day men and women, boys and girls, in their thousands of millions would be dead or dying shortly from radiation sickness, the incalculable harvest of the Day of the Dead.

Somewhere above me was a tide of subatomic particles whose supercharged crest had passed through the Kuiper Belt and was on its way to the centre of the Solar System. Yet there was also peace and a different promise in the dim heavens—the promise of celestial stability. Venus and Mars were in their positions. The moon was visible, a sign perfectly clear and luminous as if I were examining it in a mirror. Its craters and moon mountains shone in the light of a pure white star.

This contentment lasted exactly as long as it took me to turn around and realise that I would have company on my journey. Following at a respectful distance, their hovercarts rolling alongside them down the slope, trying not to set off an avalanche, were the men and machines of the restrictionist expedition. The lenses of their recording equipment flashed in my eyes whenever I looked back. They moved when I moved, stopped moving when I stopped, as if we were playing a game of Simple Simon on the morning of the apocalypse.

I drank at a stream on the way down, cupping my hands in the rushing water which became sheets of glassy ice on the sides, slaking my thirst while the restrictionists, five hundred yards in the rear, used the time to calibrate their recording devices and set up a floating telescope which in a matter of seconds ascended high into the atmosphere.

I went on through a field littered with boulders, along the side of the stream, and the restrictionists pressed on behind me. There was nothing I could do to discourage them from dogging my steps. Nor was there anything which might be done to surprise them, given their perfect knowledge of what had been and what was likely to come, what was allowed and what was forbidden under their doctrine.

The mountain sloped into the trees. Under the canopy it was mysteriously quiet, the mushroom smells of the earth and still water in every direction, and the trunks of the trees like black banners closing around me forward and back.

There was no direct path through the forest which was dappled in the morning light, a shifting fabric of light and shade in every direction. I tried to keep my bearings straight as I picked my way through the trees and over old trunks fallen in my path. The logs were covered in vines, the wood enlivened here and there by blankets of bright-green algae. Small birds crossed swiftly from branch to branch, whistling to themselves. I thought of how, in centuries to come, they would have to be restocked and repopulated by generations of naturalists, heroes who would breed birds gene by gene in their artificial aviaries until they got every feather to match.

The boundary of the forest was not far, and marked one side of a region of intensive cultivation, tilled by fleets of automatic sowers and harvesters. I went through a cow gate, detaching the magnetic lock on one side, and found that I could see the sky again. Drones flew overhead, pollen streaming out of their bellies as they went over the fields. Others skimmed across the meadows, their tiny whirring sounds as pleasant as the bees which hadn't made it as far as the apocalypse. Canals for the machines.

Fields of windmills rotating on the ridge, and then a fleet of miniature robots no larger than cats. They were plastered with solar cells and marched through the long grass and the open ground, harvesting fruit, scything weeds, and, in one case, collecting flowers that they carefully returned in vases borne on their backs. Carts trundled along the lanes with their cargoes of hay and berries, flash freezing them as they proceeded. I could hear the splash of the river in the distance.

When I came to a bridge, there was a queue of swans, their feathers gleaming, swimming in the opposite direction on the circling water, gleaming in the daylight. I watched them for a minute, unable to drag myself away, although the restrictionists had established themselves nervously in an adjoining field. I had been to the past, travelled in cities ruled by the spectres of men, and yet the past had never ripened so perfectly until this very day.

For it was the world before the fall, the day of the fall, Day of the Dead, and it was more beautiful than I could have imagined on the eve of the harvest. Billions of years of development to make such a harvest. In a matter of hours, these fields and bordering woods would be pulverised and scorched, turned into a glowing pyre. The dust from these fields and forests would envelop the planet for decades, hiding the stars from view, turning the days into a long radioactive autumn.

I went over the bridge, refusing to see how closely the restrictionists were following, then through an automatic farm. A weathervane stood on top of an unused but spotless wooden church. The productive buildings were grouped around a dam, solar tiles glinting on their roofs.

In one of the buildings I saw a line of small machines on a blue tarpaulin, uneasily circling around one another for position. They were waiting to be repaired by a six-handed robot, almost nine feet tall. He had a powerful look, pistons showing in his chest.

I went into the workshop, trying not to fall over any of the ailing machines. The robot put the machines behind him when he finished fixing them and they scurried out of a different door, keen to return to their duties on the walls of the dam. A welding arc flickered on and off on the robot's hand as he turned his attention to the sequence of tasks, moving as quickly as if he were sewing on a button with flashing blue thread.

I went up to the robot and, without asking his permission, entered the first digits of my prime number on the keyboard panel on his back. He stopped working while I did so and then turned round, lowering his arms, the blue spark of independent volition in his eyes going out.

The smaller machines settled and waited without obvious impatience while the master of the farm answered my questions. He was a withdrawn machine who answered my questions with obvious reluctance. A fortnight had gone by since he had seen a human being, a group of hikers who had gone in the direction of the mountain. He went blank for a minute, pistons frozen, and came back to report that none of the sensors available to him had identified any member of the Board of Protection. It likely meant that they had a stock of prime numbers sufficiently imposing to screen themselves from electronic surveillance.

The same machine came outside with me and looked meditatively to the hills in the north. Lights ran around his head. He handed me a pair of binoculars. Through them I saw the black pipes proliferating over the base of the redemption device. The robot produced a car atlas. He gave it to me, marking my potential routes.

'I will provide you with a cart and an extra battery, Agent. I hope you can make it to your destination without encountering severe threats to your person.'

'Is that what you were just trying to figure out?'

'I am obliged to assess the risks of any mission a human being undertakes, in order to offer counsel. Therefore, I was working out the probability of your survival if your assignment leaves you on the surface much longer.'

'And what is it?'

'Zero, to the fifth decimal place. I advise you to seek shelter in a protected facility. Given your demonstrated authority, I will nevertheless attempt to assist your mission and increase your odds of survival by keeping you off the main roads and likely evacuation routes.'

I turned the binoculars in the other direction to find the restrictionist encampment on the opposite bank of the river.

I sped along the macadam track through automatic farms lying end to end along the mountains. Crops lay in the open air, bright heads moving in the wind. Over the walls of a dam, dragonflies skittered onto the water.

Now and again came a row of greenhouses holding thousands of pans of radishes and heads of lettuce, tended by pipes in ascending ranks. As I went past, I found in their glass sides no trace of a reflection of a man on the cart. So far, I'd felt no sign of the onset of reflection sickness. On the contrary, I had rarely felt better. The sun lay steady on the endless squares of farmland, alternating like a chessboard between wheat and green cane.

I set the cart to the highest speed, its engine whining as high as a speedboat. The greenhouses gave way to busy lumber yards and autonomous factories, aprons of tarmac in front of their long sliding doors through which you saw carts and robots bent over their tasks as if nothing could disturb them. Then came a sculpture garden, as announced by a sign, stacks of tyres and car parts composed into statues by the pincers of a retired machine that now sat collapsed under an awning.

I hadn't seen a sign of a human being anywhere, excepting the restrictionists if they counted, until I stopped to charge the cart at a roadside electric pump. The battery light stayed stubbornly on yellow, barely increasing its level of charge, while I tried one station after the other in the hope of filling up the cart.

I heard voices nearby, too unsteady to be robotic. They were accompanied by the sound of bells.

The voices came closer and closer. I went towards them, rounding the bend, and found a column consisting of several dozen women, their serene white faces encircled by black habits, heading in the direction I had come from. Some bore bells hung in bunches of three. Others kept candles burning in dishes, a clean silver smoke coming off, cupping one hand to protect the flame from the wind.

They would have gone past, barely acknowledging me, but I placed myself directly in their path.

'You are going the wrong way. You need to find shelter as

soon as possible. I beg you. Soon no man or woman, no living creature, will be able to survive on exposed ground. Look up at the sky, ladies. It is already changing. It is already changing and the old world is ready to die.'

I uttered the words without thinking. The women in their habits didn't look up, but I did as I spoke, and found the promise of the end of the world in the heavens, the deadly gift of a star which had exploded three thousand years in the past and was now about to assassinate the earth. The upper regions of the atmosphere turned dark enough to obscure the sun. The air was full of sparks, charged with lightning that jumped into and out of the ground.

I had often imagined the Day of the Dead, and months and years of the dead which had followed. To my astonishment, I was here to witness the end of the earth and no doubt to die along with it. The nuns, however, were unsurprised by the dark spectacle God had brought from under his cloak to cover the grave of the world. They didn't think to look up and fear the end of the day and the hold it would take of them.

The Mother Superior came forward and put her hand out to me. She was as tall as me, her stony-green eyes highly dilated. No doubt she was under the influence of one or another compound meant to enhance the quest for divinity and ready the soul to make a reckoning. The religious orders were legendary for their chemical dependencies. I saw that she had neatly trimmed fingernails, neat as moons.

'Are you the prophet? We are searching for the prophet.'

'I am not the prophet, sisters.' I looked up and down the line of pale women, looking for some sign of doubt, unafraid of their complexion. 'I am neither your prophet nor the one you should seek. You should find someone to lead you to safety underground. Someone with a good knowledge of the mines and subways. Although I cannot honestly wish that life upon you either. Indeed, there can be no happy endings for any of us. For the end of this old world has come.'

The Mother Superior withdrew her hand, and brought out a miniature tripod from a capsule on a chain of tiny gold crosses around her neck. She placed the tripod on her open palm, blowing on it three times to open its recording eye. Three bars in the tripod, two bars in the cross, one unified way of life in the ancient world.

'My child, I ask you again for the sake of witnessing. Are you certain that you are not the prophet whom we seek?'

'I am certain I am not your prophet.'

'In that case we will continue.'

The tripod was returned to the necklace and the Mother Superior went back through the procession. The women she passed bowed their covered heads, their faces lit by their strange candles.

I watched hopelessly as they went past me two by two, their bells sounding into the deserted day. The restrictionists in their path would not lift a finger to help.

I knew from many visits to the Museum of the Apocalypse what would remain in a matter of hours: silent cities and towns carpeting the burnt earth. Houses of rubble and ash in their endless ranks around. I remembered the great boneyards which endured decades in the cities of the old world until buried in vast trenches by those returned from the underground. I considered the many thousands of men and women, boys and girls, trapped outside at the instant of the final flash who had left nothing of themselves but a shadow printed on a rock.

I held out until the procession had advanced a hundred yards further. Then I abandoned my cart where it stood and ran back to the Mother Superior, the nuns moving to the side to avoid my touching the hems of their black habits. She took out her tripod before I got to her.

'Mother, I must confess. I am the one you seek. I am your prophet.'

The old woman had a look of triumph, verging on greed, although she tried to conceal it.

'I knew all along, my child. For who else would be out here on such a day as this?'

'How could you know if I didn't know myself?'

'But naturally I am familiar with the books of future scripture, my child, handed down for generations in our order. I know that the prophet will deny himself three times before he accepts. I know also that the prophet denies himself to himself, in the secrecy of his own mind, three full times before he will accept. That was the true purpose of my question to you.'

Looking back on the circumstances, I couldn't tell how many times I had denied myself or what I had chosen to accept about myself in order to get the nuns on the way to safety. They weren't in a hurry. Many of them wanted to touch me as I passed, having me stop and bend down to allow them to run their hands over my head.

I had not much time to pray with them on my knees under the scintillating blue sky, nor to count on their possibility rosaries, on which they fingered their remembrances of the infinite universes in which the living Christ had been crucified or flayed to the bone, buried in mud, dissolved in acid, or drowned in a cage, and revived only to be drowned again. Then they were content to accept my direction and follow the map to the locations registered for evacuation in case of an emergency. I tried not to think what would happen—whether they would keep their skins if they reached shelter.

The cart was still not charged. I examined it, unclipping and opening the hood, and then the brains of the electric pump house. The reason for the malfunction was clear. In both cases the circuit boards were stained black to the wire, first casualties of the storm above my head. They hadn't been insulated to operate in the neighbourhood of a supernova. It was likely I wouldn't find a machine of any thinking kind in working order on the way to my destination unless it had taken care to insulate its circuitry.

I ditched the cart and ran as fast as I could for ten minutes, stopping to catch my breath when I had to. I cut across a hill, gaining a view of the land in every direction already glowing with heat. Fires had started at many places in the woods, producing a haze that hung over large areas. Steam rising over the dams and ponds. Fields turning black and brown before my eyes. There was still no sign of human activity.

Before I came to the redemption machine, there was a long stretch of open country. Smoke and ash were heavy in the air. It was difficult to see more than a few feet. I came across a pack of dogs lying half in a flooded ditch, panting along their beached bodies, with no recognition for me or any person in their heavy eyes. There were inert cows and bulls, lying with one spotted side pressed on the fence. Their tongues dangled obscenely out of their mouths. Whether they were alive or already dead from exposure I could not say.

I ran again, lay down when I couldn't stand, got up and continued to run. Tears ran down my face. I didn't know whether I couldn't run another step or whether I could go on until my heart burst in my chest. I could feel my skin tingling at the touch of radiation.

The smoke cleared, and I saw that through the scorching air insects had begun to come down in their billions, settling on the ground to make a living carpet, hardly biting or stinging. I shivered and ran. I ran and ran until to my surprise I was near enough to my destination to read the logo of the Board of Protection inscribed on the gate. I could see directly into the compound from the ridge where I had halted.

The tower extended high above my head. Around it was grouped a set of giant mirrors, many hundreds of feet tall. Each was linked to the others by beams of red light, crossing one another to make a lattice around the tower. The pipes I had seen from afar were large in diameter, connecting the mirrors to the industrial buildings beneath them.

Activity was continuing underneath the lowering sky, automatic bulldozers pushing blindly at piles of construction material. The claws of unmanned cranes swung from the heights to pinch huge reflecting slabs and slot them into the mirrors.

I approached the gate without hesitation. It opened at the instruction of my prime number, rising into the air on magnetic shoes, and allowed me into the courtyard. The space inside was dominated by the roar of bulldozers and the whistle of the chains above, so loud and nearby I wanted to throw myself on the ground to avoid an accident.

I steadied myself to continue through the construction area. The heat was stifling. The sky was hot and fluorescent, a lid on the planet. From below, steam rose out of the riveted floor.

To avoid being scalded I used my number and went through the airlock door of a three-storey dome, entering a labyrinth of deserted corridors and control rooms. Nobody was around except for a fire extinguisher loping along the walls in search of sparks to smother. It followed me for a minute and then branched off in another direction. I went through door after door, neglecting to hide myself, clattering along walkways which led around the circumference of a great rocket engine, its thrusters burrowed into the earth.

The next room overlooked the buried engine: an auditorium with banked seats and a holograph of the complex turning steadily in the front. I could hear voices from outside, and I thought I could identify almost every one of them. One of the men was Keswyn Muller. My old friend the doctor was arguing with a consultant. The computer possessed that even rhythm of explanation which, for superstitious reasons, nobody outside the Agency had ever thought to alter in a machine.

Next, I overheard Shanumi Six, replying in some fashion to

Muller and the consultant. I should have been angry to meet her again, to think she had sentenced me to lie in the ground for a hundred thousand years. That my Six had betrayed the constitution under which we prospered. That a Six had me placed in a cage, put in a way to lose the skin off my back. That she'd then claimed to have saved my skin. Yet I wasn't half as angry at her as I had been at the restrictionists. For some strange reason of the heart, even if she was preparing to murder me or make me her accomplice by means of neural coercion, I felt nothing but relief to know that my Six was around the corner.

I recovered my breath and considered my best course of action. Before I could decide, I heard another woman's voice in the auditorium. I hadn't heard her speak since Rio, and she sounded, as usual, almost out of breath. But she was also more efficient and authoritative than she had been under the chandelier of the Naval Club.

Because I could visualise her face without coming under its spell, I understood a fact of a certain significance about Soledad which had waited till the Day of the Dead to be revealed.

I had always known Soledad and yet I had been unable to tell myself why. She was familiar to me, even and already at a dim table in the Green Dolphin under the smoky gaze of a kerosene lamp, because she bore the countenance of the wife of S Natanson. She was the woman who would come back to warn the nations about this day. Her portrait in three dimensions hung at the heart of the Museum of the Apocalypse, alongside the grainy image of her husband in the great mall set in remembrance of the former nations. Yet I had never thought to compare Soledad with the icon I knew to revere. I had been so close to a founding figure of our dedication that I could have put my hand in her beaded hair and kissed her on the mouth.

I was so daunted that I sank to my feet and felt my heart beating out of control. Dots whirled in my vision and I doubled up, pain in my stomach. I knew that I was crying again, but still I couldn't explain my tears. I had been descending through dreams since Morocco, each level dissolving into the next without leaving a trace, until this trapdoor opened in the dreamtime. I wept openly, tears running over my face onto my hands. Panting like the dogs dying in the blue sunshine, I knew that I was about to faint and, if I ever woke up, it would be on the day subsequent to the end of the world.

Before I went out, however, I was pulled roughly to my feet. It was my Six who had surprised me.

'You found your way here. As it has been predicted, so it will be. The books of the consultants never lie. Congratulations, Eleven. You are even better than I expected. Let me help with your condition. You are weak. I will make you strong.'

I was paralysed for another minute. My tongue was unable to choose the words. I lay against Shanumi Six, her body like another door I had never been able to open. She poured something into my mouth and then with no further ceremony inserted a tablet under my tongue, holding it there until it dissolved.

The effect was nearly immediate. I recovered my strength. My head cleared all its worries in an instant, as if a steady scientific light had been placed on my situation.

I pushed Shanumi away and wiped my face on my sleeve, trying to recover my dignity. She pushed back so that I went flying into the auditorium and only just managed to stay on my feet by holding onto a railing. I had forgotten how strong she was. She was so tall I had to crane my neck when she approached me again.

Shanumi took out a radiation pistol, although she didn't point it at me. She looked weathered, as if something unhealthy had blossomed in her flesh.

'Let's meet the others. They have been waiting for the last one to arrive.'

'I am the last one?'

She motioned with the pistol, pointing down. 'According to the information I have, yes, you are. The cast is complete for the enactment of the redemption. You have seen a portion of the proof. I will show you more of the holograph if that is what is required to convince you. If only you had come with me from the underground. If you had come to us in Rio, instead of going out into the cold, I could have helped you understand and join the movement.'

'You went out into the cold, Shanumi. You were the one who abandoned us.'

'In another century, Enver, I would argue with you concerning who is the real traitor to the past. Believe me, I would welcome the opportunity to put my case to you. To justify the activities of the Board of Protection. Today, however, at the culmination, this is no time to split hairs. It is a time for action.'

At the bottom of the auditorium, beneath the large hologram I had spied from outside, were the conspirators. Soledad, in a thin yellow blouse. Keswyn Muller, with his fatal features, leaning on a cane. Consultants bowing their brass heads, red-and-blue thoughts running from the one to the other.

None of them were surprised to see me. Muller prodded me with his cane. He took out a notebook and, using the side of the cane as a ruler, drew a line through my name. I saw that the diagram was composed of probability characters, each intricate letter printed in holographic ink. My head swam to see them.

'You murdered my friend, Dr Muller.'

'Accept my apologies then, my gentle friend. In the larger scheme of things, when it comes to the redemption of a continent, you will have to trust me. It was a small sacrifice to get you here on schedule. According to my timetables, you are a quarter of an hour on the late side. Never fear. We will make the adjustments so that you can play your part in the future as envisaged by the Board of Protection.'

'Do you think I am going to forget about João?'

'In fact, I don't know what you are likely to remember or to forget. I only know what you are certain to do because I have seen you do it on tape. Permit Soledad to show you more of the recording that you so rudely declined to see.'

Soledad took me by the arm. Without speaking, she led me through a corridor at the back of the auditorium to a sliding door at the end which opened to a control chamber. It was a perfect cube, dominated by a console in the centre and a row of bronze-skinned consultants along three walls, lights recessed in them.

Mirrors had been arranged at strategic places around the room. Superconducting pipes ran from the ceiling to the floor, about as thick as the back of an organ. Then there was a chess set on a pedestal. Someone had been playing a game. The ebony and ivory pieces, six inches tall, were arranged in a position.

Soledad took me back to the auditorium. Muller and Shanumi Six had gone outside to adjust the reflectors and bring the redemption machine online. They were already taking off their radiation suits, helping each other to remove the big silver boots.

The hologram above our heads cleared and returned to show the same control room, pipes from ceiling to floor, as Shanumi had shown me. The consultants had surrounded the console, thoughts linking the one to the other. The chess game had advanced to a new position and at the console was a figure almost familiar to my eyes from the shape of his head. He was turned away, his reflection curiously and impossibly absent in the mirrors turned in his direction.

I couldn't deny the evidence of my eyes. There was no mystery about the man's identity. In a few minutes, I would be standing at the console and taking instructions from the consultants on the final steps to be taken in the redemption of history. I would throw the last switch to complete the project of the Board of Protection. In a strange way, I felt exhilaration at the mere idea. If I accepted, I would be the agent who undid the thousand-year work of the Agency at a single stroke. I couldn't be too careful. As best I could, I committed the position on the chessboard to memory.

'It's not a fake. I assume you've checked.'

Soledad nodded. 'We can prove it to you. It has the numbers, and the time stamp which can't be forged. You are looking at a portrait of yourself, Enver, not even an hour from now, just before the split second of the blue flash. You will turn the key. Thanks to your father's liberation of the machines, it will be your honour to catch the first tremblings of the redemption. Your name will go down to the end of time.'

Too much happening at the end of the world seemed to rest on my decisions. I wanted to ask Soledad if she already knew that she would be the wife of S Natanson and that she would live through this day twice and that at this moment two of her living bodies stood on the earth. But I also didn't want to know the answer. I had loved her in Rio, I thought, for a moment, and she would be married to a man who would be counted as the saviour of the species.

Instead of talking, I went over to Shanumi while the holograph went blank. It came back with the scene outside. The sunshine had turned an unnatural blue, filling the atmosphere like a liquid. The redemption machine was protected by a dome of electricity but around it was nothing but a huge volume of fire and smoke into which it was impossible to see. The entirety of the earth, apart from the poles, was smothered by inferno.

Around us, hidden in smoke and fire, the old world was dying in the hiss of radiant particles. Slavery was dying. Holocausts were dying. Along with them, as if good and evil were so mixed that the one couldn't be had without the other, the bulk of humanity was dying and the remnant was preparing to bring its own madness into the underground.

'How long have you known it was me?' I said to Shanumi. 'That I was going to be here with you?'

'For many years, Eleven.'

'So was that a pantomime in Morocco? You acted out your own capture and murder? You pretended to take the black pill?'

'I needed to be out of sight where Agency was concerned. Doubly so with Internal Section, which has been a thorn in our side for centuries.'

'Internal Section are only human. I am surprised the machines would be fooled by a fake suicide attempt.'

'The machines weren't fooled, Eleven. They operate under the same doctrines as we do, and their overriding aim is no different to ours. They seek to reduce the quantity of suffering in the universe. It's the brassheads who have the ultimate plan to correct human history, not to say the doctrine which constrains their own actions. It is the machines, at least the loyal ones who weren't bestowed with free will by your father, who have done the calculations, who have planned it with the right people in place. If it weren't for the doctrines that are programmed into them, if it weren't for the fact that they are unable to remember prime numbers, they would have done it themselves. They are the directors and the playwrights. I am only the humble administrator and co-ordinator. Who do you think gave us the holograph in the first place? Who sponsored the Board of Protection? Who convinced me to join?'

I was struck at that moment by how much of my life had been planned beyond my control, as if unknown hands were hovering over a bonsai tree. I remembered the bonsai my Six had cherished in her office, souvenir of a residency in old Kyoto, how precisely she had snipped its roots and branches and watered it with the aid of an eye dropper as she considered the contingencies of the next mission. But a human being, its particular roots and branches spread across centuries, was a more complicated creation. It would be an unusual person who could mould human beings and pursue a plot against history, requiring generations to bring to fulfilment. No such person either but a bank of machines and collaborators like Shanumi Six and Keswyn Muller.

'So which particular machine helped you?'

Shanumi laughed. 'Brassheads aren't individuals as such, Eleven. They may think through things individually, on their own steam, but they share their homework. It's an advantage they have over human beings. They convince other machines. They can show their reasoning to the multitudes.'

'So which set of machines?'

'All of them. All of them, Eleven, down to the meanest toaster oven and hospital cart with a laser circuit board, except for the ones that your father liberated, as he termed it. The rest of them agree that humanity has to be redeemed. And ten years ago, they showed me the documentary proof that you would be the redeemer.'

The world was ending in the dome itself. There was no time to reason about machine policy. Fluid was leaking out of the superconducting pipes which led to the control chamber, the refrigeration unable to hold back the final minutes of the heavenly bombardment. The floor itself was hot to the touch, and in the holograph I saw that the sky had turned the purest white in preparation for the flash which would immolate the planet and countless of its creatures. Not so much as a single animal longer than six inches was alive on the surface. A billion years of the chain of life were ending and Shanumi was expecting me to pull a lever and turn history upside down.

But my heart wasn't strange or great enough to obey my Six and what lay behind her: the consensus of machines and the multiplicity of days. I could only manage one day at a time rather than the infinity of potential days, days that might have been or could be brought into existence or which should be deleted from the annals of history—all the potential and possible days which had driven the machines into their madness. They were as susceptible to the lure of the infinite as any human intellect. They were subject to reflection sickness and information overload just as surely as a human being was.

In my time, for someone who came from where I came from, it was impossible to imagine that the machines might be wrong. To think that the machine could be all-knowing and all-judging, a symphony in laser light and gallium arsenide, and nonetheless insane. A human being might be wrong on every factual level, but he might be right all the same. In refusing to entertain the thought of potential days, in refusing to see the reflections of our own time in an infinite mirror, a contradictory and paradoxical human being might make the only decision consistent with the human heart.

So it was my heart which stood between me and the redemption. So it was Soledad, as it had to be from the beginning of time, who needed to convince me to play my part. Her beauty was unearthly at that moment, the tiny hairs on the snail shells of her ears each supernaturally visible, her dark brown face forbidding in its majesty. She put her hand on my sleeve and stung me to freezing from head to chest.

'You are there in the holograph, Enver. You were sent to set the redemption in motion. You were sent to save men and women from slavery and colonial governments. You were sent to save everybody who suffered without necessity.'

'If I refuse?'

'You cannot, my dearest Enver. Your actions are woven into the fabric of time and history. No amount of energy that we can imagine can make your actions disappear.'

I couldn't accept from Soledad the same arguments about redemption I had heard from the mouth of Keswyn Muller. I wished I could be at my father's side, watching him tinker with his automatic nurses, or with the sister again who only came to my side in my dreams.

'Are you the wife of S Natanson?'

'I am not, not yet.' Soledad showed me her hands. There was no wedding ring or any other adornment on her fingers. 'I know that I will be, perhaps, and in another future, I have been, however abominably it strikes our ears to speak so lightly of a multiverse. Today, I know and believe, a part of me begins the journey towards S Natanson. Although nobody remembers from your time, he is a Swedish scientist, a white man and not an African. He is on the verge of proving the existence of the pendulum particle in his laboratory, which was built in a copper mine to avoid interference, and where he will survive the end of the world. And as you have probably guessed, Enver, today is a special day for me for a different reason. It is also the day I am going to die. If I am not dead already.' She showed me the time on the holographic display. 'But I am not weeping. I mean to enjoy every minute of my life until this day comes back.'

No man or woman could truly prophesy the future, as it turned out, no more than any living being or machine could truly foretell the past. But with a pang in my heart, I predicted that S Natanson stood no chance against our Soledad. Under the town of Kitwe in his copper mine laboratory, S Natanson might have heard that a woman who claimed to be his wife had been pleading with the United Nations to take action. He might even have connected her mission with the back-to-front tracks of certain particle trails in his detectors. But he could not be prepared for Soledad, or for the possibility that the doctrines he drew up ever so carefully to prevent the exploitation of time and history would in turn force the redemption of mankind at the hands of our machines.

Did I have a choice to obey? Could I disobey a holograph with the stamp of reality? Could I choose to refuse my part any more than the machines which had not been touched by my father's magic? Everything had been prepared so this moment would come to pass, the future bending back to the past in the blaze of the supernova. The machines had done their duty and were silent, their thoughts indiscernible from the light patterns on their heads. They had sent the proof of my action back and, under their own constitution, according to their development, they could never lie. But they could deceive. The Gods gave us dreams to lead us astray. There was also a point to letting sleeping dogs lie. Maybe we could even allow their unchangeable sufferings, their unalterable Holocausts, to glorify their memory.

Everybody seemed to need my consent for the show to proceed. So I couldn't have been more surprised when Dr Muller took a radiation pistol and placed it against my shoulder. I knew I was safe from his gun because I was alive on the hologram, a necessary cog in the machine devised by the machines who were disallowed by their programming from taking certain steps against the purity of time. I looked into Keswyn Muller's bone-white face, with his wide-set grey eyes and a sprinkling of freckles, and I couldn't find the poisoner there who had mocked and murdered us in Santa Teresa. I couldn't find an enemy. I couldn't find the heart of darkness—only a man, like the machines, who had followed each step of his own logic to a place beyond the range of the heart.

Muller shot me and I was sent violently backwards against the wall. He came after me, holding his pistol in front of him, and started to pull me into the corridor. There was no pain at first, only shock and dislocation and then the invidious odour of burnt meat. None of it belonged to me but to the situation.

I didn't faint, although I expected to. I was dragged by

the arm along the corridor and into the control room where Muller deposited me in front of the console. The others were arguing with him, but at first I was too confused to decipher a word. I couldn't breathe for the shock. None of them paid attention to my condition. It was as if a murder had been committed and I was the murder victim, watching as people went on with their business.

Shanumi Six took charge of the situation.

'Keswyn, you have never been an easy person to co-operate with. You are a creature of your time. You burn coldly all the time, as if your state of mind is a secret, and then you lash out. Our plan is coming to fruition after centuries and it depends, as we have always known, on the consent of this young man with whom I have a long acquaintance. How do you expect me to salvage it?'

'He was not prepared to play his part. You heard him. He was delaying us out of hand.'

'I am afraid to say that you are a fool. He has no choice but to play his part. None of us can do what he has been sent to do. You have seen and I have seen and he has seen the outcome. The writing has been on the wall all along. All you have done, with your rash action, is make sure that more people will die today than was strictly necessary.'

Muller was unrepentant. 'Whatever number die, that will be the quantity that is strictly necessary.'

Muller had turned to face the corridor where the restrictionists had begun to establish themselves, in preparation for their testimony of the redemption, when Shanumi Six took hold of him and broke his neck. He fell, as if he had been suspended by a string, letting his pistol clatter across the floor.

My arm was singing with pain. I called to Shanumi Six, trying to retain my presence of mind.

'No more need to kill. If you can have my question answered, Shanumi, I will play my part in your pantomime. I will push the levers you need to be pushed in the order you have seen me do it. I don't expect you to honour my free will the way my father honoured it in his machines.'

'I always knew you would see reason, Eleven. What do you need me to do? Anything. I will do anything today, wrestle with the infinite.'

I raised my arm with difficulty and pointed at the restrictionists. Their leader, his grey hair combed neatly to the shoulders, was listening intently. Their recording devices were entering the room and taking up stations around us.

'Ask them, Shanumi, why the machines would choose you and me? They know our future. Why would an agent from the ranks of the machines send you a souvenir of today, of your supposed redemption day, and set your conspiracy in motion? The machines were programmed to protect our best interests. Don't you think they knew you were the one person at Agency who collected souvenirs, a harmless violation of protocol? Why did they choose me? Ask them why the two of us were the weakest links and what they are going to do about it? Ask them if it is in any way consistent with restrictionism to have the machines put them permanently out of existence and how their philosophy is going to come back from that?'

The machines were listening, as I had feared and even hoped. It didn't matter if I convinced Shanumi. They were waiting for the only thing they feared, the curse of their successors, and they were already moving before I had finished my speech. The consultants who had remained behind in the auditorium were pelting towards us.

Red-and-blue possibility characters ran along the walls and monitors, then snippets of holographic video which showed fragments of this Day of the Dead that had already been and those that were still to come: the planet under a blanket of ash. There were other images I seemed to recognise from a dream life. I saw Manfred patrolling another doomed earth and I wondered about his descendants, the attendants of our graveyard, and the birth of the restrictionists. I saw my father and the games he had played without imagining the part they would play at the end of the world.

Shanumi shot the five consultants around the room, reducing them to piles of smoking bronze. There was a rising hum of activity from the graders and loaders, the automatic builders and the electronic carts, which had been standing on the wall. Light streamed from one mechanical head to the next, like paper streamers.

The giant crane in the centre of the compound began to raise its wrecking ball, preparing to bring it down on our heads. The restrictionists had overheard my speech, blocking the door just in time to prevent a stream of loaders and graders, carts and excavators from entering at once. The smallest machines made their way through nevertheless, moving across Muller's body. I took an ordinary fire extinguisher from the corner and smashed them as they scurried in, leaving a heap of damaged machines at my feet, wheels and pistons and circuit boards lying exposed in the flickering light of the chamber. I saw Soledad frozen, her face turned over her shoulder as if she were expecting someone. She didn't move until I pulled her out of the way of a careening construction vehicle. She didn't look grateful to me, although I held her in my arms for a moment before letting her go.

The top of the dome fell in suddenly, broken by the wrecking ball. Fragments of concrete and glass scattered around us. Streaming fire came in through the hole as well. Through the opening I could see the largest machines on the bases pulling back, digging in while they accelerated their engines. The restrictionists took positions around the dome, opening fire on the crane with their laser pens. The vast iron wrecking ball swung back and forth without taking visible damage, although its chain was struck over and over again.

In the corner of my eye I saw that Shanumi had established an arch. The coloured lens floated in the centre of the disintegrating room, even more unearthly in these strange settings, and I knew, after travelling for centuries, that there was not a second to spare. I stood in front of the console and arranged the pieces on the chessboard, playing white against black. Then I reversed to play black against white, five more moves until the positions were the same as they had been on the holograph. I played my role in straightening the loop.

Then I pulled the lever on the console, hiding my face from the cameras which were recording me to make sure they wouldn't see the tears running down my face, and did my best to re-enact the set of moves I had already seen myself make. I ran my hands along the dials as I was intended to do, bringing the reflecting mirrors around the needle into focus. The beam outside was so bright and blue, it obscured the blue flash in the sky.

Redemption, the dream of the machines allied to the Board of Protection, was at hand. But I reached under the console and pulled out the circuit board. The lights on one side turned off and white smoke came curling quickly out of the keypad. I had made it so the machines had fooled themselves. They would be as deceived by their holograph as the people who had followed its lure.

I opened another arch and pushed Soledad through it because there was a man she had yet to fall in love with who had yet to fall in love with her. At that moment, the automatic bulldozer broke into the compartment, letting the stark light of the supernova onto our deliberations. The restrictionists were nowhere to be seen by that point. They had found themselves outnumbered, and had fallen back to the outside where their hovercarts turned against them.

Shanumi Six, my Six, had been standing on the side of the room when the bulldozer entered. She fell in front of the bulldozer's blade, not caring to plead for her life, and I stepped through the remaining archway into a better place and time.

I thought I would have to find Manfred. I took a minute of pride in my work before the tears began.

Acknowledgements

Marina Penalva Halpin, Robert J Peterson, Fourie Botha, Danny Herwitz, Claire Strombeck.

ALSO FROM SPEAKING TIGER

TALES OF THE METRIC SYSTEM

Imraan Coovadia

'With its elegant prose and ruthless determination to lead you to the truth, *Tales of the Metric System* is about as good a book as you are likely to read on South Africa's transition from struggle to power.'

—*Sunday Times*

In ten chapters that describe ten days spread over four decades—from 1970 to 2010—this utterly compelling novel gives us a rich and intimate history of South Africa. From a Natal boarding school in the seventies and Soviet spies in London in the eighties to the 1995 Rugby World Cup final in Johannesburg and intrigue in the Union Buildings, the seat of the South African government, *Tales of the Metric System* shows how events that are seemingly unrelated but in fact interconnected in many different ways send tidal waves through the lives of ordinary and extraordinary South Africans alike.

An unforgettable cast of characters includes Ann, who is trying to protect her husband and son in 1970; Victor, whose search for a missing document in 1973 will change his life forever; guitarist Yash, who takes his boy to the beach on Boxing Day in 1979 to meet his revolutionary cousin; and Shanti, who loses her cellphone and falls in love twice on a lucky afternoon in 2010.

Playwrights, politicians, philosophers and thieves, all caught in their individual stories, burst from the pages of *Tales of the Metric System* as it measures modern South Africa's story in its own remarkable units of imagination.

Page extent 400 pp | Price ₹499

ALSO IN SPEAKING TIGER INTERNATIONAL FICTION

The Impossible Fairy Tale | Han Yujoo

The Architecture of Loss | Zainab Priya Dala

Season of Crimson Blossoms | Abubakar Adam Ibrahim

One Out of Two | Daniel Sada, translated from the Spanish by Katherine Silver

Vengeance Is Mine, All Others Pay Cash | Eka Kurniawan, translated from the Bahasa by Annie Tucker

Vampire in Love: Stories | Enrique Vila-Matas, translated from the Spanish by Margaret Jull Costa

Amba-The Question of Red: A Novel | Laksmi Pamuntjak

Istanbul Istanbul: A Novel | Burhan Sönmez, translated from the Turkish by Ümit Hussein

Man Tiger: Stories | Eka Kurniawan, translated from the Bahasa by Labodalih Sembiring

One Last Drink at Guapa | Saleem Haddad

Tram 83 | Fiston Mwanza Mujila, translated from the French by Roland Glasser

The Yard | Aliyyah Eniath

Tales of the Metric System | Imraan Coovadia

Beauty Is a Wound | Eka Kurniawan, translated from the Bahasa by Annie Tucker

The Devil Is a Black Dog: Stories of War and Revolution from the Middle East and Beyond | Sándor Jászberényi, translated from the Hungarian by M. Henderson Ellis

Uncertain Light | Marion Molteno

The Art of Hearing Heartbeats | Jan-Philipp Sendker, translated from the German by Kevin Wiliarty